FAKE THE GAME

JULIA JARRETT

CONTENTS

CHAPTER ONE

Maverick

Hospitals are hell. They're too bright, too loud, and too full of desperation with a sprinkling of hope.

Two emotions that never mix well.

I don't fucking want to be here. I don't want to put on a fake smile and try to be all motivational and shit for these kids. Hell, no one should be motivated by me at the best of times, much less right now. I don't want to be surrounded by people looking at me with stars in their eyes, thinking I'm some amazing person.

I don't want to be surrounded by people, period.

I want to be at home, in the dark, by myself. My ribs hurt, my collarbone hurts, and *I don't fucking want to be here*.

When my brother who is also my agent told me to show up at the children's hospital this morning to sign some merch and take photos, I laughed at him. But Colin just ignored me, pointing out the fact that I don't have the luxury of saying no right now. I gotta kiss some ass and do whatever the fuck the team asks me to do while I'm on the injured list to try and save face. So here I am. Even if I'm not the player they usually ask to come to the children's hospital. Ever since my accident four weeks ago, all bets are off. I'm at the mercy of my agent and the media relations people from the Vancouver Tridents who are trying to salvage what's left of my image. They say jump, I say how high.

Some teenage-looking kid walks up to me with a bald head and tubes poking out of his shirt. "When you gonna be back on the field?" he asks, getting straight to it.

I shift on my feet, wishing like hell I could answer him. But fuck if I know. Doc said eight to ten weeks, if I rehab properly. It's already been four weeks and I'm going fucking crazy.

"Dunno," I answer curtly. Then in my head, I hear the voice of Willow Lawson, director of the media relations team, chastising me and reminding me to put on my game face. There's not a lot of people that could get away with that kind of shit, but Willow's good people. So I give what I hope is a convincing smile. "Gotta take care of my body, y'know?"

"Why did you crash that car, anyway?"

You think I fucking did that on purpose? But I don't say that. Willow should be proud. All that goddamn media training she forces on us might be paying off.

"I made a mistake. Everyone does sometimes, just gotta do better next time." There. That's a good bullshit answer. But the kid isn't buying it.

"My dad said it was an illegal street race."

Swear to fucking God, if this kid wasn't fighting cancer, I'd walk away right now. Last thing I need is some punk-ass kid coming here and telling me everything I already know about my most recent fuckup. I normally like kids. But right now, the lack of filter is not working for me.

My phone starts to vibrate, saving me from responding. Looking at it, I see my brother's name. "Sorry kid, gotta go. My agent's calling."

I stride away from him without a backward look, seeking out a stairwell where maybe I can get some privacy to listen to Colin yell at me some more. At least I'm guessing that's why he's calling when he knows I'm in the middle of this community service shit.

"What?"

"Nice to talk to you, too, brother. Me? Oh, I'm fine. Thanks for asking." Colin's sarcasm has me rolling my eyes as I lean against the concrete wall of the stairwell.

"Fuck off. You know I'm busy."

Maybe other players wouldn't talk to their agents like that, but for me and Col, it's different. As my agent, he doesn't always have to put up with my shit, but he does. That's because, as the closest thing to a brother I'll ever have, he *understands* my shit. More than anyone.

"You're done for today. Head home." His tone is sober, no trace of sarcasm remaining. That alone means I'm not gonna like what he's about to say. "Hydroboost is pulling your deal."

"What?" I growl, pushing off from the wall. I pace the length of the landing as I let that news sink in. "What do you mean they're pulling it?"

"I mean they don't want their brand associated with an asshole who participates in alleged street races and crashes cars," Colin fires back.

"No one has proof it was a race."

"Not the point, brother, and you know it."

I rip my Tridents hat off my head and chuck it to the ground, raking my fingers through my hair as I continue to pace. "For fuck's sake. I had to do it, Col. You know I did."

"I know you think you had to bail him out again, but you didn't," he barks at me. "You got yourself in this fucking mess with your goddamn saviour complex. When are you gonna learn? Eli is never going to stop causing shit. Not while you keep enabling him. He's on the path to self-destruction, and it's not your responsibility to save him from it."

I exhale a curse and stoop to pick up my hat, wincing as the move makes my ribs feel like they're on fire.

"You know I can't just walk away." Even if he's right and me stepping in to save our other foster brother every time his drug use gets him in trouble is only making things worse, I can't just abandon Eli.

"I know you *should*, because next time you might not get away with only a fracture, some bruised ribs, and ten weeks on the injured reserve list."

My jaw clenches. "Can we salvage the deal?"

Colin doesn't answer right away, which tells me everything. My fist tightens, the pull of muscles tugging on my still-healing clavicle.

"No, Mav. We can't. It's done."

"Fuck!" I shout, the word echoing in the concrete stairwell. I lift my fist to slam it into the wall, but pain shoots through my arm just from the motion of lifting it. Even *I'm* smart enough to know punching a wall would be a bad fucking idea. Last thing I need is to add a broken hand to the mix.

"I gotta go," I growl into the phone, ending the call with a jab of the button and shoving the device back in my pocket. I pace back and forth several more times, cursing under my breath. The walls feel like they're closing in on me, in all parts of my fucked-up life. Losing an endorsement is the first domino falling down on my career. Next could be my fucking contract.

And if I lose baseball...

There's a chair on the landing with a piece of paper taped to it stating it's there for cardiac patients. I sag down onto it, my arms falling to my sides as I slump back. Thank fuck there's no one around to witness my breakdown.

Of course, I should be so lucky. Because that's when I hear it. The soft shuffle of feet. I look up one flight of stairs to the next landing, to see a woman clutching the railing, looking like she'd rather be anywhere but here.

Join the club, sweetheart.

I should care about what she may or may not have just seen or heard. Hell, for all I know, she recorded the whole damn thing and my outburst is about to go viral. Then again, taking a longer look at her, she doesn't look like the gossip-spreading type. Her shockingly bright red hair is pulled back from her face in a bun, glasses perched on her nose. She's short, but holy hell, she's got a body I'd like to sink my hands into. Even if her outfit is more appropriate for a woman three times her age and I can't see an inch of skin, aside from the long column of her neck, her face, and small hands that are now fluttering nervously in front of her.

I'm momentarily distracted from my rage by envisioning pulling her hair down from the bun and letting it cascade over my hands. I wonder how pink her cheeks would get if I did...

Jesus.

But fast on the heels of lust comes something wholly unexpected from me. The sudden urge to reassure her, that I'm not gonna hurt her. Because that's the energy she's giving off. Nerves, bordering on fear. And I fucking hate that it's because of me and my temper.

Her lips part, she clears her throat, and I watch her straighten her spine as she slowly walks down the stairs toward me. "Sorry to disturb you." She speaks so softly I almost miss the musical lilt to her voice.

But I definitely don't miss the way she skirts around me, leaving as much space between us as she possibly can when she pulls open the door and slips through, leaving me alone in my fucking misery again.

Nothing new there, but why do I wish she hadn't left before I had a chance to apologize for my behaviour?

CHAPTER TWO

Sadie

When I was coming down the stairs and heard that angry voice, I stopped in my tracks, uncertain what I would find. It's not exactly uncommon for parents or other visitors to the Vancouver Children's Hospital to be in the stairwells taking phone calls, and with the stress they're often under, high emotions are to be expected.

But as soon as I laid eyes on the man, something in me knew this was different. I hate to admit, I judged a book by its cover, especially when it's something I have been subjected to myself. But I did. He was young; in his late twenties, same as me if I had to guess. Every inch of his muscular arms not covered by a tight-fitting T-shirt was covered in tattoos. Dirty blond hair curled out from under a black ball cap, and even with the space between us I could see the crystal blue of his eyes.

Back in my office, away from him, I rationalized it was still possible he was here with a patient, but something about his energy told me he wasn't. Which begged the question of why he's here, in a hospital stairwell, yelling into his phone. When I saw him lift his arm as if he was going to hit something, I almost turned around to go find security.

Then I watched him slump into a chair, obviously unaware that I was watching. The raw vulnerability of that moment, the anguish and despair on his face as he closed his eyes, made my heart hurt for him.

Honestly, the roller coaster of emotions I witnessed in those few minutes was the most interesting thing to happen to me in a long time. Something about him was captivating, exciting in an illicit way.

Which is why, for the last three hours, I've had to stop myself from thinking of him. He's a distraction I don't need pulling me from the mountain of work waiting. With the hospital foundation's main gala happening in just over a month, my job as the head of fundraising for the foundation is demanding, to say the least.

And right now, getting through the rest of my to-do list is taking a lot of mental fortitude. Even the mundane tasks that I can usually do while listening to an audiobook require my full attention to stop my mind from wandering. Which is odd since I'm not normally the kind of woman to drool over tight T-shirts and baseball hats.

I scribble my signature again, ignoring the cramp in my hand as I sign off on another purchase order for the event, sliding the paper into my outgoing mailbox for the foundation's admin assistant to pick up later. There's so much to do for the upcoming gala, I really don't have time to be thinking about tattooed men in stairwells, even if they are mouthwateringly hot.

And that! It's the other thing that has me confused and distracted. Since when am I attracted to messy hair and scowls? He's nothing like any of the men I've dated before, and the complete opposite of my ex, Dirk.

My head falls forward with a groan. I had to go and think of *him*. For two months now, my life has been in shambles because of him. Well, him and his wandering dick. Walking in on him having sex with his paralegal was the start of a downward mental spiral I haven't been able to stop. Maybe if he'd just admitted to cheating and left me alone, I could move on. But no, he has to dig the knife even deeper by trying to make it seem like it was my fault.

"I was bored, Sadie. That's all. When was the last time you sucked my dick? Weeks. I have needs, for Christ's sake. When you're ready to meet those needs, come and find me."

Bored. He was *bored*. As if that's justification for cheating.

Besides, if anyone had the right to feel bored with our sex life, it was me. The reason for the lack of blow jobs? It was due to his absolutely terrible, not to mention selfish, skills in bed. Why should I bother getting him off when I could count on one hand the number of times he repaid the favour.

I have needs, too, and he most definitely wasn't meeting them. Honestly, even though being forced to find an apartment in a hurry sucked almost as much as having to go to my doctor to ask for an STD panel given his infidelity, I was relieved to be done with the relationship.

Even if now I find myself alone, struggling to figure out where my life went so wrong, and why I feel so...empty. Maybe Dirk was right and I am boring.

Sitting up straight, I grab my phone. My friend Willow works for the local professional baseball team. We connected because she often brings players by for meet and greet sessions with our patients, and it's always a good boost to our donation dollars when that hits the media. She's the exact opposite of me, and I can guarantee she'd never consider her life boring, so maybe spending some time with her will rub off on me.

I type out a quick text asking if she wants to get a drink after work. It's something we used to do once a month or so, but ever since she started dating one of the guys on the team she works for, her time has been limited. Thankfully, she answers with an enthusiastic yes, and we make plans to meet at our favourite bar later.

Feeling slightly better with that modicum of control back over my immediate future, I turn back to work.

When I reach the bar where we agreed to meet a couple of hours later, it's packed, surprisingly so for a Wednesday night. I weave my way through the crowd until I find a small table tucked in the back. Setting my purse down on the bar top, I climb up into the tall stool and check my phone. Willow had said she might be a little late but to go ahead and order for her. Looking around, I realize the chance of getting a waitress's attention are slim to none tonight, meaning I need to risk losing my table by going up to the bar to order.

I drape my coat over the back of a chair in hopes of deterring anyone from sitting down and make my way to the bar. When

I see a familiar face staring back at me from a stool at the very end of the bar, tucked into a dark corner, I come up short with a stumble. The tattooed mystery man from the stairwell...

"Hello again," he rumbles with a smirk that doesn't quite soften the hard lines of his jaw.

I blink once, twice, then realize I must look like a fool standing there staring at him. "H-hi."

"I'll keep an eye on your table." The rasp of his voice filters through the background noise of the bar, raising the hairs on my arm.

"Thanks," I say, still staring. He breaks eye contact, looking back down at the glass of clear liquid in front of him.

Of all the flipping bars in town, he had to come here? So much for not thinking about him. The bartender's voice steals my attention, and I order two glasses of wine for Willow and me, then carry the drinks carefully back to my table.

He's so close to my seat, I don't know why I didn't notice him sooner. But now that I know he's right there behind me, every part of my body feels attuned to him. Which makes absolutely zero sense. This man gives off *don't mess with me* vibes like no one else. He's got trouble written all over him. And the last thing I want is trouble. Maybe my idea of excitement isn't tattoos and bad boys, and sure, I could probably do with a little more fun, but I like my safe, simple little life. I like my routines and calm and predictable days.

And he seems anything but calm and predictable.

Checking my phone again as I take a sip of the crisp white wine, my lips turn down at Willow's latest message. She can no longer meet for a drink, thanks to an urgent issue at work.

Great.

I'm not really wanting to sit here alone, but wasting two perfectly good glasses of wine also feels wrong.

My finger runs around the base of my wine glass as I try to decide what to do. I'm acutely aware of the man behind me, and while I can't confirm he's looking at me, I feel as though he is. It's so distracting, I don't realize trouble is heading my way and not coming from the direction of the man at the bar.

Someone else slides into the seat across from me and my head shoots up, my mood instantly souring even further when I see who it is.

"What are you doing here, Dirk?" I say, my grip tightening on my wine glass.

My ex leans back against the chair, his suit jacket falling open as he gives me a cocky grin. "This is where we always go for drinks, princess." He gestures at me casually and shakes his head. "C'mon. Let your hair down, why you gotta be so uptight all the time?"

How the heck did I ever think this was the right man for me? I stare at him, trying to burn holes into him with my eyes. The comments about my hair, my clothes, *me*. They're always said so casually, so offhand, like he's not really judging me, but he is.

"Leave, please." I say it quietly but firmly, hoping he'll get the message.

"Now why would I do that? You've been ignoring my messages. I just want to talk." He has the absolute audacity to sound wounded, and I scoff.

"I've been ignoring you because I have nothing to say."

"You're seriously still mad about Gina? God, Sadie. Get over it. I'm tired of waiting for you to come to your senses and come home."

I'm at a loss on how to respond. It's not the first time in the past couple of months he's hinted at thinking I'll come crawling back to him someday, but it is the most blatant he's ever said it.

Before I can say anything, Dirk's gaze drops down to the two glasses of wine in front of me, then back up at my face. "Are you waiting for someone?" The way he says it, like he can't quite believe I'd be here with someone else, grates on my nerves.

"Pretty sure she asked you to leave."

The deep rumble from behind makes me gasp. Crap, I'd forgotten he was there, obviously witnessing this humiliating mess. A heavy arm is draped over my shoulder and from the corner of my eye I can see the tattoos that cover his hand. But instead of freaking out that the man I saw almost punch a wall is currently touching me, I feel strangely relieved. He's a solid presence at my side, and while I want to say I can handle Dirk myself, the backup is nice to have.

"Who the fuck are you?" Dirk starts to puff up in defense, and then I watch him freeze, his eyes growing wide and his dumb mouth falling open. "Holy shit, wait, you're Maverick —"

He's cut off by tattoo man pivoting to step in front of me, gathering my coat and purse and taking my elbow. "Let's go somewhere else, Specs." His arm is around my waist and he's guiding me out of the bar before I can register what's even happening.

Once we're out on the sidewalk, his arm drops and I whirl around to face him, jabbing my finger into a very solid chest.

"What the hell was that?"

CHAPTER THREE

Maverick

"You're welcome," I shoot back at the redhead currently glaring at me. She's so short, it's almost comical how she's blustering. As if I didn't just save her from that jackass inside the bar.

"I didn't... I don't... I..." She steps backward, shaking her head at me.

Then, in an instant, the fire seems to abandon her, and her entire body starts to cave in, her arms wrapping around her midsection.

"Hey, hey, you're fine. I wouldn't have let him do anything." I'm closing the distance between us, my hands coming to the tops of her arms to support her.

Her choked laugh sounds way too self-deprecating. "Trust me, I can take care of myself when it comes to dirtbag Dirk."

"What?" I ask, amused at the nickname and relieved some of her spunk seems to be coming back.

She rolls her eyes behind big gold-rimmed glasses. "The guy inside. My ex-boyfriend. He's annoying. Also, pathetic and apparently delusional if he thinks cornering me at the bar is the way to win me back. Not that he *could* win me back." The last sentence is mumbled half under her breath.

Her arms are still wrapped around her middle, and I drop my hands from her shoulders, ignoring the twinge in my collarbone.

"Well, thanks for your help," she starts hesitantly, then stops, tugging her lip in between her teeth.

Don't ask me to explain why, but I want to reach up and free it. Instead, I stuff my hands in my pockets.

"It's fine. Are you gonna be okay?" I say gruffly, more than ready to leave and go home, to get away from this woman who's getting to me in a way not many ever do.

She looks up at me and catches my wince as I try to subtly rotate my shoulder that's still throbbing from me moving it in ways I shouldn't.

"I'll be fine, but are *you* okay?"

I shrug. She still doesn't seem to know me, which means she doesn't know how fucking broken I am. "Yeah, just some old injuries acting up." If four weeks is old...and if acting up means my ribs are on fire, and my fucking collarbone feels like a hot poker is being stuck into it.

"Okay. Well, thanks again. I really am sorry you had to get involved in there." She starts to move like she's going to walk away, then stops and looks back at me. "And, earlier today...at the hospital. I didn't mean to overhear anything, I hope you know that. And I hope whatever's wrong gets better soon."

It takes me by surprise that she brings up what she saw in the stairwell, and I'm at a loss. What the fuck am I meant to say? Instead, I give her a brusque nod. She's looking at me, like she's waiting for me to say something. *Too bad, babe, you'll be waiting a long-ass time.* After another few seconds of silence, she gives me a small smile, then turns and walks away.

My eyes don't leave her luscious ass until she turns the corner. As soon as she's out of sight, it's as if a haze is lifted and I can think clearly again. Which leaves me fucking baffled. Sure, I'm not one to shy away from defending a woman — any woman — if I see them being harassed. That's one thing I won't stand for, in any situation. Most of the fucking gossip about me being in fights is because of that kind of shit. But something about my redheaded Specs had me on edge more than normal, and that was before the fucker sat down across from her. The second he opened his fucking mouth, I was ready to go.

I start walking in the opposite direction she went, toward my apartment. It's not a far walk, and I'm hoping it clears my head the rest of the way. Although, if the doctor doesn't clear me to drive when I see him next, I might lose my shit.

The only good thing about this fucked-up day is that she didn't recognize me, even if her asshole ex seemed to. Last thing I need is some goody-two-shoes hero-worshipping me or getting me tangled up in her drama.

No, that's the last I'll see of her.

As soon as I let myself into my apartment, I flick on some lights and drop my shit on the counter. Going to the fridge, I grab a sparkling water and pop the top of the can before settling down on my couch, and closing my eyes.

A small weight lands on my lap a minute later, and a paw lifts to bat my cheek.

"*Mrowp.*"

I look down at the scruffy ball of fur and lift my good hand to scratch behind an ear that's missing a chunk. "Hey, Cat." I get another meow, and then he spins in a circle before settling onto my lap, his purr the only sound in my otherwise silent apartment. Grabbing the remote from the couch beside me, I turn on the TV. Sportscasters are going over the day's highlights, and I lean my head back and close my eyes again. It's not like the stats matter to me right now. I couldn't fucking care less what team won or lost today since my team was traveling, not playing.

I just need the noise.

The next thing I know, light is coming in through my living room window. The sun looks to be just coming up, which means it's still really fucking early. A glance at my phone confirms it's just after six in the morning. I don't have anywhere to be until my rehab session at the stadium later, so for a moment, I contemplate simply moving to my bed and going back to sleep. But as soon as I start to move, it becomes annoyingly evident that I won't be getting any more sleep today. Not unless I give in and take some of the untouched prescription painkillers sitting on my counter. Spending the night on my couch has made everything that was already painful yesterday hurt even worse, my entire body aching and stiff. I drag myself up and stagger down the short hall to the bathroom. Stripping down, I turn on the water as hot as it can go before stepping in.

The heat helps, slowly loosening my muscles that are really not fucking happy I fell asleep sitting upright on the goddamn couch. It wouldn't have been so bad if I was smart enough to lie down, but apparently, exhaustion makes me stupid.

I can hear my phone ringing in the kitchen but ignore it. Whoever the fuck it is, they can wait.

When I eventually step out of the shower and get dressed, I bypass my phone, still not wanting to see who or what is trying to cause shit for me today. Heading out my apartment door, I knock on the door across the hall before letting myself in with a key.

"Ralph? My man, you awake?"

The rattle of his walker across the floor has me looking toward the short hallway. "What the hell are you doing here so early?" he grumbles as he slowly makes his way to the main living area.

I go to cross my arms and then stop. I'm gonna have to wear that goddamn sling today. It's the only way to stop myself from doing shit that hurts. "Are you complaining? I'm here to make omelets."

"It ain't Saturday," he mutters.

"So?"

Ralph eases himself down into his recliner with a grunt. "Well, alright then. What are ya waitin' for?"

He can't see my lips quirk up at his grumbling. He's probably the only person around who's more grumpy than I am, but I know better than to take it personally. Guys like me and Ralph push people away. It takes someone tough to stick around.

I make my way to the kitchen and carefully start to prep the ingredients I stocked his refrigerator with earlier in the week.

"Did you take your meds, old man?" I call out, earning a grumbled "Fuck off" but then a louder "Not yet. I need my coffee."

Grabbing the instant coffee crap he insists is just fine, I prepare his mug and get the water on to boil. Minutes later, I carry it over to him, setting it down with the little container that holds his medication for the day. "Here. Take it." Back in the kitchen, I finish off the omelets, his with just some cheese and mine loaded with ham and vegetables. It takes a couple of trips since I know I shouldn't use my bad arm to carry things, but eventually, the food is set out on the coffee table.

We eat in silence, as always. That's why we get along so well. No need to talk about random shit.

"You able to play again yet?" he asks when he's finished. Ralph's just about the only person who can ask me a question about my injury without pissing me off. I finish my mouthful before answering.

"Not yet. It's only been a month, Doc says another week or two before they'll let me try some load-bearing exercises. Just working on range of motion for now."

Ralph harrumphs. "You really fucked up, boy."

I snort out a half laugh. "Yeah. Thanks." I know he's right. Just like I know Colin's right when he tells me I have to stop bailing out our former foster brother Eli every time he calls. That's how this all happened. He called, sounding beyond freaked, and I tracked his phone to some back road out in the valley. When I realized he'd somehow ended up agreeing to a fucking street race, I only intended on talking him down and somehow getting him out of it.

Then I discovered my brother was high as a motherfucking kite, and the guy who had convinced him to race was not gonna let him out of it.

Instead, he said he'd let me drive.

I thought I had it in the bag. Drive fast? Not a problem.

Until a massive pothole I didn't see knocked me off course and I ended up losing control and spinning into a fucking telephone pole.

Everyone scattered, including my drug-addicted foster brother, and I had to call 911 for myself and come up with some reason for the multiple sets of skid marks on the road.

It took some fast-talking, but with no evidence, I was in the clear. And lucky to walk away with only bruised ribs and a fractured clavicle. It could have been a hell of a lot worse.

It's not the first time I've bailed Eli out of a dumbass situation. Most of the time, I could throw some money at it, and the problem would go away. This time that didn't work.

But I still paid the fucking price.

When I get back to my apartment, I reluctantly pick up my phone when it starts to ring with a call from Colin.

"What's up?" I answer as I make my way to my own kitchen and start making a better cup of coffee than the swill Ralph drinks.

"What's fucking up? Dude. I've been calling and texting for a goddamn hour." Colin sounds stressed, and I immediately set down the mug I had in hand. "I'm on my way. Don't fucking open your phone or do anything until I'm there."

I ignore his instructions, of course, immediately unlocking my phone as soon as we hang up and see all the missed calls and texts from him. Flipping to the web browser I have set to show alerts from major news outlets when my name is mentioned, I see why he's pissed. Someone got a photo last night of me and the chick from the bar. And it looks like a lot more is going on than there actually was.

"Jesus Christ," I grumble, dropping my phone with a clatter. My front door flies open a few minutes later, courtesy of the key Colin has to my place.

"You better have some strong-ass coffee ready," he barks out, running his fingers through his close-cropped hair. He looks down at my phone, then back to me. "I know you looked, even though I told you not to. Care to explain who she is?"

"It's nothing. She's nothing. Just some woman whose ex was bugging her. I stepped in to get rid of him."

"Don't bullshit me, Mav. It doesn't look like nothing. You look like you're fucking in love." His voice is incredulous, and I snort in response.

"I don't do love."

"I know that, but to the rest of the world, that's a lie. Everyone's probably busy writing your fucking wedding vows right now. Do you know who she is, Mav?" Colin pulls out his phone and quickly starts typing. Then he spins it around so I can see the screen. I shouldn't be surprised he figured out her identity so quickly. And I try to tamp down my curiosity, because what the fuck do I care who she is?

"Sadie LeDuc. Head of fundraising for the Vancouver Children's Hospital Foundation. She's not some random chick, Mav."

Colin sinks down and looks at me with an expression that for some reason makes me nervous.

"What?" I growl, pouring the coffee into two mugs and shoving one across the counter to him. "She's nothing to me."

"Unless we make her something to you. This could be a good thing, brother." His voice has turned deceptively soft and I'm equal parts confused and concerned by it.

"What are you getting at?" I ask sharply, lifting my mug to take a small sip of the scorching hot liquid. *Hell of a lot better than the swill Ralph drinks.*

"I'm saying we need to repair your image, and what better way than a love story between you and Miss Goody Two-shoes here to feed the media with something positive for a change?"

Coffee spews from my mouth onto the counter between us. "You're fucking joking."

But Colin just shakes his head slowly. "This photo shows you as a human being, capable of having feelings for someone. That's what we need, Mav. For the world to see a side of you they've never witnessed."

I back away from him. "No. Just, no. Fuck off with that madness, bro." My hand reaches into my pocket for the small piece of metal that's always with me. I start to flip it across my fingers, a habit I picked up as a teenager when my social worker first gave me the coin-sized medal of St. Sebastian. Muny said it was to help me be brave since he's the patron saint of courage. I laughed and asked why a Sikh social worker was carrying around Catholic saint talismans, and she just arched a brow and said, "Does it matter what the source of encouragement is, as long as it has meaning for you?"

"Just listen to me, Mav. You get this Sadie chick to pretend to be with you for a little while. Show up to some charity shit with her. Give the media a few happy photos. Show the team there's more to you than liability. That you're capable of settling down and not being such a wild card."

Okay, that hurts.

"Think about it, Mav. A few months, a couple of public appearances. If she needed you last night for help with her ex, maybe she could use you again. Or we fucking pay her. I don't know, bro, we convince her somehow. But you gotta behave, and you gotta be convincing. And however it ends, we need to make sure you come out looking good." Desperation starts to thread through his words, and I realize Colin's serious. And that sobers me. "We need this. We need to get the public back on your side or..."

He doesn't have to say it. The Tridents are a great team, and I want to stay here in Vancouver. But even I know their patience for my shit is gonna run out soon. Even if all the messes I find myself in are because of my impulsive need to defend others and not because I'm truly the asshole the world thinks I am.

"I'll think about it," I say quietly, stepping forward and picking up my coffee again.

Colin nods. "Good. I'll figure out a media strategy and talk to the Tridents. We need them to believe it's all real, that she's your girl, and you're turning over a new leaf. If I can't find a home address, we'll go see her at the hospital later today."

He picks up his coffee and drinks it, as if the decision has been made and a plan has been set.

Colin's one of the very few people in this life that I trust. Hell, I pay him to manage my career and don't ever question his decisions. So why the fuck do I feel like I just agreed to let him manage my fucking love life?

Chapter Four

Sadie

Have you ever fallen off the edge of a single bed?

I don't recommend it. Zero stars.

With a groan, I heave myself up from the carpeted floor of my tiny bedroom and push back the mess of red hair from my face. Blinking sleepily, my vision becomes more clear and I instantly wish it wouldn't. Because seeing the piles and piles of boxes that surround me just reminds me of how much my life freaking sucks right now.

When I discovered Dirk and his paralegal in bed, very much naked, I had no choice but to move out. It was his apartment, and I had sold most of my furniture before I moved in with him. After two weeks at my parents' house, I needed to get out. But the Vancouver rental market is awful at the best of times.

Which is how I ended up in a sketchy but furnished one-bedroom apartment on the outskirts of downtown. Close enough to commute to work, but definitely not a great neighbourhood.

And a far cry from the high-rise apartment Dirk and I lived in for six months before everything went sideways.

Dragging my feet, I make my way into the tiny kitchen, intent on making some coffee. My phone is charging on the counter, and after the coffee maker is turned on, I pick it up to scroll the news headlines. Only, instead of a mindless scroll, I end up choking on the sip of water I've taken when I see the virtual flood of messages waiting for me.

Texts from people I haven't spoken to in months, years even. Dozens of them. Scrolling through, I see one from my sister and open that one.

> **SIENNA: OMFG YOU'RE DATING MAV-ERICK KING?! SADIEEEEEEEEEE! I NEED TO KNOW EVERYTHING!!!!!!!!**

Except her message makes absolutely no sense to me. Other than that name... Didn't Dirk call tattoo guy Maverick? Dread starts to pool in my stomach when I click a link to a gossip magazine she sent. The photo that uploads has me clapping a hand over my mouth to muffle my shriek.

It's not a great photo, clearly taken on someone's phone at the bar last night. But it's clear enough to see who's in it. Tattoo guy has his arm around me and is looking down at me with an expression on his face that I definitely don't remember him having. Instead of looking all mean and scary, he almost looks...affectionate? I'm pretty sure it's when he was giving Dirk shit, and pretending he was there with me, but dang, I didn't realize he was that good of an actor.

My musings about the photo come to an abrupt halt when the headline steals my attention: *Tridents' Third Baseman*

Maverick King Seen with Mystery Woman. Is the Bad Boy of Baseball Settling Down at Last?

"Oh my God." Suddenly Dirk's shock makes sense. He's a huge Tridents fan and used to bug me nonstop to get free tickets from Willow. It felt so icky to me, I never asked. Guess that should've been a red flag that the rest of him was just as icky.

I scan the rest of the article which tells me nothing except that he's some hotshot baseball player who's infamous for getting into trouble off the field. Then it talks about a recent car crash, and how he's on the injured list and unable to play. My hand comes up to my mouth again as I realize that's why he winced last night. I scan the text and see *bruised ribs and fractured clavicle* pop out at me. Yeah, even with my limited medical knowledge simply gleaned from working in a hospital, I can imagine those would hurt.

As I'm reading, my phone vibrates with an incoming call. I answer without looking at the number, my mind still reeling.

"Sadie LeDuc? John Tucker with *Vancouver Daily*. Can we get a statement on your relationship with Maverick King?"

My mouth gapes open, then flies shut as I hit the end button on the call. This isn't good. How on earth did they figure out who I am? Another call comes in from another unknown number. I hit decline, only for it to start ringing again. This time, it's my best friend Ali.

I answer, but don't even get a word out before she's yelling in my ear.

"Holy shit, Sadie. Good job, girlfriend! I knew you had a secret wild side, but baseball's bad boy? Damn, I'm impressed."

"For goodness' sake, don't be so gullible, it's all a misunderstanding!" I shout into the phone. Ali falls silent, and all I hear is my own pulse pounding in my ear. "It's not real. None of it. Well, I mean, I did see him at a bar last night and he did put his arm around me, but that was just to get Dirk to shut up."

"Maverick King defended you in front of dirtbag Dirk?" Amusement laces her tone. "That's honestly a better story than my bestie dating the hottest man in Vancouver and not telling me."

I groan and flop down on my bed. "Ali, help me. What do I do? The press has already found me, my sister is sending me shouty all caps text messages, and it's complete garbage."

"Okay, breathe, Sadie." Ali's teacher voice kicks on. The voice she uses to wrangle twenty kindergarteners every single day. "This isn't the end of the world. You've got a friend that works for his team, right? You can reach out to her, and I'm sure she'll be able to help clear this all up."

I'm already nodding, my breathing slowly settling. "You're right. Yes. Of course. I'll call Willow today. Thanks, Ali."

"I gotchu, bestie. But can I just say, a little romp with Maverick King could be kinda fun!"

That pulls a small laugh from me, even as the idea of a little *anything* with that man makes me shiver. "You're terrible. I better go, thanks for having my back."

"Always."

I hang up, only to have my phone immediately start ringing again, this time with an unlisted number.

"Oh my God, stop!" I groan, knowing it's futile. I decline the call and drop it on the counter. Any calm I'd found talking to Ali is gone as I watch the screen continue to light up with a never-ending barrage of calls and messages. I start to shake as I step back from the phone, staring at it in horror like it's a ticking time bomb. The tremble continues until I sink down to the floor, feeling beyond overwhelmed.

I didn't think my life could get any more out of control after the Dirk mess. But this is beyond anything I could have imagined.

Somehow, I need to make it through my work day and get a hold of Willow. Ali's right, she should be able to help me clear this all up. And then we can have a laugh about how the media actually thought for a hot minute that I, Sadie LeDuc, would be dating one of the Vancouver Tridents.

Oh, how naive I was to actually believe that making it through my work day would be the easy part. After only an hour at work, I have to close — and lock — my office door to keep nosy coworkers out. My cell phone is still blowing up with messages and phone calls to the point I think I need to figure out how to make my number unlisted.

No matter how hard I try to focus, it's not happening. My email inbox is filling up with messages from all kinds of people, some sharing more headlines and some asking if it's all true. I want so badly to respond with a resounding NO, but something is holding me back. A futile hope that this Maverick King guy will fix everything, or maybe an even more futile hope that this is all just a horribly bad dream I'm going to wake up from.

But when the phone on my desk rings, I have to answer it, praying these awful reporters haven't tracked down this number yet. Just another reason why we need call display on these antiquated phones.

"Hello, Sadie speaking," I say, impressed with how I manage to keep my tone professional.

"Do you really expect me to believe Maverick King is dating *you?*" Dirk's condescension comes through loud and clear, and I grip the phone tighter.

"Excuse me? My personal life is none of your damn business," I hiss, grateful my office door is already closed. My eyes flutter closed as the sick feeling that took root in my stomach this morning grows. "Just leave me alone, Dirk."

"Knock it off, Sadie," he scoffs. "I don't know what that was last night, but your stunt failed. You're not dating him. There's no way. Honestly, I'm surprised. I didn't think you had it in you to lie like that. So if you're trying to make me jealous, just give up. It's not going to work."

For the second time today, my mouth falls open in disbelief as my eyes fly open. "Are you... Are you serious? You think this is about me wanting to make you jealous?" My voice rises near the end, even as a wild desire to shove it to Dirk and lie, and say it absolutely is real, crosses my mind. God, the look on his face would be priceless if he actually believed I moved on from him to one of his baseball idols.

But I can't drag this out just to possibly get Dirk to leave me alone... Can I? What would happen if I went to Maverick's people and asked them... No. It's crazy. Dirk's an ass, but he's not wrong. A guy like Maverick won't want anything to do with me. He's probably already sent his statement refuting this madness to the press, meaning it's only a matter of time before Dirk's phoning me back to rub it in my face.

"Goodbye Dirk," I say, hanging the phone up before I lose it completely.

What a flipping mess. The very fact that I entertained the idea of trying to get a professional athlete to pretend to be with me just to make my cheating ex-boyfriend go away is absurd and proof of how low I've sunk.

My hands reach out blindly, grabbing papers and shuffling them into a pile. Anything to try and bring some order into this mess. But it's a lost cause.

Dropping my head to the desk with a groan, I give in to my personal pity party. For someone who thrives on an organized, controlled life, I've never before felt so totally out of control. My head is spinning, the room closing in on me. There's not enough oxygen in the air, and I start to gasp, desperate for a full breath.

Pressure in my chest builds and builds, and I force myself to stand, somehow knowing I need to move and snap out of this panic spiral. As I pace closer to my office door, I can hear muffled voices outside. Focusing in on them, I'm relieved to hear they're not talking about me or the photo. Words filter through about budgets and equipment requests from various departments. Typical topics for the foundation office. The pacing and focusing on the innocuous chatter outside helps calm my racing heart. Not everyone is gossiping about me and this insanity about Maverick King, even if my cell phone's call log and email inbox say otherwise.

Moving back to my desk, I sit down and perform a few breathing exercises. I just need to get through the next few hours. Then I can go home, take a long hot bath in the small but at least functional bathtub, and call Willow. I need to beg her to help me figure out a way to clear this all up.

My mind always feels better with a plan in place, so I turn my attention to the list of charitable donors I still need to reach out to for our upcoming gala.

The rest of my day passes with me ignoring phone calls and focusing on sending emails and letters to our donors. But as I push back from my computer, ready to go home and bring this insane day to a close, a knock on my door stops me.

"Come in," I say, pulling on my cardigan over the sleeveless blouse I wore today. My boss, the chair of the foundation, steps in, a perturbed look on his face.

"Sadie, I realize the situation may be beyond your control, and far be it for me to participate in any interoffice gossip. But you need to know that hospital security has had to escort multiple members of the press off the hospital premises today, all of whom were trying to get to you."

"What?" I gasp, sinking back down in my chair, any calm I'd managed to pull together gone in an instant. "I'm so sorry, Gus."

His lined face softens to resemble the likable man he normally is. "I'm guessing you and your" — he clears his throat — "*friend* didn't anticipate this type of response to this morning's news. Perhaps you should start your weekend early, and consider working from home next week. At least until the excitement dies down."

I nod robotically. Working from my crappy apartment? Sure. That'll be fun... I suppress a shudder. But he's got a point. The patients and families don't need to be wading through a sea of ravenous reporters just to get here.

Gus shifts on his feet, and I know he has more he wants to say.

"Can I do anything else for you today, Gus?" I ask, hoping he says no and leaves me alone.

"Actually, it's more a suggestion than anything. But perhaps you could ask your friend to lend his influence to the gala? Maybe a donation to the silent auction or some publicity to boost ticket sales?"

Part of me is stunned Gus is asking me this. It's not much better than when dirtbag Dirk tried to get me to ask Willow for Tridents' tickets. But he's my boss, not my ex, so I can't tell him no quite as easily.

"I'll see what I can do," I say hoarsely. Thankfully, Gus seems to accept that answer.

"Right. Well. Take care getting out of here, and we'll see you back in a few days when the excitement dies down." He moves to the door, and all I can think is that once he's gone I can get out of here and give in to the tears that are trying to build behind my eyes. *Keep it together, Sadie, just until you're home.*

Then there's another knock on my office door. Gus is closest, so he opens it. And when I look up to see who it is, I have to accept it's going to be a while before I can go home and give in to the breakdown I desperately want to have.

CHAPTER FIVE

Maverick

We should have come earlier. That's all I can think when I finally make it past the fucking vultures outside the hospital. I didn't expect them to be this aggressive, that they'd hunt her down at work. Hell, how did they even figure out who she is? Then again, Colin managed to do so with a quick internet search; maybe it's not that hard. We'll have to up her privacy settings and security if I can get her to agree to this madness.

I get shown to Sadie's office and *fuck*. I wasn't prepared for my reaction to seeing her again. Even dressed like a goddamn librarian, there's no denying she's a beautiful woman, with endless curves and that fiery red hair I still want to see wrapped around my fist. But the panic she's just barely managing to hide makes me want to turn around and storm back outside to rage at those fuckers trying to get their goddamn sound bites even more. Thank fuck Colin basically shoved me inside and is handling them for me.

"Let's go, Specs," I say gruffly, ignoring the wide-eyed stare of the old guy standing across from Sadie. "We gotta talk."

She stands up, not meeting my eyes.

"Gus, I'll touch base from home tomorrow," she says coolly to the older man. He gives her a nod and me an inscrutable look before walking out. She follows him to the door, closing it behind him before turning to look at me. Exhaustion is etched across her face, and it hits me like a punch to the gut.

"I guess you've seen the news."

She lets out a choked laugh and starts to pace the small space between me and the door. "The news. Is that what we're calling it? How about salacious gossip? Slander? Misrepresentation?" Her hands are flailing in the air as she talks, strands of red hair flying loose from her bun.

"Would you stop?" I rasp, putting out my good arm to bring her movements to a halt. "We can figure this out. We just gotta get out of here."

Another harsh laugh escapes her, the hard sound jarring to my ears.

"Easier said than done, buddy. Apparently, your reporter friends are waiting outside."

"I know," I answer calmly, as if I'm facing down a wild animal instead of a short redhead in another fucking sweater set. "My agent is outside getting rid of them so we can leave."

"What's he saying to them?" she asks me sharply, her vibrant green eyes narrowing behind those glasses. "Clearing up this misunderstanding, I hope?"

"That's what we need to discuss," I say mildly, intentionally keeping it vague. If I can't get her on board with Colin's insanity, this is gonna get ugly.

My phone vibrates, and it can only be one person since everyone else is blocked right now. Mindful of the daggers she's shooting my way, I pull it from my pocket and glance down quickly.

COLIN: Coast is clear. Is she in?

My gaze darts back up to Sadie standing in front of me with her hands on her hips, her small chest heaving with every breath. I thumb out a short response.

MAV: Not yet.

"Can we go somewhere to talk?" I ask again, stuffing my phone back in my pocket. Her gaze travels to my left arm that's back in the fucking sling, courtesy of Colin, then back to my face before she gives me a brusque shake of her head. *Well, shit.* I mentally try to scramble together a way to convince her to at least talk to me when she beats me to the punch.

"We can talk right here. I'm not leaving this office until this mess is dealt with. I don't even *know* you and the press thinks we're together. Good grief, before this morning I didn't even know your name!"

"Okay..." I take a deep breath, walk over to one of the chairs, and sit down before gesturing to the other. "Can we at least sit?" I pull off my ball cap and smooth my hand over my hair before setting it back on, backward now.

She waits several seconds before marching over and sitting down across from me. Her feet are folded at the ankle and swear to fucking Christ, she's living up to her *Specs* nickname right now with how prim and proper she looks.

"Listen. You're right, we don't know each other. And this situation is fucked-up. I realize that." I suck in a breath. I fucking hate talking. "But it could also be good. In a way."

Her eyebrows lift as she stares at me in disbelief. "Good?"

I nod slowly. "Your ex, the asshole last night. I'm guessing he's already tried to get in touch today?" I phrase it as a question, even though instinctively, I know the answer. Guys like that want what they can't have. And me staking my claim last night was like a red flag to a bull. Sure enough, after a second, she nods, her shoulders sagging slightly.

"And unless I misunderstood you last night, you have no interest in him anymore."

Another nod.

This isn't exactly how Colin suggested I approach things, but his idea of offering her money was an instant no. I don't know this chick, but I do know she's not the type to be bought like that. Which is why I'm leaning on his other idea and tapping into the ex angle.

"Then we let the public believe the lie for a little while. Get him to realize you've moved on to someone else and he'll leave you alone. He knew who I was last night, so I'm guessing he's a baseball fan. Trust me, nothing will piss him off more than seeing you date a player from his favourite team."

Her arms cross over her chest as she studies me for a several minutes. I try not to let it show how much I fucking hate being under scrutiny.

"What's in it for you?" she finally asks.

And this is where it could all fall apart. If I tell her the truth, that I need her good girl image to clean up mine, she could laugh in my face. Or if she decides being connected to someone like me is a bad idea, then I've got nothing. Because it probably is a really fucking bad idea. But I refuse to lie to her.

"My recent accident put me in a bad position, image wise. My agent thinks the media's reaction to that one photo was a good thing and could turn things around for me. If they think I'm happily in love, especially with someone like you, it could help."

She just keeps staring. And staring. "You don't seem like the kind of guy to care about your image."

I shrug, already over the whole talking part of today. I want out of here, and I need her by my side. "I care about my team and my career. And if this helps both of those things, then I'm in."

Sadie draws in a ragged breath, her face so expressive I swear I can see the wheels turning. She's gonna need a better poker face if we're going to pull this off. "Okay. Here's the deal. I'll stay quiet and not try to set the record straight. In return, you will come with me to my foundation's big gala in four weeks. My ex will be there since his law firm is a major sponsor, and I'd rather not deal with him alone."

I'm already nodding. Four weeks sounds good to me, but she's apparently not done.

"We need to set some ground rules, though. If your image is so bad, there must be a reason, and I don't need my own reputation being dragged down with it."

I never give a shit about defending myself when the media twists things around to make me the villain, but for some reason right now, I do. I care a hell of a lot that this woman doesn't think I'm the asshole everyone else believes I am.

"Just so we're clear, I'm not a bad guy," I start, my voice gravelly. "I do shit the media loves to spin into me being an asshole, but they don't bother looking at *why* I do it."

Her lips tip up in a small smile. "You're saying you're a bad boy with a good moral code?"

A short laugh escapes me, and the sound is rusty and unfamiliar to my ears. "Guess so."

We both fall silent again, but her arms have relaxed, and she's not looking at me like I'm crazy anymore.

"Four weeks. I'll play along for four weeks, you'll come to the gala with me, and then we figure a way to end this without anymore drama."

I put out my good hand to shake on it, then pull it back. "You should know, my agent will probably try to get us to do some appearances and shit."

"Control the narrative, I get it." She's nodding and doesn't seem concerned. "And if I need you to do something for me, to keep my ex off my back or whatever, I'll let you know."

My hand reaches out again and she takes it, shaking it firmly. When our hands fall, I'm at a loss as to what to do next. She said yes, Colin's plan worked.

What now?

"Well, first order of business is getting to know each other, don't you think?" Sadie says, her tone sounding somewhat forced. But I latch onto it, grateful she's at least capable of figuring out our next steps.

"Why don't you give me your number, and we can set up some time to talk." She rubs her forehead, and I don't miss her grimace. "Just not today. It's been a heck of a day."

When she holds out her phone expectantly, I stare at it. My phone has exactly five contacts in it.

Colin, Eli, the owner of the Tridents, my head coach, and Ralph.

Those are also the only five people that have my direct number.

And now, this stranger who's just agreed to pretend to be my girlfriend is about to become number six.

As I type my info into her phone, knowing she's doing the same on mine, a part of me wonders why this doesn't feel more uncomfortable.

Why it feels almost...right.

CHAPTER SIX

Sadie

SADIE: Okay, let's share the basics. I'm born and raised here in the Vancouver area. My parents live out in Langley, I'm the oldest of two siblings. I love animals, reading, and swimming. Oh and I'm allergic to bees.

MAVERICK: Got it.

SADIE: It would help if you told me something about you?

MAVERICK: I'm from up north. No family. Baseball is my life. No allergies.

SADIE: Wow, I feel like I know you so well...

MAVERICK: Sarcasm isn't a good look for you Specs.

SADIE: Don't call me that. Anyway, moving on. How did we meet?

MAVERICK: Don't care. Make it up. I hate text messages by the way.

I stare at my phone, wanting to scream and hit something. He's worse than my younger brother at communicating, and that's saying something since Simon communicates mostly in grunts.

I avoided contacting Maverick all weekend, needing a day to wrap my head around everything. But when I woke up today and realized I wouldn't be heading into the office, I knew I couldn't put everything off any longer.

Getting things started with Maverick is the only way out of this mess, and two days trapped in this crappy apartment worried the vultures that found me at work would find me anywhere, has me going crazy. To say nothing of the guilt I feel, as I ignore the pull to check my phone for anymore headlines and the curious calls and messages from the few family and friends I actually care about.

Honestly, that second part has been the hardest. I hate lying, abhor it, really. Which is going to make talking to my family and friends painful. But Maverick insisted that no one can know. I haven't had the guts to tell him that Ali already knows... But since his agent-brother person does, I figure it's all fair.

My phone pings with a new text message. I let myself glance at who sent it, and when I see who it is, I click immediately to open.

> **WILLOW: Girl! Care to share why I came back from a weekend away with my family to have the mother of all news bombs dropped in my lap?**

> **WILLOW: WHY DIDN'T YOU TELL ME?! Setting aside the whole, I'm head of media relations and this kinda stuff is literally my job to know, I thought we were friends... How could you not say you started dating one of my guys. I'm not mad, promise. Just surprised. Meet me at the diner by the stadium for lunch?**

> **SADIE: The one the players go to?**

I chew on my thumbnail as I wait for her to answer. On one hand, I'd love to see her. But I also have to keep up the lie. And there's the media to contend with...

> **WILLOW: Yep. The owner, Maura, is great at keeping any press far away, she's got a zero tolerance rule. You'll be safe from the cameras.**

Well, that's reassuring. And I guess I can't avoid her forever.

SADIE: Okay. See you around noon?

WILLOW: It's a date. Can't wait to hear
ALL ABOUT IT!

I groan to myself. Freaking Maverick and his inability to hold a conversation. I have no idea what to say to Willow. What kind of a story to spin. And he's useless. I debate texting Colin since Maverick gave me his number as well. But no, I'm going to have to figure this out on my own.

At least I have a good reason to leave my apartment. And if anyone can handle the press, should it be needed, it's Willow.

When I reach the diner that's right next to the Tridents' stadium an hour later, Willow is waving at me from inside, a huge smile on her face. I walk in, hoping I don't look as deer-in-the-headlights as I feel.

"Oh my God, I am in shock!" Willow says by way of greeting, dragging me in for a hug when I reach the booth. "You tamed Maverick King. Wonders will never cease."

It baffles me how she could possibly believe it's all real, but as we sit down, I see the excitement on her face, and I have to reconcile that what seems insane to me isn't that way to everyone else.

"I wouldn't say I tamed him," I start slowly, and Willow giggles.

"Of course not. Where's the fun in that?" Her expression sobers as she reaches one hand across the table to cover mine. "In all seriousness, I'm glad someone as good and kind as you managed to see the real Maverick. He's not what the media portrays him to be, but so few people bother to find that out."

My eyes widen. "I...I know. He's a bad boy with a moral code," I blurt out, repeating what I said to Maverick in my office last week. And Willow throws her head back in laughter.

"Oh my God, yes. That's exactly it. It took me a while to see it, but Uncle Mike always did. That's why he's had such a hard time trying to decide what to do with Mav. I mean" — Willow leans forward, her voice dropping low — "Mav's recklessness can't continue, even if those of us that know him realize it's coming from a good place. It's not prudent for the team to be seen supporting it or even allowing it. But the last thing we want to do is abandon him. He's a good guy and a great player. He just needs to stop making dumb decisions."

I nod along with her, pretending I know exactly what she's talking about. But inside, my head is spinning. I'm realizing I truly have no clue what I've gotten myself into.

A waitress comes over and takes our orders, and as soon as she leaves, Willow leans back in. "Alright, spill. When did you two start dating? Wait, did you meet at the hospital?" Her hands lift to cover her heart. "That's so romantic."

"Okay, slow down, lady," I say, shaking my head. "Just because you're happy and in love doesn't mean everyone else is surrounded by hearts and rainbows."

Willow looks confused and I immediately try to backpedal from that unintentional cynicism.

"I just mean, it's new between Maverick and me. Yes, we met at the hospital, but we're so different. We didn't want anyone to know until we figured out if it was going to work between us."

There. That's as close to the truth as I can make it.

"You know they say, opposites attract." Willow smiles. "You're just what Maverick needs. Someone calm and steady to show him he can relax and let down his guard."

Our lunch is delivered, saving me from having to fabricate a response to that. But part of me wonders what Maverick is guarding himself from.

Willow fills the time while we're eating with updates on her relationship with Ronan Sinclair, the new first baseman for the Tridents. They're so happy together, even though I know they had a couple of bumps in the road not that long ago.

When we're finished, Willow grabs the bill with a wink aimed my way. "Business expense, girlfriend. We discussed the media situation surrounding one of my players."

I choke out a laugh, but don't argue with a free lunch. As we leave the diner, I start to turn toward my parked car when Willow gestures toward the large stadium. "Are you coming to see Mav? When I left, he was almost done with his rehab session. I can show you where to find him if you want."

"Oh, um," I try to come up with an excuse but fail as Willow looks at me expectantly. "Yeah, sure. That would be great, thanks."

I fall in step beside her, and we cross the short distance to the stadium grounds. She opens a back door and leads me through a maze of corridors that has me feeling dizzy. But then we come to a stop outside large glass doors with the Tridents' logo. And there he is.

Walking toward us, his shirt is wet with sweat and a towel is draped over his neck. His arm is in a sling again, and a scowl is etched across his face. His intense masculinity has me swallowing down the rush of unwelcome attraction I feel. Fine, he's an attractive man. Doesn't mean I want to do anything about it.

"Mav, look who I found," Willow calls out, and his head snaps up to look at us. To his credit, he doesn't falter, walking straight to us with an emotionless face.

"Hi," I say softly, waiting to see what he does.

"Hey, Specs," is his gruff reply. Then, to my utter shock, he leans in and his lips graze my cheek, making me shiver. He moves beside me, and as if I wasn't stunned enough, I feel his hand grasp mine. "Hi, Willow. I didn't realize you know Sadie."

How the hell is he so calm right now? I look at his face, and it's still unreadable. Willow, on the other hand, is grinning so wide, I can't imagine her face doesn't hurt.

"Okay, I'm sorry, but this is freaking adorable. I'm so happy for you two." She claps her hands together.

"Who are we happy for?"

We all turn at the new voice, and an unfamiliar older man wearing a suit comes striding down the hall.

"Hi, my girl. Mav," he greets Willow and Maverick, then turns to me, his hand outstretched. "Mike Cartwright. Are you one of Willow's friends?"

"She's dating Mav!" Willow blurts out before I can say anything, and I feel Maverick's hand tighten around mine.

The man, Mike, raises his eyebrows as he glances from me to the man next to me. Then his eyes drop down to where Maverick is still holding my hand.

"Right. You're the one from the photo."

Just then, everything clicks. This is *Mike Cartwright*. As in, Willow's uncle. As in, the owner of the team. I gulp and nod.

"Yes, I am. Nice to meet you." Everything is on the line for Maverick. I have to sell this. Dropping his hand, I lift mine to shake Mike's hand.

"Well, I hope our guy treats you right." There's no mistaking the intense stare he turns on Maverick, and I slip my arm around his waist, leaning in with what I hope is a smitten expression.

"He does, I promise."

Mike's face softens as he looks back at me. "Good. Nice to see you, Mav. I hear I'll be getting an update on your recovery from the team later today. Hope it's good news. I'd better run, Willow, we have that budget meeting. Are you coming?"

"Yup." Willow wraps me in a hug, whispering in my ear, "So, so, so happy for you. We'll catch up soon."

Then she's gone, along with her uncle, and I'm left standing there, arm in arm with Maverick. I step away instantly, and to my surprise, I miss the feel of his solid body against mine.

"Sorry, I didn't mean to ambush you here. Willow and I were out for lunch and she assumed I was coming to see you. I couldn't figure a way to get out of it."

"Sadie, stop." Maverick's firm tone halts my ramble. "It's fine. It's honestly probably a good thing. They seemed to buy it, that we're together."

My head bobs up and down. "Okay. Cool. Yay! Mission accomplished."

He gives me a hard look. "Not yet."

I gulp again. "I know. But it's a good start."

At that, he seems to deflate slightly. "Yeah." Lifting his hat from his head, he runs his fingers through dark blond hair before setting the hat back down. "C'mon, I'll walk you to your car."

He's silent the entire way back to where I parked outside the diner. But once I'm sitting down, instead of walking away, Maverick stops and leans down to look at me. "What did you tell Willow about us?"

I raise my eyebrows. "Oh, so now you want to discuss our backstory?"

His lips actually tip up for the briefest of seconds. "Just so we're on the same page."

I click my seat belt in place before answering with a wry smirk of my own.

"I'll text you."

Chapter Seven

Sadie

"Nope. You're not wearing that." Ali snatches the blouse out of my hand and shoves it back in my closet. "The email from what's his face, the agent guy, said 'casual shopping excursion.' You don't wear a freaking blouse and dress pants to spend the afternoon with your boyfriend."

I drop back down on my bed, already exhausted, and it's not even noon. "This is crazy, isn't it? A staged outing to a farmer's market with a man who would probably rather be doing anything else with his Wednesday evening."

"A *hot* man who *needs* you. Don't sell yourself short." Ali tosses a tank top at me that I catch at the last minute.

I look at it with a frown. "I can't wear this."

"Yes, you can." She passes over a pair of shorts that I've worn exactly once, last summer when we went to the beach for the day.

"Ali, these barely cover my butt," I protest, but my alleged best friend is ignoring me, whipping out a sheer kimono and throwing that at me as well.

"Listen, babe, I know you're used to covering up and blending in, but it's okay to let loose a little. Relax and have a good time," she says, trying to be soothing, but honestly, it just makes me feel defensive.

"Blending in is safer," I grumble.

"Blending in is boring," Ali fires back. "And that's the last thing you want to be called ever again. Right?"

I huff, but nod. "Right." But it's not really that easy. A lifetime of never wanting to cause trouble or draw attention to myself isn't so simple to move on from. Still, I'll let her win this time.

"You're going to look hot as hell. Maverick King will be tripping over his own feet."

"I don't want him tripping, I just want him not laughing," I mumble half to myself as I pull on the darn shorts.

"No one is going to laugh." Ali's hands land on my shoulders, and I look into her eyes. Obviously, the anxiety I'm feeling is clear on my face because she pulls me in for a long hug. "You're beautiful, smart, kind, and all-around amazing. Is it crazy to pretend to date Maverick freaking King? Yeah, maybe. But think of what a cool story you'll always have."

"NDA, remember?"

Ali just snorts. "Okay, fine, so when we're eighty and in our rocking chairs on the porch of an old folks' home, we can let everyone think we've lost our marbles when we talk about those few weeks you had the hottest guy in baseball on your arm."

We both dissolve into giggles. "Fine, let's get this over with." I quickly finish dressing and go to braid my hair, but Ali's already shaking her head.

"Leave it down. Trust me."

I certainly don't trust my own judgment right now, so I do as she says, grabbing a small purse and stuffing my keys, wallet, and sunglasses in it. We make our way to my door, and I check my phone to confirm nothing's changed, although why it would've in the past half hour, I don't know.

Sure enough, the last message about today is the email from Colin.

```
Sadie and Mav,
You'll meet one street over from
the market at 5pm. Hold hands,
look cute. This is a casual
outing, not a planned PR event,
which means you need to act like
no one's watching. But they are.
I've got photographers staged
to grab a couple of shots that
we can control, but guaranteed
there will be more taken that
we don't know about.
It's showtime, kids.
Colin
```

Look cute. Act natural. Sure, that sounds simple enough. And I repeat that to myself the entire short drive to where I'm meeting Maverick. But when I see him leaning against a black SUV, any semblance of calm I had dissipates in seconds. My hands are still gripping the steering wheel so tight my knuckles are white, and I'm staring straight ahead when I hear a light knock on my window. Gulping in a breath, I let go and unlock the door.

Maverick takes that for the invitation it is and opens the door before crouching down beside me. "Hey, Specs."

"Don't call me that," I whisper, but it's a feeble request. Part of me kind of likes the pet name, even if I suspect he initially meant it in a derogatory sense.

"You ready for this?" he asks, not even acknowledging my request. I should be mad at the dismissal of my complaint, but all I can focus on is how good he smells.

Like a walk in a forest after it's rained, with a hint of something deeper that has me leaning forward before I can stop myself.

Then he stands up and backs away, and I catch myself before I start to fall out of my darn car. I put my purse over my shoulder and climb out of my car.

There's no missing the way his gaze travels up and down my body when I'm upright, and I inwardly thank Ali for pushing me to wear the shorts when he pauses on my legs. I had a growth spurt when I hit puberty, but instead of growing taller, I developed curves. It took me a long time to hit a point of acceptance for my midsize body. But seeing Maverick stare at my legs with unmistakable heat in his eyes, longer than he probably should, is doing a lot for my self-esteem.

Of course, he doesn't say anything, not even when he realizes I've caught him staring. Instead, he just turns in the direction of the market and starts walking.

Here goes nothing.

We slowly walk over to the rows of stalls that make up the local farmer's market. I love coming here on the weekend and taking my time wandering through while looking at everything. But being here today with this man at my side has all of my senses heightened. The sun is brighter, even from behind my sunglasses, the sounds and voices sharper in my ears. I find myself tightening my hold on Maverick's hand, my gaze darting around, trying to see if I can catch anyone paying attention to us. When it's not overtly obvious in the first few minutes, I force myself to relax.

But in order to sell this, we have to do more than walk around hand in hand with what feels like ten feet of distance between us. Maverick is stiff next to me, not looking at me or saying anything. Spying my favourite florist stall, I tug him in that direction. "This vendor always has stunning flowers, I'd love to get some for my office," I say brightly, hoping my cheery tone doesn't sound as forced as it feels.

I spend a few minutes *oohing* and *aahing* over the bright dahlias and sunflowers. Maverick is a wall of silence behind me, and it's becoming more and more clear that he's not just uncomfortable, he genuinely doesn't know how to act.

Has this man seriously never had a girlfriend or gone on a date? It's baffling, really. But Colin's words are in my ear. Act natural, look cute. And assume anyone and everyone is watching.

I pretend to be busy choosing between two bouquets as I try to come up with a plan of action. Somehow, I need him to relax and at least try to pretend he's enjoying himself. But as I settle on a riotous mix of dahlias, a small voice reaches us.

"'Scuse me, are you Maverick King?"

I turn to see the big, tattooed man crouch down in front of a kid who can't be more than six.

"Yeah, I am." His voice sounds gruff but kind.

"You're a really good player. I wanna be on the Tridents when I grow up."

Oh my God, this kid is adorable. There's no avoiding the smile growing on my face as I watch them interact. A woman is standing to the side, watching the kid like a hawk. She catches my eye and smiles nervously. I try to give a reassuring grin back to her.

"You want an autograph?" Maverick asks, and the way the kid's eyes light up makes me want to melt.

He nods eagerly, and the mom steps forward, a pen and note pad already out and ready. A few minutes later and Maverick's waving goodbye as he straightens from his crouch, turning back to me.

"Sorry."

My head is moving side to side as I just clutch the bouquet of flowers to my chest. "Don't be, that was really sweet."

To my utter shock, pink colours his cheeks as he stuff his hands into the pockets of his shorts. "Kids don't come up to me that often. The tattoos, I guess."

I take a chance he won't push me away, and slip my arm back through his good one and lean in. "You're not so scary, Maverick."

His head turns sharply as he looks down at me, something like disbelief flashing over his face. It's gone in an instant, but I saw it. And it makes me wonder when he last had someone tell him something like that.

Tell him that he's not a bad guy.

"You gettin' those?" he asks and I nod. Then he takes the bouquet from me and looks to the vendor. "How much?"

Before I can protest, he hands the vendor some cash, and then leads me out of the stall, the flowers tucked into his arm.

"Thank you," I say quietly. "I'll pay you back."

The hard look he gives me is obvious even from under the brim of his ball cap. "I can handle getting you some flowers, Specs."

I gulp at the low rumble to his words. Maybe he's not such a lost cause on this whole dating thing after all.

For the next hour, we wander through the market, sampling and buying a few things here and there. Maverick isn't approached again, but I start to notice the stares we get from some people and catch more than a couple of phones pointed our way. Even though I know one or two of them could be the photographers Colin arranged, it still makes my skin crawl, having all this unwanted attention on me.

Maverick seems unaffected, his gaze straight forward, ignoring the whispers and finger pointing.

"How do you stand it?" I whisper as we stand off to the side, waiting for the coffee cart to finish our iced drinks.

To his credit, he doesn't ask me what I mean. I guess he wasn't as immune to the stares and murmurs as he seemed.

"Comes with the job. If it weren't for the fans, I wouldn't get paid to do the one thing I'm good at."

His response makes me pause. "But they're not always friendly like that little boy, are they?"

Again, he just shrugs. "Nope. Can't please everybody."

There's so much he isn't saying, but this isn't the time to push him to explain. We get our iced coffees and continue wandering through the market once again in silence. But at least Maverick's body language has relaxed. He's holding his coffee with his good hand but crooked his other elbow to the side for me to slide my arm through it. I try to be gentle, aware this is his injured side, but if there's any discomfort, he doesn't let it show.

Until someone bumps into me, hard, making me collide with his bad arm.

His grunt of pain is brief, then he's stepping forward, his hand on the shoulder of the man who knocked into me.

"Watch where you're going," he growls. The guy turns around, a scowl on his face that deepens when he obviously recognizes Maverick.

"Hey, it's fine," I say quickly, sliding between the two. It's probably not the smartest place to be, but the last thing we need is a scene. "I'm fine, it was an accident."

But Maverick ignores me, glaring at the other man for a second. Thank goodness, he backs off first, raising his hands. "Whatever. Sorry." He turns and is gone, disappearing into the crowd of marketgoers.

Tentatively, I reach out and touch Maverick's side. "Come on, let's go." His Adam's apple bobs up and down as he swallows, but I watch his jaw unclench. He's still stiff as he pivots on his foot and starts to walk toward the street we parked on. He's a step ahead of me, but I wait until we're a little farther away from the market before I call out to him.

"Slow down, please."

He comes to an abrupt stop, and when I reach him, his stare is hard, unflinching. Immediately, I worry it's because of his injury. "Are you hurt? I'm so sorry, I shouldn't have been holding on to your bad side." My gaze roves over him, as if I could see the evidence of his discomfort.

But he steps back, looking at me like he can't quite understand me. "I'm fucking fine, Specs."

I raise my hand in surrender. "Okay, good."

We stand there staring at each other for a minute before Maverick's phone chirps. He pulls it out of his pocket and looks down at it for a long second. "Well, it worked." Turning the phone around to face me, he exhales slowly.

It's a text from Colin with a screenshot of a tabloid site and two words. *Good job.* The photo is convincing, even to me. Maverick has the flowers in his arms and I'm at his side, smiling. We look every bit the happy couple. It's startling how fast the press moves, seeing as that photo can't have been taken more than an hour ago.

We've reached our cars by now, and an awkwardness descends, as if neither one of us knows how to end this. We might not be at the market any longer, but that doesn't mean no one is watching. There could be people in the houses surrounding us or anyone walking down the street.

"I guess we should hug?" I say quietly when it becomes clear that once again, he has no idea what to do. Given Maverick's jerky nod of agreement, he's feeling just as weird about this as I am.

But he pulls me in against his chest, and the steady thump of his heartbeat is somehow soothing and familiar. His strong arms feel normal, safe. Even though he's holding me somewhat stiffly, it feels good to just be held.

He lets me go and I step back. Feeling bold, I rise up on my toes and kiss the scruff of his cheek. That pink colour comes back, and I hide my smile.

"See you later, babe," I say loudly, biting back a giggle at the slow blink he gives me. I open the back door of my car and set my bags inside, and when I turn back around, he's already at his own car.

One fake date down, four more weeks of fake dates to go.

Chapter Eight

Maverick

"She's meant to be your girlfriend. You can't act like a fucking robot."

Colin continues pacing in front of me while I sip coffee on my couch, trying to tune him out and failing. I know he's right, I was too stiff yesterday, too caught up in my own fucking head.

I wasn't ready for her to climb out of that car looking like a fucking pinup girl. Gone were the frumpy clothes that hid everything. Hell, she didn't even have those glasses on. Instead, it was curves for days, held in by a tiny pair of jean shorts and a tank top that showed a hell of a lot more skin than I was expecting to see.

I'm not blind. I thought Sadie was pretty the second I saw her in the stairwell at the hospital. But I also dismissed that notion really fucking fast. I don't do relationships, and she's not the kind of woman to hook up with a guy like me one night and be done with it. She's the kind of woman that wants to get to know a guy, have feelings and shit. And that will never be me.

So I overcompensated. I tamped down the wave of goddamn lust I felt when I saw her and put a wall between us to make sure she didn't realize how I was affected.

Apparently, that wall was noticeable to everyone but her.

"Okay, I get it," I grumble, draining the rest of my coffee from the cup. "What do we have to do next?"

Colin drops down into the chair across from me and fixes me with a hard stare. "Another date. This time, you gotta play it up more. I'm not saying sleep with her..." He drops his head in his hands, shaking it from side to side. "In fact, please, for the love of God, don't sleep with her. But you need to make everyone else think you're intimate with her. We need you smiling, hugging, looking like you actually want to be around her."

I heave a sigh and let my head fall back against the couch. "This is bullshit. Serious fucking bullshit. I don't understand why me appearing to date some do-gooder is gonna be the key to making everyone believe I'm not just an asshole who gets in fights."

"And crashes cars in street races," Colin adds wryly. "Don't forget that."

I sit up and glare at him. "As if I could."

My phone vibrates on the table between us. We both see the name, and I'm not fast enough to grab it before he does.

"What the hell does he want now?" Colin growls, opening the text from Eli.

"Don't fucking read my messages, asshole," I say, moving swiftly to try and take it from him. But even though I'm the pro athlete, not him, he moves fast enough to dodge me.

"For fuck's sake, Mav. How often does he text you asking for money?" Colin's voice is dripping with rage. "Tell me you don't still give it to him. You know what he wants it for."

I grind my teeth together, refusing to answer.

"Holy shit, you do." Colin tosses my phone down on the couch. "This is why you're stuck. This is why everyone thinks you're an asshole. Because you refuse to believe you can be anything more. Because he's got you trapped, thinking all of his shit is your fault and it's fucking not. You're enabling his habits, Mav. You're not helping him, you're making it worse."

"Enough!" I roar, my fists tight at my sides. The pain in my shoulder is welcome, fueling my anger. This isn't the first time we've had this fight and it won't be the last. "I'm doing what you asked. I'm pretending to date Sadie. I'm staying out of trouble. Now you go do your fucking job and make sure my career is safe."

We stare at each other for a long minute. He breaks first, shaking his head at me one more time. "Fine. I'll email the two of you details for tonight. Make it believable, brother."

I give him a brusque nod, staying where I stand until my door closes behind him. Only then do I exhale sharply. I know he *is* doing his job. Just as I know there's no one else I'd trust to have my back. But *fuck.*

Swiping my phone off the couch, I open the message from Eli. Sure enough, he's asking for money. Never mind that he still hasn't checked to see if I'm okay after the fucking car crash that I got in because of him.

I drop the phone back down and head to the bathroom instead, turning on the shower as hot as it can go. I'm due at the stadium for a physical therapy session in just over an hour, and I know Lark, the trainer who's working on my rehab, isn't going to take it easy on me. Not with my return to the field hinging on how the next couple of weeks go.

And I need to get back on the field.

Which means I need to make sure my future with the Tridents is safe. If making the world think I'm dating Sadie is the key to that, then I'll do whatever it fucking takes. Colin wants it to be believable? I'll show him.

Just have to remember, this can't ever be real, and that means making sure she knows it's all for show.

When she pulls up at the restaurant where we're having dinner tonight, I walk over to her car, mentally preparing myself for seeing her dressed up. I open her door and have to choke back a frustrated laugh.

Gone is the sexy-girl-next-door look from yesterday. We're back to frumpy librarian, it seems.

"Hey," I say, intentionally leaving off the *Specs*. She says she doesn't like it, but I see the way her eyes flare when I say it, and I call bullshit. Sure enough, her pert lips tip down ever so slightly. She steps out of her car and her hands twist around the strap of her bag.

"Hi."

The dress she's wearing swallows her whole. Those luscious curves are hidden under way too much fabric. The glasses are back in place, as is the bun.

We walk to the front of the restaurant without saying anything else. It's awkward, just like yesterday, and Colin's voice is in my head, reminding me to do better. I reach to open the door, my hand falling to her lower back as we walk inside. It's easy for him to say *do better*, he's at least been in a relationship or two. Me, I've got no fucking clue how to act on a goddamn date, even if it is all just pretend.

"Have you eaten here before?" Sadie asks in a nervous whisper as we're guided to our table. I'm guessing she's noticed the furtive looks we're getting from other patrons, and the way we're seated by the front window is intentional on Colin's part. I hold her chair out, and once she's seated, I take my own seat and answer her. "No. Colin booked it. Something about this being the hot place to be seen."

"That's such a weird concept. Planning where to eat based on visibility."

"Welcome to public relations, I guess. It's all a fucking game." My wry response has her tilting her head to the side and I brace myself for the incoming questions.

"You don't like the media attention, I'm guessing."

There's no judgment in her tone, and I find myself wanting to answer as honestly as I can.

"The press has a habit of being particularly shitty with how they spin things. I think they give us all an identity that meets their needs, no matter how far off base it is. I got the label of being the bad boy because I didn't want to cooperate with their bullshit. So, no. I don't like the media. But it's a necessary evil."

I can see her fighting back a smile, which doesn't make sense since none of what I just said was funny. "What?" I ask gruffly.

"It's just, I think that's the most words you've ever said to me at one time." Now her smile breaks free as she giggles, and to my surprise, I feel my own mouth curving up in response.

"Don't get used to it, Specs."

Her eyes are dancing, and fuck, she's pretty. Even in that god-awful dress. There's something about her that shines no matter what she's wearing. And goddamn it, I grudgingly admit, I like seeing her smile.

The moment is broken by the arrival of a waiter. And as soon as her eyes aren't on me, I miss them. That's fucking dangerous. I inhale deeply, taking the minute while she's placing her order to remind myself, I can't let the lines be blurred. No matter what. I have to play the part of infatuated boyfriend, but I have to make it damn clear she knows that's not reality.

The waiter leaves, and Sadie leans forward. "You know, if we're going to pull this off, it would really help if I knew some more about you. Like, now I know you hate the press. What else is there to Maverick King?"

Mentally, I groan. I don't want to get to know her, and I sure as shit don't want her to get to know me. But once again, I hear my brother lecturing me about being believable. Which means I can't be silent the entire meal.

"What do you want to know?"

Sadie looks pleased by my question, as she should. Little minx is getting her way. "We could start with the basics. What's your favourite food?"

"Burgers."

"Okay, favourite place to visit?"

"Don't know."

Her lips turn down in a slight frown. "You've never gone on vacation?"

I lift my good shoulder in a shrug. "Nope."

She lets out a frustrated huff. "Do you always answer your date's questions in one-word answers?"

"*Don't know* is two words," I fire back, and she purses her lips, trying to hide a smile.

"Fine."

But instead of asking another question, Sadie slumps back in her chair. And I find myself leaning forward instead. "I don't go on dates. I occasionally find women to have sex, but there's no hand holding, no farmer's markets, and no get-to-know-you questions. Just orgasms."

Her mouth falls open, and before I can stop myself, my hand is reaching out and one finger is pushing gently on her chin to close it.

"Relax, Specs. Your virtue is safe with me." I ignore the flash of disappointment that crosses her face. "But you're right. We do have to make this look real. My brother pointed out that some of the photos from yesterday didn't look all that believable. I've been instructed to step it up in the acting department."

Sadie sips her wine slowly, and when she sets it down, her eyes meet mine. "Which means what, exactly?"

For once in my life, I pause and think before I answer her. "Which means we need to make it look convincing. Colin says we need a little more affection and a little less scowling from me."

Her short burst of laughter is deserved. "He's not wrong."

I didn't even realize I wanted to see her relax until I notice her shoulders drop down ever so slightly. The thing is, I don't know how to act. I don't know what couples do on dates like this. I've never been in this position before, and I fucking hate it. But I'm not the only one with something at stake, which means I need to man the fuck up.

"Tell me about your ex."

Sadie's eyes widen in confusion. "Why?"

"Because. He's the reason you're here, isn't he? Seems I should know about the jackass I'm showing up."

She takes another sip of her wine, sets it down, and stares at the glass. "We were together a few years. Looking back now, I don't know why I actually thought he could be the one, but when I was in it, I guess I was blind. Couldn't see that I could do better."

Her voice is harsh, unkind, and directed at herself if I'm not mistaken. It makes my jaw clench.

"I walked in on him and his paralegal having sex in our bed. Well. His bed." She lets out a sharp laugh, even though there's nothing funny about what she just said. "He made me get rid of my furniture when I moved in, insisting his was better quality. God, he was so arrogant, and I just went along with it like an idiot."

"You're not an idiot. Men like him don't deserve to fucking walk this earth," I growl, and her eyes shoot up to meet mine. "He's an asshole. A fucking stupid asshole."

"Th-thank you," she whispers.

Our dinner arrives and thank fuck, Sadie drops the questions. In fact, she barely says another word the entire meal. It leaves me thinking I'm in for another fucking lecture from Colin.

When we're done, we leave the restaurant, my hand on her lower back again. I know we haven't done enough. Even with my complete ignorance of how to date, I know tonight didn't go well. Then we reach her car, and something out of the corner of my eye has me looking to the side.

There.

A fucking camera.

My lips are on hers in an instant, turning so her back is to the photographer. My hands are on her, one in the curve above her ass and one at the base of her neck. Holding her tightly.

She's stiff underneath me at first, and I'm thinking this was a fucking huge mistake. I should have said something, but no. In typical Maverick fashion, I acted first and thought later. That approach has landed me in trouble more times than I can count, and for all I know, it's fucking things up now, too.

But then Sadie lets out a little moan, and suddenly, she's pressing into me, too, not to push me away, but to get closer. Her arms come around my neck, and she gives in to the kiss.

My ribs are screaming at me, but I ignore them. The pain is worth it.

We break apart and reality hits me when I see the dazed look on her face. *Shit*. This is why I've been giving her whiplash, as she called it. Because girls like Sadie don't know how to keep feelings apart from the physical.

"What was that for?" she asks, reaching her hand up to brush across her lips.

"Photographer behind the tree," I say sharply, and the dazed look falls away immediately.

"Oh."

Her tongue darts out to swipe her lips, and fucking hell if I don't want to kiss her again. But we gave the pap his shot, and that's all this is for.

A photo op. Nothing more.

CHAPTER NINE

Maverick

"I don't have much experience with relationships, but I'm pretty sure the guy normally picks his girl up to go places."

"Hello to you, too," Sadie replies to my grumble with a smile as she gets out of her car. She's not dressed as a librarian today, although the dress she's got on is still pretty modest, covering up a lot of her curves. But her hair is down, flowing over her shoulders, and I'm annoyed at myself for noticing and for liking it.

It doesn't slip my attention that she ignores my statement about picking her up. But this is the fifth time we've met up over the past week and a half, and every time she's insisted on driving herself. I can't figure out why, and it's frustrating.

"Okay, remind me. Who do we have to focus on today?"

"Everyone," I retort as we walk toward the restaurant where most of my teammates and their significant others are waiting.

Every year, at the end of the All-Star break, the guys rent out a local restaurant for a team dinner. And every year, I come up with a reason not to go.

This year, I was given no choice but to come with Sadie. And it's make-or-break time. The press has been surprisingly easy to fool so far. The photos Colin's arranged to be leaked have painted a pretty picture. But tonight, we've got to convince twenty baseball players and their respective partners. Up close and personal, they'll notice everything.

I take her hand, lacing our fingers together as we walk inside. The room is already loud with boisterous conversation and laughter, and I immediately want to leave.

"It's okay, we got this," Sadie whispers, leaning into me slightly as she squeezes my hand. And I feel my breathing even out.

"Mav!"

Monty, one of the catchers, weaves his way through the tables and chairs to reach us, a goofy grin on his face. The guy is permanently happy, and while I'd never admit it, I admire that about him. Even if I secretly wonder just how legit his good mood is. I mean, how can someone be so fucking happy all the time?

"Hey, Monty. This is Sadie. Sadie, Dan Montgomery, catch-er."

"Oh, we know each other." Monty grins at Sadie. "She always stops by when we visit the children's hospital. But I gotta say, you've become somewhat of a legend around here." Monty smiles again.

"I have?" she asks, looking from him to me with a confused smile on her face. "Why?"

"Because you got our boy Mav smiling. It's a fucking mira-cle."

"Fuck off, I smile," I grumble, but Monty and Sadie are both just laughing at me. Which stings a little. Am I really that grumpy, even around my team?

Who the fuck am I kidding? Yeah. I am.

"Come on, Sadie. Let's introduce you around to the players you don't know yet so this guy can go get a drink and find a quiet corner to chill."

Monty gestures to lead Sadie away, but I pull her back to my side. "I can take her around."

He looks at me, surprised. "Of course, man. Sorry. Not trying to overstep. I just figured with how you don't love crowds, I'd do you a solid and handle the intros."

Well, now I feel like an ass. "It's fine."

"Okay, cool." Monty gives Sadie one more quick grin before walking over to another group of guys. Sadie steps in front of me, her big eyes staring up at me. She's not wearing her glasses today, making them seem even larger than normal.

"What was that all about?"

"I didn't know you already knew some of the guys."

She tilts her head as she looks at me, tucking a strand of hair behind her ear. "Not well, but yeah, I sometimes stop by to see Willow when they come for a visit. The relationship between the Tridents and the hospital is good for the foundation; they help bring in a lot of money."

"Well. You're here with me. I'll introduce you to everyone, not Monty." It comes off sounding more controlling than I mean it to, but damn it, I don't need Monty charming her.

"Fine." Her easy acceptance makes me breathe a little easier until she shifts in closer. "But I'm asking what Monty meant when he said you don't like crowds."

I shrug. "It's not a big deal. I'm just not a fan of socializing with big groups."

"You're a professional athlete. You're surrounded by crowds all day, every day."

Goddamn it, she's way too insightful. "Yeah but playing in front of a crowd is different from having to talk to them."

Her eyebrows draw together as she chews on her lower lip, staring at me like I'm a puzzle she wants to solve.

Good fucking luck, Specs.

"You're an introvert."

Well, fuck. It took the guys on the team an entire season to figure that out and stop inviting me to everything. At first, they didn't understand it wasn't because I didn't want to hang out. It was because I was so fucking drained from the social energy it took to perform at games, hell, even at practice sometimes, that when it was done, I just needed to go home and be by myself.

Monty was actually the first one to figure it out, which makes me feel even more guilty for snapping at him earlier. The guy was just trying to give me a break. Of course, he'd assume my girlfriend would know how uncomfortable these types of situations make me.

"Don't make a big deal out of it. Let's just go meet the guys," I say, looking away from her all-too-knowing stare.

I lead her toward one group, and pushing down my discomfort, introduce her around. This group of players don't do the children's hospital stuff, so they don't know Sadie. There's a lot of questions about our relationship, and to my immense relief, Sadie steps up and handles them. She's fucking amazing, spinning stories, laughing with the guys, and charming them all. I play my part of boyfriend with my arm around her waist. And slowly, I start to relax.

We drift around the room, stopping at the bar to get a glass of wine for her and a club soda for me. She takes it with a smile of thanks to the bartender before turning to me.

"You don't want a drink?"

I've already revealed enough of myself for the night so I just shake my head.

"Sadie, you're here!" Willow's excited squeal has us turning around, and I mentally thank her for the interruption.

I stand back as the two women hug, giving Ronan Sinclair, Willow's boyfriend and the starting first baseman, a nod.

"How's the shoulder?" he asks, taking a drink of his beer.

"Fine. Hoping to be back in a few weeks."

"Good. It's not the same without you out there."

"Diaz is a solid player."

"His arm isn't like yours."

Okay, I can't lie, that feels good to hear. "Thanks."

Ronan leans against the bar and looks from the women to me. "Sadie's a good person. Willow thinks very highly of her."

I sip my soda water, waiting to see where he's going with this.

He takes a minute, studying me intently. "I know I'm the new guy, and with all the shit Willow and I dealt with recently, I probably shouldn't be the one to say this. But I'm going to anyway. Because Willow also thinks highly of you."

That takes me by surprise. But he's not done.

"Take it from someone who recently fucked up and had to spend several days worrying he'd lost one of the most important people in his life. Treat her well, put her first, and don't be a dumbass."

I was there in the days after Ronan and Willow's relationship suddenly became public knowledge, after he punched out a player from another team that harassed her. It wasn't pretty. I don't know the details, but I saw how devastated he was those few days before they worked it out, so I know what he's getting at. Hell, I was the one to sit next to him on the bus and tell him to get his head out of his ass and fix things.

The difference is, he loves Willow. Their relationship was at stake.

For me, the stakes are different. I don't have a relationship on the line, it's my career.

Choosing my words carefully, I respond, "Tell Willow I have no intention of doing anything to hurt Sadie."

The women in question turn back to us in that second, and Sadie's smile is warmer and more relaxed than I think I've ever seen. She slides her arm around my waist and snuggles into my good side, and fuck, if it doesn't feel good.

Too good.

I shift slightly so she can't feel exactly how my body reacts to having her pressed close to me.

"How are you doing?" She lifts up to whisper in my ear, and the fact that she's checking in on me when she's the one who is surrounded by strangers stirs something else inside of me.

"I'm good, Specs."

And that is not a lie. Not fake, not pretend. Somehow, tonight has already been easier than I anticipated. And it's all because of her.

CHAPTER TEN

Sadie

If you had told me two weeks ago that I would be the constant subject of media scrutiny, I would have laughed and told you to get your head checked because insanity was clearly setting in.

Yet here I am, staring at another freaking gossip page headline. "At least the photos are decent," I mutter to myself as I close the browser window. It wouldn't be so bad if it weren't for my sister, my friends, heck, even my mom sending me links all the time. My colleagues seem to have settled; perhaps Gus wasn't wrong to tell me to work from home for the last while. But family and friends don't have the same boundaries.

Of course, part of it is because in my family, I've never been the one in the limelight. Sienna and Simon were the ones who loved the attention, Simon moving to LA to pursue acting, and Sienna taking the synchronized swimming world by storm. I've always been content to let them be the bold, outgoing ones. It was easier for me to be the smart one, the helpful one.

Okay, fine, the boring one.

But I can't dodge my mother's not-so-subtle insinuation that she would like to meet Maverick for long. Only that's a conversation I'm not looking forward to broaching with him. He's a tough nut to crack, and even after two weeks of spending time together several days a week, I barely feel like I know him.

What I do know is that he's not the jerk the media makes him out to be. His teammates know that, his brother knows that, and I know that. I've watched him overtip waitstaff, hold open doors, and swoop in to pick up a book someone dropped the other day. I've seen him be friendly with kids who come up to him, and it makes me wonder how no one else can see that underneath the reckless behaviour is a good man.

He's also an incredibly sexy man who smells like heaven and makes me feel so safe and protected, even when we're approached by strangers or media.

Standing up from my lumpy couch, I stretch my arms overhead. I stayed up late last night working, meaning I had little to do today, and I just finished my last task. Wandering into my kitchen, I open the fridge and examine the contents. It's meager. Maverick and I had another fake date last night and we went out for dinner. The night before, Ali and I had a girls night. So I haven't cooked in several days, and the lack of food is proof.

I grab an apple and a yogurt, and make my way back to the horrible couch, still thinking about how nice Maverick's arm feels around me. And how I really need to not get used to it. We've got just two weeks to go until the foundation gala, which was the agreed-upon end date for our little situation.

I'm busy trying not to think about why that thought makes me a little disappointed when my phone starts to vibrate with an incoming call, and I glare at it. But my sense of responsibility wins out over my desire to live like a hermit and ignore the world. Then I see who's calling.

Heidi Morgan used to work as a nurse on the oncology ward until she decided to go back to school to become a doctor, and then moved to Vancouver Island to finish out her residency. She fell in love with another pediatrician, and they're engaged. It startles me to realize her wedding is this coming weekend. With all the Maverick insanity, the date crept up on me.

"Hi, bride-to-be," I say, answering the call with a genuine smile on my face. This is one call I don't want to ignore. "If you're calling to tell me you have cold feet, I'm going to say you're nuts and to stick them in warm water."

Heidi's giggle is full of so much joy. "Heck, no. No cold feet here. I can't wait to marry Max."

The love dripping from her words makes me smile for her. She deserves to be happy.

"Good. So what's up?"

"Well, when you and Dirk broke up, I know you decided to just get a hotel room in Westport for the weekend. But with Maverick in the picture, I thought you might want something better."

I arrange my legs underneath me on the couch, frowning slightly as I try to figure out what she's getting at. Thankfully, she doesn't keep me in suspense for long.

"The resort finished the renovations on two more cabins, which means there's one available for you! You don't need to stay in a boring hotel after the wedding, you and your new man can have a romantic night in your own little cabin. How perfect is that!"

"Perfect," I manage to croak out. Oh no. Oh *freaking* no. How did I not think about the fact that Heidi would automatically assume Maverick would come with me to the wedding? The whole country knows he's still not back playing ball, so why wouldn't he accompany his girlfriend on a weekend getaway.

Except he doesn't know about the wedding, and he's not my real boyfriend. We've never spent more than a couple of hours together, and that's always been for show. Going to my friend's wedding and having to play the part of a happy couple for an entire weekend? There's no way he'd say yes to that.

Especially not the part where we have to spend two nights in a romantic beachfront cabin together...

"Listen, Heidi, I've got to run, work call in a couple of minutes." It's upsetting how easily the lie falls from my lips, but then again, I've had plenty of practice spinning tales these days.

"No worries, I just couldn't wait to tell you. We're so excited to see you on Saturday! Oh, and I promise, we've already told Sawyer to tone down the fanboy around Mav."

I give a pained laugh in response to her much more excited one. Max's younger brother, who's dating Willow's best friend, is a huge Tridents fan. This situation just got even more complicated for Maverick.

"Thanks, Heidi. I'll see you soon."

I hang up the phone and drop my head in my hands, letting out a rare curse. "Holy shit."

I don't call Maverick right away.

In fact, I don't even call him that day. Nope, my big ole chicken self waits a full twenty-four hours after Heidi's call before I even get up the courage to open our text messages.

And then I stare at my phone for several minutes, typing and deleting, trying to figure out how to bring up the subject.

This is why, when my phone suddenly vibrates with an incoming message from him, I yelp and drop my phone in surprise.

> **MAVERICK: Colin thinks we need to do something this weekend. I guess we can go to that market again if its open.**

It's the perfect opening for me to bring up the wedding. We could easily get some photos on the ferry ride to the island. When we all met for coffee earlier in the week to check in, Colin said we needed to post more on social media, to which Maverick just laughed. Apparently, he doesn't have a social media presence except for the one Colin manages for him. I agreed to share a few photos but have yet to do so.

Okay, Sadie. Time to just rip off the Band-Aid. The worst that could happen is he says no and you have to come up with an excuse for Heidi.

> **SADIE: Actually, I won't be in town this weekend. My friend is getting married over on Vancouver Island.**

> **MAVERICK: Oh. Okay.**

> **SADIE: They're expecting you to come with me. If you want to.**

I wait for him to respond, sitting on my hand so I don't chew my nails from the stress of it all. When he finally does, I exhale in relief.

> **MAVERICK: Fine. Send me details. Colin says we need to make sure people see us doing shit.**

I'll save the whole *only one cabin* thing until later, I guess. Switching over to my email, I send a quick message to Maverick and Colin with details for the weekend. Then I get up, go to my bedroom, and pull on some comfy clothes before grabbing my keys and a bottle of wine from my fridge and heading out to my car.

Twenty minutes later, I'm knocking on Ali's door. She opens it, her eyebrows raising as she takes in my harried expression and the wine.

"What's going on?"

I push past her, not answering until I've opened the wine, poured some into a coffee mug, and taken a long drink.

"Maverick is coming to the island with me for Heidi's wedding. We have to share a teeny-tiny cabin. And I haven't even booked a leg wax."

She approaches me slowly, taking the bottle of wine, and pouring some for herself. I drain my mug and make grabby hands at the bottle, needing a refill.

"Let me get this straight. You're spending the weekend with your hot fake boyfriend, in a romantic cabin, and you're worrying about a leg wax."

I give her a hard look. "The leg wax is just one of my many problems."

"I mean, I get it. Priorities. Last thing you need is your hottie baseball boyfriend thinking you're a Sasquatch with hairy legs. But that's an easy fix, one phone call. No big deal. So what's really going on."

I move to Ali's not-lumpy couch and slump into the corner. "He's a good guy, Ali."

"Yeah, you've said that." She sits down next to me and sets the bottle on the table. Such a good friend. "And?"

"And he's really hot."

"Still stating the obvious, babe."

"And even though I only said yes to this insanity because I wanted to make Dirk suffer, I also want this to work out for him. I want to help him fix his image and get the public to see he's not who the media makes him out to be."

Ali's still looking at me, waiting for me to get to the point.

"So far, all of our dates together have been carefully planned PR stunts, designed for media exposure. They've all been for him. For his career. Now I'm asking him to spend an entire weekend with me, convincing people he doesn't know or care about that he's actually with me. What if...what if he can't? What if it all falls apart this weekend? Then his career will be ruined, and it'll be my fault. And Dirk will find out I'm a pathetic loser that agreed to fake date a baseball player for revenge."

"Holy hell, you're spiraling, girlfriend." Ali lifts my glass to my mouth. "Drink up, calm down, and let's talk."

I dutifully take a drink, then stare down at the glass. "People are going to be watching. Not photographers, not his teammates, but people that will recognize him, know who he is. Then they'll look at me, see how different we are, and wonder what the heck is going on. We have to spend forty-eight hours sharing the same living space and constantly being *on* in front of these people. What if he can't do it? What if he can't pretend to like me for that long?"

"Sadie LeDuc. You've gone from 'I need a leg wax,' to 'I might destroy his career,' in two point five seconds. Take a breath, girlfriend. And remember this is not just on you. He's got skin in this game, and if he wants this to work, he's gonna have to step up. It'll be his own damn fault if his career implodes. Don't forget, you've held up your end of this deal for the last couple of weeks. Now it's his turn to show that he can do it. It's not your responsibility alone to convince people this relationship is real. You wanted him to help get Dirk off your back, and part of that is continuing to have everyone think you're happy together. And as for him pretending to like you, how hard can it be?"

My best friend sounds offended on my behalf, and I finally crack a smile.

"You're amazing. You're beautiful, smart, funny, kind, and basically the most generous person I know. There's absolutely nothing about you not to like, which means this is the easiest job he's ever gonna have."

I pick at invisible lint on the couch beside me, trying not to let my insecurities get the better of me.

"Dirk was right, I'm boring. I live a boring, normal life. I wear boring clothes. I'm not a supermodel, or some beautiful, elegant, perfect woman. I'm not the kind of girl professional athletes date." I hold up my hand when I can sense Ali about to protest. "And I'm okay with that. Honestly. But we're so different. It's a lot to ask of him, to put aside those differences and somehow be believable in his attraction to me for this long. And if he can't do it, then everything we're trying to accomplish with this farce is at risk. Because I asked him to come to a wedding."

Even as I say it, I know Ali's right and I'm spiraling, taking on all the responsibility for something that wasn't even my idea to begin with. But now that we're in this, I feel so much pressure to do it right. To make this work for Maverick. There's so much on the line, and I've just upped the stakes.

CHAPTER ELEVEN

Maverick

Sadie and I agreed to meet at the ferry terminal. I'm not sure why she won't just let me pick her up from her place, but whatever. Not my concern. At least that's what I keep reminding myself, even as some annoying part of me wonders if it's because she doesn't trust me, or if there's something she's hiding.

I put my SUV in park and roll my shoulders, feeling out the twinge in my arm. After six weeks, things are feeling better. But not better enough to let me play, according to the team doctors. I'm getting antsy. I need to be on the field, shagging balls. Not playing PR puppet and going to fucking farmer's markets.

Then again, as I watch Sadie approach, rolling a suitcase behind her, I have to admit, there are worse people to spend time with. She somehow makes it tolerable. Makes me feel comfortable, which isn't an easy thing to do. I don't open up to people. I don't let them in. Hell, even guys I've played with for the last couple of years barely know anything about me. And that's not because they haven't tried. It's because I don't do that shit. Getting close to people only means they have the ability to hurt you.

"Hi," Sadie says in a forced cheerful tone as she opens the back of my SUV. Belatedly, I realize I'm an ass and should probably be helping her load her stuff, but before I can even get out of the car, she's done and opening the passenger door.

"Hey." My voice sounds more gruff than intended, because I'm pissed at myself for not even having the basic decency to help a woman. Jesus Christ, I'm a lost fucking cause.

"Thanks again for agreeing to this, I know going to a wedding between two strangers is probably not high on your list of fun weekend plans." I glance over before turning the engine on and see her hands in her lap, eyes downcast behind those big glasses. She's dressed casually today in khaki shorts and some kinda shirt that looks like a button-up but with a tie at the bottom. Honestly, it looks like something you'd see on a bible camp counselor, but on Sadie, the innocent looks fucking indecent.

I really am a piece of shit. Lusting over my fake girlfriend who's so far out of my league, we might as well be on different planets. A woman I can't have, because if I fuck this up, my career could be over.

"It's fine."

I turn the engine on and drive out of the parking lot where we're leaving her car, heading down the causeway toward the ferry terminal. I've only been to the island a couple of times, and in my opinion, the best part is the boat ride over. I fucking love being on the water. It's why I've never wanted to live anywhere but here. Surrounded by mountains and oceans. The few years I spent with teams not on the coast were awful, and as soon as I hired Colin, I told him to get me back to Vancouver.

The guy in the ticket booth does a double take when he recognizes me, but thankfully, doesn't say anything. Then we're pulling into the long lineup of cars.

"Do you want anything to eat or drink?" Sadie asks, finally lifting her eyes to meet mine. "I can go inside the terminal and get it if you don't want to."

She just can't seem to stop herself from bending over backward for me, and I don't know how to convince her it isn't necessary. Once again, my lack of social skills has me at a loss, and I fucking hate this feeling.

"I'm fine."

"Oh, okay."

Fuck. Now she's staring down at her lap again. If this entire weekend is gonna consist of her feeling bad for me being here, then I might need a drink. And seeing as I've never had a drop of alcohol my entire life, that's saying something. I know I've got to do something to get her to unwind.

"Sadie." Her eyes shoot up to mine, wide and nervous. I try to soften my tone. "You gotta relax. You're acting like you've fucking kidnapped me or forced me into this. You didn't, okay? This is part of our deal. Anything you need to convince your friends and family that you're good after the dirtbag breakup, I'm here for it. Right?"

Finally, I see the tiniest give in her shoulders. She gives me the barest of nods, but it's enough. I recline my seat slightly. "We've got some time before we gotta load onto the boat. Let's just chill."

Spinning my hat bill around to face front, I pull it down to cover my eyes and try to settle. But I can feel her stare, and after a moment, I push the hat up and arch my brow at her. "What?"

Her pretty blush makes my dick stir in my pants, but I ignore it. Then she bites her plump lower lip and I want to tug it out of her teeth with my own. *Fucking fuck. No.* I might be attracted to the woman sitting next to me, but nothing, I mean nothing, can ever happen. She holds my career in her hands. One wrong word from her, and I could go from slowly reforming my bad boy image to a total write-off.

The fact that she is still giving off nervous-as-shit vibes has me blurting out, "Sadie, if you don't want me here, say the word and I'll go."

Her eyes widen as, thank God, she shakes her head. "No, Maverick. I'm sorry. That's not it. I'm just nervous."

I bring my seat back to upright and turn to look at her, trying not to clench my jaw. She needs to talk. Great.

"About what."

Her gaze dips down again, and it's about all I can handle. I've seen her be confident and secure. That dinner with all my teammates? She had them eating out of her hands. So who is this shy, insecure person? And what did I do to make her feel that way around me?

Reaching out, I tip her chin up to make her look at me. "Specs. What's wrong."

I don't know if it was the nickname or me touching her, but the floodgates open.

"We have to spend forty-eight hours together, Maverick. We have to fake being into each other in front of my friend and her entire family. People who know you, who are probably your fans. They're going to look at you and look at me, and if we aren't convincing enough, they're going to question everything. This isn't just a two-hour dinner date, this is an entire weekend with the same group of people, trying to make them believe we're truly dating."

Her voice is nearing hysteria pitch and it's got me grinding my teeth because I fucking hate seeing her upset.

"So? Do you think you can't do it?" I fire at her.

I don't know what I was expecting for a reaction, but a scoff of disbelief isn't it. "Can I act like I'm attracted to you and want to be near you? Yeah, Maverick, I can. It's not like it's hard. I mean, look at you." She waves her hands in my direction. "But can *you* do it? Can you drop the scowl for that long and actually look like you're having a good time with me? Like you want to be here?"

There's so much she's not saying, and my first reaction is to want to just fucking kiss her. She thinks I can't pretend to be into her for a weekend? Holy hell, it's going to be hard to hide the fact that I *am* into her if I have to be around her for that long.

"Trust me, Specs. I'll be fine," I grit out.

Yeah. Fine. Totally fine.

We're *fine* the entire ferry ride and drive up the island to the town of Dogwood Cove where her friend lives.

And by fine, I mean totally silent until we're driving down the highway and she finally decides to speak to me.

"I guess I should tell you about my friend, so it seems like we talk and know stuff about each other. Like a normal couple."

There's a sharp point to her words, and I know it's directed at me and my recalcitrance any time she tries to get me to talk about myself.

"Heidi used to work at the hospital, in the oncology ward. Then she went back to school to become a pediatric surgeon. She went to Dogwood Cove to do her final residency and fell in love with a doctor there. He's got a huge family. They're all lovely, but also, a lot. Be prepared for his brother Sawyer, especially. He's apparently a huge fan of the Tridents, and from what I remember when I met him last year, he's kind of intense in this goofy, fun way. The weekend is a mixture of planned wedding events and free time if you want to explore the area. It's really beautiful, I get why Heidi loves it."

She's rambling, and I chance a quick look over to see her staring out the window. At least she's talking to me now.

"Tonight is the cocktail hour after they finish the rehearsal. We should have about an hour to settle in before that starts. Then tomorrow, the ceremony isn't until the late afternoon, which means we have the morning free. Ceremony, reception after, then an optional breakfast the next morning before we head home. It's all happening at this resort right on the beach that has cabins and a new main lodge. But if you want to go off and do your own thing at any point, you can totally just leave me there, I'll be fine."

"I'm not gonna leave you alone."

Her eyes slant over to me. "You say that now…"

I glance back over at her again at that cryptic statement, but she turns to face forward without saying anything else. I take the next turn onto the driveway for Oceanside Resort and travel down the winding track until it opens up. Pulling into an open spot, we climb out of the car and I take a look around. Holy shit, she wasn't kidding, it's beautiful here.

Cabins line the beach to one side of a low building that has a dock jutting out from it. There's a boat launch, and behind us, I can see more cabins and a newer three-story building that must be the lodge Sadie mentioned.

The fresh sea air is amazing, and I can feel myself relaxing just standing here soaking it in. Honestly? Two days of peace and quiet away from the city, the stress of my rehab, and managing the press is gonna be fucking amazing.

"I'll go get our cabin key," Sadie says, hurrying off.

She's back shortly, brandishing a key. We move my car down to the designated spot behind one of the cabins that overlooks the ocean. This time, I'm prepared, and move quickly to the back to unload the bags.

"Maverick, your arm." Sadie hovers behind me, sounding way too much like my physical therapists.

"I'm fine." I lift her bag out, then my own, all using my good arm only. Turning to her, I give her a look. "See? Fine."

"You keep using that word. And I hate that word," she says, narrowing her eyes at me. "It never means you're actually fine."

That makes a rough laugh escape me as I let her take the handle of her suitcase. "Okay, how about this. My arm is healed enough to lift a bag out of my car."

"Better," she says primly, but her mouth is fighting a smile.

But that smile falls as we round the corner to the front of the cabin, and a nervous expression once again covers her face.

I don't have the fucking energy left in me to ask what's wrong now, so I choose to ignore it, letting her unlock the door and push it open. The second I step inside, I see the reason for Sadie's nerves. And judging by the guilty look on her face, she knew about this situation and chose not to mention it.

A quick look around the small studio cabin makes two things stand out.

There's no couch, just a couple of comfortable-looking chairs. Comfortable, yes. Good for sleeping, no.

Which brings me to the second thing.

There's only one bed.

This is definitely not *fine*.

CHAPTER TWELVE

Sadie

Guess I should've checked exactly how small these cabins are before dragging Maverick here. The look on his face makes it clear he wasn't expecting a place so...*cozy*. We could stand at either end of the living space with one hand on the wall and still touch each other with our arms outstretched.

"Hmm, this is a bit tighter than I was expecting," I say brightly, moving into the room and setting my suitcase down. "But it's fine. I can sleep in one of the chairs, they look super comfortable." I gesture wildly to one, not meeting Maverick's gaze. "Or I bet the resort has air mattresses or something we could borrow."

"And when you ask for the air mattress, you don't think they're gonna wonder why Maverick King's girlfriend won't just share a bed with him?" he asks acerbically.

I wince, knowing he's right. "Fine. The chair, then. It'll be fine."

"Right. Fine." Again with the sarcasm-laced tone, and I know he's referring to my earlier comment about what fine actually means.

I breathe in and out slowly and turn to face him. "I'm sorry, alright? I didn't know it would be this kind of set up or I never would've made you come."

He brushes past me, setting his bag down on the low dresser next to the queen-sized bed. "I'll sleep on the floor. I've had worse."

I open my mouth to protest but he shoots me a hard look before walking toward the door.

"I'm gonna go for a walk before we have to go to the cocktail thing. You said we had an hour, right?"

All I can do is nod.

"Good. I'll be back in a bit to get ready."

The door closes behind him, and I sink down into one of the chairs and try to envision falling asleep in it. *Ugh,* there's no way. But making Maverick sleep on the floor feels incredibly wrong. *We could share the bed...*

No. Absolutely not. It's bad enough I'm attracted to a man I absolutely, one hundred percent cannot have in real life. And I've dragged him to a wedding where the pressure is on to convince everyone we're the real deal for an entire weekend. The last thing I can do is make him any more uncomfortable by even suggesting we share the bed. Heaven forbid I talk in my sleep or end up touching him somehow.

Nope. Not happening.

Standing up, I brush my hands down the front of my shorts. Might as well get myself ready for tonight so whenever he gets back, Maverick can have the bathroom to himself.

Twenty minutes later, I'm out of the shower, listening to see if he's returned. When I'm met with silence, I chance it and dart out of the bathroom to where my suitcase is still against the wall. If I'd been smart, I would have brought my outfit for tonight into the bathroom. But the bed situation clearly scrambled my brain. I grab my underwear, bra, and the dress I planned to wear, and dart back into the safety of the bathroom. With this being the only separate space, I suppose we'll be taking turns getting dressed all weekend.

Although the idea of seeing Maverick in, well, any state of undress has me clenching my thighs together. I wonder how far his tattoos go in covering his body…

Slipping on my underwear and bra, I pull the gray dress I planned to wear tonight over my head. It's a simple sheath dress, light gray with a subtle floral pattern. The cap sleeves are pretty, I think, and the neckline is high enough to not draw attention. But as I stare at myself in the mirror and try to picture Maverick next to me, the only reaction I have is *blah*.

I do have options. There's the dress I have for the wedding and reception tomorrow, and Ali insisted on sliding in a lavender dress she made me buy in the spring that I've never had the bravery to actually wear. I tried to tell her there wasn't a chance I'd put it on, especially not in front of Maverick, but she just shrugged and tucked it in my suitcase anyway.

As I try to envision myself in the figure-hugging dress that flares just a little from my hips, I hear the door open and close.

Lavender dress forgotten, I hurry through the rest of my makeup, then open the bathroom door. Slouched in one of the chairs, Maverick doesn't even lift his head when I walk out. "Bathroom's yours," I say quietly, and get the barest of nods in response.

I guess I really don't have any right to be disappointed in his behaviour. There's no reason he has to engage with me when we're not in front of people, and knowing that he's an introvert, I should understand if he needs some time to himself right now. But it's never fun feeling ignored, and as I move into the main living space, his eyes remain on his phone. Stifling my sigh, I spy a bottle of wine and glasses sitting on the table with a card from Max and Heidi indicating they're a gift. Perfect.

Pouring myself a glass, I turn back and catch Maverick staring at me. He looks away immediately, standing and moving to his bag. "I'll be ready soon."

He disappears into the bathroom, leaving me wondering if I imagined the fact that his gaze seemed pointed at my ass.

I try sitting on one of the chairs with my drink, but the shower is on, and now all I can picture is Maverick under the water, naked. So I get up, go outside, and sip my wine while watching the water lap at the shore. After several minutes, my ability to focus on the water is nonexistent, and I keep thinking about the gorgeous man in the shower.

I need my phone. A few rounds of sudoku or scrolling social media will help distract me. But as I open the door of the cabin, the door to the bathroom also opens and out steps Maverick, wearing dress pants and...nothing else.

I'd blame my clumsiness on what happens next, but the truth is, the sight of him half naked with his hair still wet made me forget how to work my own feet. I stumble forward, and the small amount of wine left in my glass sloshes up and somehow lands on the front of my dress.

"Crap!"

I hurry to the table and set down my glass, plucking at the front of my dress. At least the mess diverts my attention from Maverick and on to myself. But my stomach churns. I can't wear a stained dress.

When I look back up, Maverick is buttoning a light blue shirt that already has the sleeves rolled up to show off his ink-covered forearms.

"You got anything else to wear?"

His question seems genuine. Although, is it because he's concerned about me having something to wear or concerned about having to show up with his fake girlfriend wearing a stained dress? I'd like to believe it's the former, but with my nerves shot to hell, I can't push away the kernel of self-doubt that wonders the latter.

"Yes." My clipped reply gets no response from him except to move out of my way as I go to my suitcase. My gaze falls upon the two options. The dress I planned to wear tomorrow, a romantic blush-coloured one with a sweetheart neckline, or the sexy lavender dress.

If ever there was a time to be brave, it's now. Grabbing the lavender dress, I stand up and hurry to the bathroom. "Just give me a couple minutes."

Once the door closes behind me, I take a better look at myself in the mirror and wince. The wine splatter is going to be a bitch to get out, and even if it's not the most stylish, I did really like this dress. But that's a problem for later. I quickly pull it off and step into the lavender one. But once I pull the straps up over my shoulders, I realize my next problem. The zipper is in the back, and it dips down low to the point I can't reach it myself.

"Be brave," I whisper to the reflection staring back at me. My cheeks are flushed, but hopefully, he assumes that's from the stress of my last-minute change and not any other reason.

This time, I open the door slowly, steeling myself for whatever I might see. But there's no surprises waiting for me, just Maverick leaning against the wall by the window, looking out at the water. He turns as I walk out of the bathroom, and this time, there's no mistaking the way his eyes widen as he looks at me.

We stand there, watching each other for what feels like an eternity but is probably less than five seconds before I remember what I need from him. Walking over, I gather my hair over one shoulder and turn my back to him.

"Could you help me with the zipper?" I ask, breaking the charged silence. For another long minute, he doesn't move. Then I feel his hand on my back, barely touching me as he slowly slides the zipper up.

I feel him step away. "Thanks."

When I turn around, he's staring at me. He breaks first, walking over to the door. I quickly slip on my low-heeled sandals and make my way to him. But as I go to walk past, his hand lands on my lower back, and I freeze. His head lowers just a bit and suddenly, I can't breathe.

"This is the dress you should've been wearing all along. You look beautiful."

I'm speechless. My head turns toward him ever so slightly, but he guides me out of the cabin, sliding his hand off my back and down to take my hand, lacing our fingers together.

The walk to the large pier that juts off from the main resort building is short, not long enough for me to get control of my racing pulse. And then someone's calling my name, and I'm turning to see my friend hurrying toward me with the smile of someone happy and in love etched across her face.

"Oh my God, you're here!" Heidi folds me into a hug, forcing me to drop Maverick's hand. I sink into her embrace, letting it ground me back in reality.

"Of course, I am. I wouldn't miss it."

We pull apart just in time to see Max, Heidi's handsome fiancé, shaking hands with Maverick.

"Glad you could make it. How's the arm?"

This is it. The moment where I find out if Maverick can step up and fake it well enough when there's no camera on us, and it's not his team watching or his career on the line. It's only my friends and my pride we have to worry about if he can't be convincing enough to pretend to be attracted to me.

"It's good. Hoping to be back playing soon. But I'm happy to be here with my beautiful girl. Thanks for including me."

Maverick's arm snakes around my waist, tugging me into his side, and I stare up at him. He seems relaxed, and his response to Max was so believable I almost bought it. And judging by the happy expressions on my friends' faces, they did, too.

"That's great. Well, I'd say we can introduce you around but I think you'll find everyone knows who you are." Max grins. "They'll be cool, though, I promise. My brother Jude used to play in the NHL so everyone knows better than to go crazy."

"Well, no promises with Sawyer." Heidi laughs, and when I steal another look up at Maverick, he's still got that perfectly relaxed smile on his face.

"No problem. Don't worry about us, you two should just enjoy the evening."

I'm still wondering who this friendly, relaxed man is when Heidi pulls me in for another quick hug. "Girl. He's even hotter in person, and oh my God, he's so smitten! He can't stop looking at you," she whispers. Pulling back, she grins at me. "I'm so happy for you. You looking freaking incredible. So happy and so freaking sexy in that dress. He's good for you, babe." After one final squeeze, she whirls away with Max at her side.

"They seem nice," Maverick says mildly, reaching for my hand again. I let him lead me over to a table with drinks on it, accepting the glass of white wine he hands me.

I spend the rest of the evening trying to make sense of how the introverted, gruff man I've become used to on our dates so far has somehow morphed into this relaxed, charming person.

And trying not to let myself fall for him with every touch and every smile. He's playing the role we agreed upon, and he's playing it well.

If anything, I should be relieved.

Not disappointed.

CHAPTER THIRTEEN

Sadie

Blinking my eyes open, it takes me a second to register where I am. Right. The tiny cabin on Vancouver Island. Heidi and Max's wedding. *Maverick.*

Okay, that last one I register as soon as I hear a pained grunt and my gaze flies to where he's slowly standing up from the floor where he insisted on sleeping last night. He moves through a few stretches, rotating his arms slowly, and there's no mistaking the grimaces of pain.

Throwing off the covers, I stand up and walk over to him. "Tonight, you're taking the bed," I say firmly. He glares at me but doesn't argue. I move to the kitchen area, sending up a prayer of thanks that the cabins come with coffee makers. I hear Maverick move into the bathroom and the shower turns on. Guess it's a good thing I don't have to pee...although, I can't be mad at him. I'm guessing he's hoping the hot water will ease what has to be a very stiff and sore body from sleeping on the floor.

I should've made him take the bed last night, but when I tried, the look of complete disbelief he gave me left no room to try and convince him. At least he took the blankets and extra pillows we found in a closet and tried to make something of a bed, but clearly, it wasn't enough.

Once my coffee's made, I step outside to soak in the view and try to gather myself for the day ahead.

Maverick surprised me last night. He was friendly, albeit quiet, and charming to everyone, even Max's brother Sawyer who definitely went a little fanboy. He recognized Cooper, whose mom Tori is friends with Willow, and spent a lot of time chatting with the young kid. I'm having to admit it wasn't all that fair of me to worry he wouldn't live up to his end of things and be convincing in front of my friends. After all, he'd suffer more than me if we didn't pull this weekend off.

And away from the limelight and the pressure of the city, the media, the team, all of it, Maverick seems different. Like he's able to let go, ever so slightly, of the heavy pressure he seems to always be under.

The problem is, with every layer I'm peeling back to discover, I find myself falling just a little bit more for him. At first, he was just a hot baseball player with a bad attitude who needed my help.

Now I see someone different. I see a man who won't let anyone get close to him, who has built walls ten feet tall and five feet deep to keep everyone away. But also, a man who cares deeply. Who rises to expectations, even when everyone around him, including me, thinks he won't.

There's just two weeks left in our arrangement. Two weeks when I have to continue to pretend to date a man I could very easily develop feelings for if I let myself go there. But I can't.

Because there's no way those feelings would ever be returned. And if Dirk taught me anything, it's that I will no longer settle for a man who doesn't love and respect me without fail.

Several hours later, and I find myself anxiously waiting for Maverick to hit his limit. This morning he went for a hike, leaving me in the cabin alone. I didn't mind and took the time to relax and read, watching the waves from inside. When he returned, it wasn't empty-handed. He'd stopped by a local bakery and picked up a box full of incredible treats that he handed to me wordlessly before going back into the bathroom and turning on the shower again.

At least the man cares about personal hygiene.

But the reception is in full swing now, with the dinner plates cleared and the dance floor full of happy couples. Maverick held my hand throughout the ceremony, not saying a word when I started to cry at how Max and Heidi are clearly happy and in love. He was polite to everyone at our table throughout dinner, and now he's beside me, nursing a glass of clear liquid.

I smile up at another couple that walks past us with a curious look thrown our way. So far, no one has been too intense around Maverick. I guess it has something to do with Max's brother being a former pro hockey player. This crowd is used to famous athletes and don't get worked up about it. But the two of us are definitely getting some looks. I shift in my seat, trying not to worry if it's because my supposed boyfriend isn't touching me at all, or if it's because it's obvious we don't belong together.

"Can I steal your girl away for a few minutes?" Heidi smiles down at Maverick as she takes my hand and tugs me out of my chair. How out of it was I to not even realize she had walked up to us?

Maverick raises his eyebrows at me but gives Heidi a nod. She seems to take that as enough of an answer and sweeps me away from the dance floor, not stopping until we reach a pair of Adirondack-style chairs facing the water. Dropping into one with a loud sigh, Heidi tips her head to the side, facing me, and smiles. "Finally."

"Everything okay?" I ask, unsure what she means.

"Oh, everything's perfect. I'm now married, and everyone I love is here and happy. I meant, finally, I get a chance to talk to you!"

I shift on the chair, not loving the way I suddenly feel like a spotlight is shining down on me, interrogation style. "Oh, um. What do you want to talk about?"

"Gosh, Sadie, I don't know, what could we possibly talk about." She's teasing, I know it, but I'm still tense with worry. The only other time I've had to spend with a friend one-on-one since this whole thing started was with Willow that second day of my arrangement with Maverick. And it was still so new, I was in shock and fumbled my way through somehow. But Heidi knows me better than Willow. Which is going to make this a lot harder, I just know it.

"Max's family is lovely, and I see why you love it here. This part of the island is gorgeous," I say, trying to deflect. But Heidi sees right through me.

"Nice try, girlfriend. We're not talking about my amazing in-laws or this slice of heaven I get to call home. We're talking about the broody tattooed bad boy of baseball that is so obviously falling in love with you."

A wave of guilt crashes over me. I hate having to lie to anyone, but hearing my friends be so happy about something that isn't even real makes me sick to my stomach.

"I don't know if I'd go that far," I say, perhaps a little too quickly when I hear Heidi's sound of surprise. "I mean, it's not really serious or anything. We're just, I mean..." *Crap.* Heidi's face is a picture of dismay and disbelief and I know I'm screwing up big-time. "We're taking it slow. That's all."

Her face clears, and I breathe a secret sigh of relief.

"Of course. I get it, it can't be easy dating someone who's so much in the public eye. He doesn't exactly have a great reputation." Heidi frowns. "But he's got to be more than what the media shows, or you wouldn't be with him. The Sadie I know is way too smart to fall for someone who's not good for her."

Now that guilt is souring even further in my stomach. She's right, Maverick is much more than what the media shows. But she's also wrong. Because apparently, I'm not smart enough to not fall for a man like him.

"Exactly," I say, clearing my throat. "The media paints a picture, but it's not the whole picture, you know?"

"I knew it. So has he told you what happened the night of his accident?"

Um, no. That would require him talking to me. Opening up to me. And that's never going to happen.

But I can't tell Heidi that. "It's kind of a sensitive subject. Sorry, Heidi." I give her an apologetic smile, hoping she'll accept my nonanswer.

"Oh my gosh, of course. I'm sorry, here I am being all nosy when you're just trying to protect your man. Well, as long as he treats you well, he's good in my book." She pats my hand just as we hear someone calling her name.

"There you are, love." Max leans down to kiss his bride, and that small gesture is so overflowing with love, it makes my cheeks heat. "Sorry to interrupt your girl chat, but they want to do the bouquet toss."

Heidi jumps to her feet, taking Max's hand and gesturing to me with the other. "C'mon, Sadie, I'll try to aim it at you." She gives me a wink as I try to think up a way to get out of this, but Heidi Morgan — no, Heidi Donnelly now — is a force of nature when she wants to be. And the next thing I know, I'm being dragged back into the reception and to a small group of women all laughing and smiling. I glance around but don't see Maverick anywhere. Good, maybe he'll miss this embarrassing moment.

I duck behind someone, hoping Heidi's aim is terrible. But the next minute, flowers are flying through the air, straight at me, and I instinctively put my hands up. Not to catch them, just to avoid a face full of wildflowers.

But when a cheer goes up, I realize I have, in fact, caught the damn bouquet. And of course, when I look to the side, there's Maverick, his hands in his charcoal dress pants, looking like the sexiest cover model ever with his messy curly hair, tattoos peeking out from under the shirt that strains to cover his muscles. He's staring at me, an unreadable expression on his face.

Then I'm being gently pushed in his direction and someone — I think it's Max's sister Kat — is whispering to me, "Go and dance with your man."

I reach his side and look up at him, the flowers in my hand forgotten. "We don't have to do this," I whisper, unsure if the intense look he's giving me is annoyance, discomfort, or something else. Either way, I feel compelled to give him an out, an excuse if this is not okay with him.

"Sadie. I'm gonna dance with you."

His rumbling voice makes me inhale sharply. Slowly, methodically, he takes the flowers from me and sets them down on the table next to us. Then, taking my hand in his, he leads us out onto the dance floor where a few couples are slow dancing to Ed Sheeran's voice. Maverick lifts my hand to his shoulder, giving me a small quirk of his lips. "Just don't hold too tightly on that side."

I move to snatch my hand away when I realize it's his injured side, but he just takes it and puts my hand right back. "It's fine, Specs. Just wanted you to be aware."

"Maverick, we don't have to do this," I whisper, only to get a narrowing of his eyes back at me.

"Yeah. We do. I'm not the kind of guy to come to a wedding with my girl and not dance with her."

My mouth goes dry at hearing him say *my girl* even though I know he meant it hypothetically. Lord, this is bad. My feelings are like a runaway train, but there's no station on this track.

No final destination that could possibly result in anything but heartache.

Still, I let him take my other hand and interlace our fingers. And then I let him draw me close, his hand on the small of my back, fingers spread wide, holding me against him. The heat from his hand burns through my dress. I feel surrounded by him, consumed by him. And when his lips graze my ear, I know he feels me shiver.

"Relax, Specs. Try to look like you want to be here. In my arms."

I choke out a laugh at the ridiculousness of this. Here I was, worried he wouldn't be able to make it believable in front of everyone for the weekend, and instead, I'm the one holding back and acting stiff and uncomfortable. His thumb starts to stroke up and down on my back, and that small movement somehow settles me.

To my surprise, when the song ends, Maverick doesn't let go. He keeps me there in his arms for two more songs until the tempo changes to something more upbeat and we finally draw apart. Glancing around, I realize at least half of the guests have already left. Exhaustion hits me like a Mack truck.

"Do you want to call it a night?" I ask, and there's no mistaking the relief on his face.

"Yeah."

We make quick work of saying goodnight to Heidi and Max, then make our way back to our cabin. The moonlight on the water and the soft sounds of music and laughter from what's left of the reception make for one heck of a romantic moment, but I keep my hands to myself and a foot of distance between Maverick and me the entire walk.

When we reach the cabin, neither of us says a word, simply orbiting around each other as we take turns in the bathroom. I emerge in my pajamas to see him wearing the same thing he did last night, a T-shirt and shorts. Grabbing a pillow from the bed, I move to one of the chairs and settle in, tugging a blanket over my legs.

"What the fuck are you doing?"

I look up to see Maverick glaring at me. "Going to bed?"

"Like hell you are, not in that chair. Get in the bed."

I cross my arms and glare right back. "No. Don't think I didn't notice how much pain you were in this morning after sleeping on the floor. It's only fair, you get the bed tonight, and it's my choice to take the chair, not the floor."

"For fuck's sake, Sadie. You're not sleeping in a goddamn chair."

"Um, yes, I am."

His nostrils flare as we stare at each other in some weird standoff. Then suddenly, he strides over to me and yanks the blanket off.

"Maverick!" I shriek as he chucks it on the bed. I jump up, planning to get my blanket and return to the chair, but Maverick moves to stand in front of me.

He scoffs, still glowering down at me. "You want a blanket, get in the bed. You're not sleeping on the chair."

"Well, you're not sleeping on the floor."

We stare at each other for another second before a yawn overtakes me. "Fine. You know what, this will be fine. We're adults." I climb into the bed, moving all the way over to the edge. "You stay on your side, I'll stay on mine. Everything will be *fine*." To make my point, I flip over, facing the wall away from Maverick and screw my eyes shut. Another minute passes before I feel the bed dip and Maverick lying down beside me. I hold myself perfectly still, not wanting to move an inch.

After a while, he shifts and settles, turning off the bedside light and plunging the cabin into darkness. Only then do I let my eyes open and try to remember to breathe normally. Until he speaks again.

"What was it you said about that word *fine*? It never means what you want it to mean, does it, Specs?"

Chapter Fourteen

Maverick

I don't want to wake up. For once, I feel comfortable, warm, and relaxed. My brain is oddly quiet and peaceful. But it feels as if there's a weight on my chest, which probably isn't a good thing for bruised ribs that are only just healed. Except when I try to move, it doesn't go away.

Wait.

I slowly blink my eyes open. Silky red hair is spread across my chest, and the soft sounds I couldn't place are coming from the woman draped over half of my body.

Like a goddamn koala, Sadie has her arms wrapped around me and one leg over top of mine. As I come fully awake, I'm aware of another major problem, other than the pressure on my ribs. My semi-hard dick is trapped underneath Sadie's thigh, and the heat from her body is making the problem worse.

I've got to get out of here, and fast. Before she wakes up to find my dick pressing into her leg.

If the little snores are anything to go by, she's still deeply asleep. It's not easy, but I manage to shift her leg off mine first, then slowly slide out from underneath her. She makes some snuffling sounds that are fucking cute as hell, but once I'm out, her breathing stays steady, and she simply curls in on herself.

Fuck. I stand there watching her, telling myself it's just to make sure she's asleep, but the reality is, I can't look away. She's beautiful. Peaceful. And I have to admit, I didn't hate the feeling of her wrapped around me.

Which is why I make myself turn around, grab my runners and a cabin key on my way out the door, and head out into the warm morning for a run along the trails I found yesterday.

The rhythmic pounding of my feet on the ground does a little bit to help ease my confusing frustration. And I try to lose myself in the exercise, focusing on my breathing, on my steady pulse, and on how my body feels as I push it just slightly more than I have so far since the accident. Anything to put some distance between me and the tempting redhead I apparently just spent the night cuddling.

A short while later, the five or so kilometer route I took brings me back to the cabins, and I slow to a walk as I approach ours. Maybe she's still asleep and I can sneak into the shower and rub one out before she wakes up. Because after my run, I'm still hard underneath my shorts, and I can't fully blame it on the usual morning wood.

When I slowly open the door, my eyes go instantly to the bed. It looks like Sadie hasn't moved, the blankets are still moving up and down slowly. Thank fuck. I toe off my shoes and walk as silently as I can to my bag to grab some clean clothes before sneaking into the bathroom and closing the door behind me. I can't do anything about the noise of the shower, but maybe it'll be like those white noise machines Monty swears by on road trips, and it won't wake her.

I keep the water cold and step in, stifling my groan. Grabbing my dick, I try not to think about the woman on the other side the door. Swear to fucking God, I try not to be that guy. But when she's the reason I'm in this predicament, with a raging hard-on and a head full of conflicting thoughts, it's impossible.

My hand starts to move up and down, tugging far more aggressively than normal. My frustration at Sadie, at fucking everything, is mounting. She wasn't meant to get to me. She wasn't meant to be anything more than a means to an end. A tool to convince my team and my fans that I'm not the asshole they think I am. To show them there's more to me than the twisted shit the media portrays.

It's not fucking fair. So what if I can be reckless and impulsive sometimes. So what if I go overboard when I'm defending someone. I've never once acted out against anyone who didn't deserve it. Hell, there's players in the league that do way worse shit than me. They get drunk and stupid and go on social media. Cheat on their wives. Prey on other women. Just look at what happened to Willow right before my accident. That fucker deserves to rot in hell.

Why am I being tortured with a fake girlfriend that's making me start to want things I have no business wanting? Why am I facing lost endorsements and potentially rocky contract negotiations? Why does life just keep shitting on me, throwing nonstop curve balls that are impossible to field without taking damage of some kind. Why has it been this way for as long as I can remember? Me against the whole fucking world.

My release is just out of reach, and if I grind my teeth together any harder I'm gonna need a fucking mouth guard. For fuck's sake, can't I even have this? Can't I just quickly fucking jerk myself off and be done with this shit, and move on with my day, my life?

I grunt out a quiet "fuck" when I finally feel my balls draw up, and then I'm shooting cum onto the floor of the shower, screwing my eyes shut to try and banish the image of Sadie on her knees, catching it in her mouth.

When I'm done, I feel drained. And not in a good way. Guilt, shame, and anger all wash over me. Hell, maybe I am the asshole the press wants to make me out to be. Why the fuck am I feeling sorry for myself with my high-paying career, playing a game I love, when ten years ago, I didn't know if I'd even manage to graduate from high school. So what if I feel misunderstood by just about everyone? I'm living a life most only dream of. Yet here I am, dragging an innocent woman into my fucked-up life just to try and repair damage done by my own stupid actions.

Yeah. I am the asshole.

The self-condemnation monologue continues as I shower off, not feeling any better despite the physical release. Fucking hell. I need this weekend to be over. I need to go back to my apartment, to my solitude, and not be around friendly people asking polite questions, and not be around soft-hearted, redheads.

Once I'm dried off and dressed, I put my hand on the doorknob and take several slow breaths. Chances are good she's awake by now. Sure enough, when I open the door, she's sitting up in bed, her hair a messy halo around her head. She's blinking sleepily, and my gaze immediately drops to the points of her nipples poking against the T-shirt she wore to bed. *Fuck, no.* I look away immediately, hoping she didn't catch me leering at her breasts like that.

She deserves a hell of a lot better than some fucked-up baseball player with limited social skills and a bad reputation staring at her like a fucking asshole.

She deserves better than me, period. Suddenly, I want to let her out of this. Out of all of it. I want her to be free from this insanity, not tied to pretending to be into me just to save my career. It all feels so wrong, so unfair.

"Morning," she says softly, interrupting my spiral. "Hope you're not as sore this morning as you were yesterday." She gives me a gentle smile and fuck, it does something to me.

"I'm good."

Her smile grows just a little as she climbs off the bed. But when she turns and bends over to get something out of her suitcase, I inwardly groan at the sight of her curvy ass that my hands itch to grab onto.

Why. Why do I have to be attracted to her? God-fucking-damn it.

She straightens up and turns back around, that smile still on her face. I'm frozen as she walks my way, and logically, I know she's heading to the bathroom, but the dumbass part of me wishes she was heading toward me, instead. At the door to the bathroom, she pauses and looks over at me.

"You know, I have to say, I'm impressed with us. I think we did a good job convincing everyone this weekend. It went better than I expected." She pauses, looking down at her clothes.

When her gaze lifts again, the raw vulnerability in her expression floors me and makes me long to reach out and pull her into my arms, to protect her from whatever she's about to say. "And I just want to say thank you for being here with me. I was prepared to come by myself, even if it would be awkward flying solo at a wedding where I don't know anyone except the bride and groom. But you...you made it easier. Made me feel not quite so alone. And after what Dirk did to me, I'm just really happy I didn't have to be alone."

She slips into the bathroom, closing the door quietly behind her, and I just stand there like an idiot, staring at the door.

I did that? I made something easier for her?

I've had women thank me before when I step in and deal with assholes bugging them. But this moment, that quiet little speech, her obviously genuine appreciation and warmth, that somehow means more to me than anything anyone has ever said to me.

We end up skipping the brunch, opting instead for an earlier ferry — Sadie's idea, not mine, but I'm happy to avoid another social event. My battery is lower than low. Maybe she's realized that, or maybe she's also just tired. Whatever the reason, we're quiet the entire trip home, only speaking briefly to check in about food options and ferry schedules. But instead of feeling uncomfortable, it's peaceful. Easy.

Later that evening, after I've checked in with Ralph, brought Cat back over to my apartment, and unpacked from the weekend, Sadie's words still haven't left me.

You made it easier...I'm really happy I didn't have to be alone.

I like being alone. After years growing up in crowded foster homes, I crave solitude. But being alone and feeling lonely are two separate things. And after a weekend around Sadie, my quiet apartment seems oddly empty. The clink of my fork against the plate of food I just heated up for dinner echoes in the silence.

I finish eating and stand up to clear away my dishes when my phone vibrates on the table. Like a fucking putz, I snatch it up, eager to see if it's Sadie.

It's not.

> **COLIN: Saw the pics Sadie put on social media. You should share some too. Looks like the weekend wasn't so terrible. Don't forget about that dinner Tuesday night with Velocity. You gotta pour on the charm, brother. I think they're solid, but show them your good side. I can't be there, gotta go down to Seattle for one of my other guys, so it's all on you.**

I stare at his text for several seconds. I hate this shit. Dinners where I have to shmooze with sponsors, trying to get them to take me on. Normally, Colin would come and I'd just sit back and let him talk. The fact that he won't be there is unsettling. How the hell does he expect me to pull this off alone?

Unless...I didn't have to do it alone.

Instead of replying to Colin, I switch over to a different message thread and hover my thumbs over the keyboard, trying to decide what to write. How to ask without it sounding weird. Up until now, Colin arranged all of our "dates," with the exception of her asking me to the wedding.

If she can do that, I can do this.

> **MAVERICK: Hey. Are you free Tuesday night? I've got a dinner with some people from one of my endorsements. Colin was meant to come but can't now.**

I hit send before I have time to second-guess what I wrote. Rereading it, I cringe a little. It sounds cold, but then again, that's what I need. To keep it clear this is all part of our deal, and not me wanting her by my side simply because she, too, makes it easier.

CHAPTER FIFTEEN

Sadie

Maverick has been full radio silence since the message Sunday night, asking me to attend this dinner. I replied that I would come, and then that was it. Nothing more except a time and location.

I agonized all day over what to wear, almost breaking down and messaging Willow for advice. But in the end, I remembered his reaction to my purple dress on the weekend and decided to be brave once again. Tonight I'm wearing a deep royal blue blouse and pants that are tighter than I usually would wear, and while the outfit is nowhere near as revealing as the cocktail dress from the weekend, it's still a bold choice for me.

As I do my makeup and hair, I stare at myself in the mirror. I've never given much thought to my appearance. Part of fading into the background was simply choosing comfortable and functional clothes, not caring too much for style. There were other things that seemed more important, like doing well in school, making everyone around me happy, and maintaining control over my life to ensure things moved in the right direction.

Only, I never stopped to think about where that direction was headed. And now, with so much of my life in shambles, where is that control? What even are my priorities anymore? And why do I need to stay in the background? My siblings and I are all grown adults, living our own lives. Who's to say I can't step out of the shadows and live my life for myself.

Of course, who would have ever imagined that living my own life would include fake dating a professional baseball player.

The longer I look in the mirror, the more I come to face the truth I've been reluctant to admit. Ever since I caught Dirk in bed with another woman, I've felt adrift. It's not that he was the love of my life and I'm devastated and lost without him. It's more that our relationship was a tether I didn't realize was holding me down. Until that tether was gone. And maybe I'm a little afraid of what I might find if I look too closely at myself and try to open up to what I want out of life.

What if the fulfilling career, respectable husband, and happy family in a perfect-looking life isn't what I want like I thought it was? That's the life I believed I was working toward with Dirk, and now I don't know if that's actually what I ever wanted, or if that's just what I believed I *should* want.

How much of my life, decisions, and actions were because I did what I thought I should do, instead of what I wanted to do?

My stomach flip-flops at this overwhelming question that doesn't have a clear answer. Right now, with less than an hour before I have to be at the restaurant to meet Maverick, is hardly the time for an existential life crisis. With one final check of my lip stain, I decide I'm as ready as I'll ever be.

The sounds my car is making when I pull into the restaurant parking lot are a little concerning, but again, not something I can deal with right now. I get out of my car and see Maverick waiting by the door. Aware that anyone could be watching, and only a little bit because I want to, I walk over to him, lift up on my toes, and press a kiss to his cheek. "Hi," I murmur as his hand lands on my lower back.

"Hi, Specs," he says, a small, surprised-but-in-a-good-way, I think, smile on his face. He guides me inside, keeping his hand firmly in place. We're shown to a table for four, but no one else is there yet. Maverick pulls out my seat, and as I sit down, his hands land on my shoulder and he leans down. "You look beautiful."

He takes the seat next to me and I face him. "You haven't told me much about tonight. Who are we shmoozing?"

The short laugh that escapes him makes me inwardly cheer. But my question was a serious one. I need to know more about what we're doing tonight because I feel woefully unprepared.

"Just two guys from one of my sponsors, Maximum Velocity Activewear. We meet up whenever they're in town. They like to wine and dine their athletes."

I nod slowly. "You said Colin normally comes with you?"

Maverick's jaw clenches. "Yeah. I don't know if you've noticed, but I'm not normally good at the *shmoozing*, as you call it," he says wryly. "Colin's good at charming them while I sit here and just nod along."

A waiter comes by to take our drink orders, and I start to order a glass of wine, then stop. "Actually, take his order first," I say pleasantly, my eyes skimming the cocktail menu. Maverick orders a sparkling water and then turns to me, his arm reaching across the back of my chair, his thumb landing on the bare skin just above the collar of my blouse. My breath catches as my brain goes fuzzy.

"White wine. Pinot grigio please," I stutter out, closing the menu and giving it to the waiter. How does one small touch undo me?

Maverick leans in again, and I stifle a moan at the fresh scent that after two days of sharing a living space, I will forever associate with him and nothing else reaches me. "If you want a cocktail instead of your usual wine, you should get one. Live a little, Specs."

Before I can think of a response, or question how he knows my usual drink of choice is wine, or that I was truly considering something else before he scrambled my ability to think with that thumb on my back, a tall man with a significantly large belly walks up.

"Mav fucking King, my man!" He grabs Maverick's hand, pumping it up and down.

My eyes widen because it's his injured side, but Maverick's face is impassive, showing no sign of discomfort.

"Hey, Chip. This is my girl Sadie. Hope you don't mind she's joining us."

"Of course not." The man, Chip, turns to me with a smile that's just a little too wide to be genuine. "Lovely to meet you, Sadie. You're the one keeping this guy in check, aren't you? My wife is loving the pictures of you two."

"Hello, nice to meet you," I manage to force out, already uncomfortable.

It's immediately obvious why Maverick lets Colin take the lead in these situations. Knowing the little I do about him, his introverted nature and preference for low-key interactions, someone like Chip must be a lot.

But proving once again that Maverick can rise to the occasion, he holds his own. The conversation flows, and when I can, I contribute. But truthfully, when Chip starts droning on about the latest line of compression wear his company is launching that apparently, Maverick is the face for, I lose track. While they're deep in conversation about photo shoots and design concepts, I glance around the restaurant. There's been a few times I've noticed people darting looks our way, but our table is near the back, in a corner, giving us some semblance of privacy.

A hand landing on my thigh startles me. My head whips around to see Maverick eyeing me. "Specs?" he murmurs quietly, and I realize they must have asked me a question.

"I'm so sorry, what was that?" I give Chip and his partner a smile.

"Chip was generously offering you a set from the latest women's line if you want it."

My eyebrows lift. "Me? Oh, that's not necessary, really. Thank you, but —"

"Nonsense." Chip waves his hand at me. "You're Mav's girl, you're in all his photos, so really, it benefits us. Hell, we should probably sign you your own endorsement deal." He chortles, and I force out a laugh along with him even though I really don't know what's so funny. "Anyway. Email my assistant your size and colour preferences and we'll set you up."

Maverick's hand is still resting on my thigh, and he squeezes gently. "Thanks, Chip. That's good of you."

"Y-yes. Thanks." I'm still trying to reconcile the fact that Maverick's hand is on my leg, burning through the fabric, and now that damn thumb is slowly moving up and down. It could almost be an unconscious movement if not for the way he's still looking at me, like he knows what his touch is doing to me.

It's heating me up from the inside out. It's making me want to clench my thighs together, but then also shift them to move his hand higher. It's making me think of things, dirty things, that I have no business thinking of with Maverick King.

My tongue darts out to lick my lips, and his gaze drops to them, following the motion. His hold on me tightens ever so slightly.

Our food arrives and Maverick is forced to let go. I can't decide if I'm relieved or disappointed. Either way, I'm also confused. The rest of dinner goes by in somewhat of a blur, for me, at least. And then, finally, after what feels like hours of torture waiting for Maverick's next touch, we're standing up from the table, moving to the door, and saying goodnight to Maverick's sponsor.

"I'm glad you could join us tonight, Sadie. You're good for this guy. Keep it up." I give Chip a faint smile, not wanting him to see how desperate I am to get out of here.

"Thank you for letting me join, Chip. I hope you have a nice evening."

Maverick shakes their hands, then walks me out to the parking lot and over to my car.

"Thanks. For coming tonight, I mean." His voice is low and rumbly, and the sound of it only adds fuel to the fire of my arousal after tonight. I'm honestly embarrassed at how turned on I managed to get from nothing but a few touches of his hands. He probably meant nothing by it, simply playing the role of doting boyfriend. But there's no avoiding the truth that as soon as I get home, I'm pulling out my box of toys and giving myself some relief.

"No problem. Have a good night." I give him what's probably too big of a smile and climb into my car, hoping he'll walk over to his vehicle. No such luck. Taking a few steps back, hands in his pockets, he waits to make sure I get on my way home before leaving. It's sweet and doesn't help the whole *turned on by everything he does* situation I'm fighting.

I put the key in the ignition and turn it, but nothing happens.

"Shit." I turn the key again. Still nothing. Not even a click. I want to drop my head to the steering wheel in frustration, but I know Maverick's watching me. Mustering up what I hope is a calm expression, I open my door and climb out. "Well, not sure what's going on here, but my car won't start. It's fine," I say as he starts to walk over to me. "I've got roadside assistance. I'll call them and just wait at the coffee shop across the street."

"I'll wait with you."

"No, no, that's not necessary." Oh Lord, no. I'm barely holding it together right now. I need Maverick King far away from me, or I don't know what I'll do. My body is still tingling just from his touch all through dinner. His hand on my leg, the whisper of his breath on my neck, all of it has me feeling like a live wire is running through my body.

"Sadie. I'm waiting with you, or I'm driving you home. You choose."

I choose to ignore him and dial roadside assistance. But when the recorded voice tells me my estimated wait time is more than two hours, I know I'm in trouble. I take a deep breath, hold it, and exhale slowly.

"Fine. I'll take a ride home."

The last thing I want is Maverick seeing where I currently live. That thought alone manages to douse every shred of arousal that was coursing through me minutes ago.

CHAPTER SIXTEEN

Maverick

As the GPS in my car directs me to Sadie's apartment, I can feel my frown growing deeper. What the actual fuck is she doing living in this part of town? Graffiti adorns most of the buildings and there's a steady sound of the nearby trains mixed with constant sirens. The people walking down the sidewalk this late in the evening are not exactly family-friendly. Yeah, I'm no snob; hell, I've lived in shittier places, but this is not the kind of place a single woman should be staying.

When I pull up to the front of her building, my anger and confusion only grows. "Specs, what the fuck are we doing here."

But instead of answering me, Sadie unbuckles and climbs out of the SUV so fast, I'm scrambling to turn off the car and follow her.

"Thanks for the ride, Maverick," she calls out as she moves to the front door, sidestepping a pile of garbage.

"Stop," I say, and I guess she can tell from my tone, I'm not fucking around. "Sadie. What the hell."

She turns slowly, defiance sparking in her eyes. But I can see the tremble, the embarrassment hiding underneath. I'm familiar with that feeling. Shame over where you live, or how, or what things you own, or don't. I grew up in that world. I recognize those emotions even as she tries to hide them.

"It's fine, Maverick. Good night." She turns to walk away and I reach out and grab her arm.

"Fuck that, I'm walking you up to your apartment."

Pressing the button to lock my vehicle with one hand, I keep the other firmly on her elbow, not missing a step as we walk into her building. The musty smell of damp carpets and lingering cigarette smoke permeates the air. A guy wearing a stained white tank top and shorts comes shuffling down the hall, bringing with him a waft of stale alcohol. He leers at Sadie and given the fact that she's all dressed up from dinner, I know exactly what kind of shit he's thinking. I glare at him, the promise of pain in my gaze if he doesn't back off. He sees me and stumbles, rightfully reading the rage I'm pushing at him. He gives us a wide berth as he walks out the front door, but I notice how he turns back to look at us. He notices me watching him and darts away.

Sadie bypasses the elevator for the stairs, and we make our way up to the third floor. The stairwell stinks like a dirty locker room if the players all smoked and pissed in the corners.

When we reach what I assume is her apartment, she stops and turns to me. "There. You walked me up. Now will you leave?"

I simply arch my brow. She lets out a little huff, and if I wasn't so unamused, I'd probably smile. But she doesn't force me to go, turning back to unlock her door.

"Just so you know, the Vancouver rental market is awful right now. It was either this or staying with my parents for another month, and I could only take so much of their badly concealed pity. They loved Dirk, and even though they know what he did is unforgivable, they've got it in their heads that my life is now ruined because I'm not with him."

I'm not touching that statement with a ten-foot pole. But as soon as we walk into her apartment, I start shaking my head.

"No. What the hell, Sadie. You can't live here."

I turn slowly, taking in the water damage on the ceiling and the loud hum of a refrigerator that is probably about to die. There's a rickety table and two chairs, a nasty-looking couch, and that's it for furniture. A glance at the door shows me it doesn't even have a security chain, just a deadbolt. How the fuck does a woman with a successful career end up in a place like this? Jesus fucking Christ.

"Pack a bag, Specs. Whatever you need for a couple of days. We'll get the rest of your shit later."

"Excuse me?"

I turn at her incredulous tone to see her standing with her hands on her hips, eyes narrowed at me.

"What part of that wasn't clear?"

I'm being a demanding, controlling ass, but I don't fucking care. The sooner she packs, the sooner we can get out of this shithole.

"The bit where you decided you have the right to dictate where I live. That was *not* part of the agreement."

I fold my arms across my chest and stare back at her. "You're telling me you like living here?"

It takes a few seconds before I see her resignation. "No. I hate it. But I'm not joking when I say it was the best I could find in my budget. I needed something fully furnished because when I moved in with Dirk, he convinced me to sell almost everything I owned. And furnished apartments in the city are hard to come by."

Fuck. She sounds broken, and I hate the thought that at least some of it might be from me being too heavy-handed. Lowering my arms, I move closer, cautiously, as if she's a feral animal and not a woman I'm starting to care for a little too much. Lifting one hand, I move painfully slow, giving her time to step back. But she doesn't, her eyes now showing more of that vulnerability and less defiance. I tuck a strand of red hair behind her ear and drift my hand down until it reaches hers. Picking it up, I hold it softly. "Come on. Let's pack some shit up and get out of here."

Her tongue swipes across her lips as she considers my words, and as I wait for her to accept or reject my offer, my heart pounds loudly in my ears. If she says no, I'll have to stay here. I'll camp out on her couch or in the hallway. I'm not leaving her here alone.

"Okay."

She says it quietly, but I can hear the relief in that one word, and I know she's grateful for me getting her out of here. Without dropping my hand, she turns, and I let her lead me into the bedroom. I keep my eyes turned away from her bed where a pair of panties is sitting on the sheets. When I hear her muffled curse, my lips quirk up, knowing she's spotted them.

Barely five minutes later, she's standing in front of me with a suitcase and a duffle bag. "Alright, I'm ready." I take the suitcase and let her lead me to the front door.

On the way out, she grabs a pair of runners from the closet, but other than that, Sadie doesn't hesitate in leaving her slum of an apartment behind. When her hand slips in mine after locking the door, I don't react. At least, not outwardly. But inside, something in me cracks open at the trust she's placed in me, at the way she's seeking and accepting comfort and security from me.

We're silent the entire drive across the city to my building. I don't live in a fancy high-rise like some of my teammates, but my place is nice. When I bought it in my first season with the Tridents, all I cared about was having somewhere safe and comfortable to lay my head at night. I didn't give a shit about amenities or the view. But compared to the shithole Sadie was living in, my place feels like a fucking palace.

When I hold open the door for her, letting her walk in first, I watch to see her reaction, but all I detect is barely-concealed curiosity.

"So, there's only one bedroom. And before you even try to say anything about that, let me tell you, I've slept on my couch many times and it's perfectly comfortable." I walk past her, heading toward the bedroom to grab a pillow for myself. "The sheets are clean as of this morning, my housekeeper was here."

"If the couch is so comfortable, then it'll be fine for me." Sadie arches a brow at me. But I'm not doing this shit again. And there's no goddamn chance I'm gonna be able to sleep in *my bed* with her. And her defiance is ruined when she can't completely hide her yawn.

"Go to bed, Sadie. You're falling asleep on your fucking feet. We can discuss sleeping arrangements tomorrow."

The standoff is broken by the sound of Cat chirping and meowing as he prowls out from the bedroom.

"Well, who is this?" Sadie asks, her voice sounding happy for the first time all evening as she drops down into a crouch to pet the damn animal. "What a gorgeous kitty. Hello there, what's your name?"

Cat just purrs, arching into her touch.

"That's Cat. He used to hang out in the bushes out front, then one day snuck in with me. I can't get rid of him," I say gruffly.

The beaming smile Sadie turns on me almost makes me stumble back. It's such a sudden change from the emotionally spent woman who walked in here a few minutes ago.

"Are you serious? Are you a secret softie when it comes to animals?" She turns back to the goddamn cat and starts cooing at him. "I think he is, don't you? Big bad Maverick King is actually a total marshmallow. Can't help but rescue damsels in distress." She giggles, and the sound is pure fucking sunshine. "Well, I guess you're not a damsel, are you? No, you're not, you big handsome boy."

She stands up, scooping Cat into her arms. He drapes himself over her shoulder and I can hear the purring from here. Looking over at me, Sadie blushes, I'm guessing because she realizes what she just said about me rescuing her. Little does she know, my chest fucking puffed with pride when she said that, making me almost blush right along with her.

I clear my throat and look away. "Right. So. Bathroom is there." I gesture down the hall. "Help yourself to anything in the kitchen. I'll just grab some stuff from my room, then it's all yours."

Moving swiftly to put some distance between me and the far-too-fucking-tempting redhead cuddling my damn cat, I reach my bedroom. Placing my hands on the dresser, I let my head hang forward and take in a few deep breaths. What the fuck am I doing?

No one has been in my apartment except for Colin, my housekeeper, Ralph, and Eli on a couple of occasions.

I don't have guests over. I sure as fuck don't have women over.

Yet standing in my living room is a woman who has managed to get under my skin and made her way into a part of me I didn't think existed.

I care about Sadie LeDuc.

And I don't usually let myself get close enough to *anyone* to care about them.

Fucking hell, I'm in trouble.

As if to drive home that point, my phone vibrates. I pull it out of my pocket and immediately wish I hadn't as guilt mixed with anger washes over me.

> **ELI: Bro. Where you at? I msgd you like weeks ago. I need cash, man. Hit me back.**

I lock my phone and slide it back into my pocket without answering. But the damage is done. I've been reminded that my feelings for Sadie aren't exactly the only *trouble* in my life right now.

Chapter Seventeen

Maverick

The sound of someone in my kitchen pulls me from asleep to awake. My groggy brain assumes it's Colin; he's the only one with a key other than my housekeeper, and she was just here. Then a distinctly feminine voice starts murmuring something to Cat, and reality slams into me.

Sadie.

Sitting up, I push off the blanket draped over my legs and look over the back of the couch toward the kitchen. She's got Cat in her arms again and is slowly swaying back and forth with that fucking animal snuggled right in against her neck.

Great, now I'm jealous of a goddamn cat. And my dick is taking notice of the way she looks all adorably rumpled in a set of pajama shorts and a T-shirt that is falling off her shoulder, showing way too much of that pale smooth skin. Fucking hell.

A frustrated noise slips out and Sadie's head darts up, her gaze meeting mine.

"Morning, I hope I didn't wake you." She gives me a hesitant smile, no longer swaying but still holding my cat in her arms.

"You didn't." I clear my throat to get rid of the sleepy gravel sound. Turning back around so I'm not looking at her, I recite as many of my youth stats as I can remember to try and get things to settle down so I can stand up without freaking her out.

But my self-control is put to the test when I hear her set Cat down and the familiar sound of coffee being poured. Then it's shot to hell when she walks over and sets two coffee mugs on the table. I just barely have time to grab the blanket and throw it over my lap before she sits down at the opposite end of the couch.

Picking up her own coffee, she takes a sip and lets out a sound of contentment that does nothing to help my situation.

For ten years, I've woken up alone. Even at training camp, or on away game trips, I have my own room. Ever since leaving the group home at eighteen, I've lived by myself. I like silence. Solitude. I like not having to deal with people first thing in the morning.

But Sadie doesn't say anything, just sits there sipping coffee in the quiet. And slowly, surprisingly, I find myself relaxing back into the couch. I lean forward, pick up my coffee, and take a sip, then look at her. "This is good. Thanks."

She gives me a quick smile, but still doesn't say anything. Just drinks her coffee at the opposite end of the couch, gently stroking Cat who hopped up between us to curl into a ball.

And fuck, it's actually kind of nice.

Sadie finishes first and stands up from the couch. "I'll just take a quick shower if that's okay. I can go find a café to work at today."

My confusion must be clear because she goes on.

"I haven't been to the office since this started. The reporters...it got a little crazy that first day so my boss suggested I work from home."

In an instant, that confusion is replaced with indignation. "Are you serious?" She nods. "You were working out of that shithole? For the last three weeks?"

Her eyes fill with fire. "Listen. That shithole was my home. I get that it's not up to your millionaire athlete standards, and I'm not saying I love it there, but it was home. I did what I had to do, after *a man* turned my entire life upside down. And yeah, I hated working from home. Being stuck there all day, every day. But once again, it was what I had to do after *another man* messed up my life even more."

The way she's glaring at me makes it clear who she's referring to. And I guess I'm a sick bastard because the way she's standing up and pushing back at me is fucking hot as hell. It's not hard to see that Sadie tends to think of everyone but herself. That what she wants comes second to what everyone around her wants. And I wish so badly I could tell her to stop. To put herself first because fuck knows no one else will. It's a lesson I learned the hard way.

But seeing that fire in her, even as she's giving me hell, is a relief. Because maybe she won't have to go through anymore shit to realize she's worth being a priority in her own life.

"Sorry, Specs," I reply, and I mean it. I am sorry my notoriety made things messy for her. But I'm not sorry for stepping up when her ex was being a fucker.

Sinking back down onto the couch, she lets out a long sigh. "No, don't apologize. You haven't done anything wrong. Heck, you've been nothing but good to me." She grimaces, looking down at her empty coffee mug. "My life was a mess before you showed up, and you were just trying to help that night."

I say nothing as she stands up again and reaches out for my mug. "Anyway. I'll shower, then get out of here for the day so you can have some peace and quiet. I could probably just take my stuff back to my parents' place for a while or go stay with my friend."

"If those were good options, you'd have done them already, wouldn't you?"

I see her swallow before she answers. "It's not ideal, but I can't crash here forever, either."

I stand up to join her, taking both mugs and moving into the kitchen. "No, but you don't have to go anywhere yet." Reaching into a drawer, I withdraw something and make my way back to her. "Stay. I've got to go to a rehab session at the stadium anyway. But if you do leave, for the day or whatever, come back here after." I take her hand and place the spare key in her palm.

She stares at it, then slowly lifts her head to meet my gaze. "Why?"

Her soft question hits me, and I don't know how to answer. I shrug instead. "Why not."

Walking away, I go into my room, grab some clothes, and then walk back out. She's still standing in the spot where I left her, staring down at the key in her hand. "I'll just get changed quickly, then the place is yours."

I get the barest of nods, and that's it. By the time I finish getting changed and brushing my teeth, the door to my bedroom is closed.

I have no idea if she'll stay or not. But I do know if I find out she's back in that fucking apartment, I'm gonna lose my shit. And then Colin would be mad at me.

She better be here when I get back from the stadium...

My entire body is aching the entire drive home from the ball-park several hours later. Lark and the rest of the training staff fucking tortured me, and holy fuck, am I feeling the exhaustion, but Doc made my goddamn day when he said I can start throwing again in a week.

I pull into my spot in the underground parking garage and ride the elevator up to my floor, slowly rolling my shoulders.

As I approach my apartment, the door across the hall opens.

"There's a woman in your apartment."

I give Ralph a rare grin. "Yeah, I know."

"What's that all about?"

"I'll let you know when I do."

Ralph harrumphs and closes his door again. But my grin doesn't go anywhere. *She's still here.* It's weird as fuck how excited I am by that, and when I unlock the door and push it open, I'm hit with an incredible aroma of tomato and basil. She's here...and she cooked?

But Sadie's not in the kitchen, where I look first. Then I spy her red hair piled on top of her head, peeking out over the back of the couch.

Setting my keys down, I walk around the end of the sofa and find her with Cat tucked into her side, her laptop on her legs, and an adorable look of concentration on her face. Her lack of acknowledgment makes sense when I see the earbuds tucked in her ears.

"Holy crap!" She slams her computer shut when she notices me.

"Sorry, didn't realize you couldn't hear me come in." I glance down at her computer. "You don't have to stop working on my account."

She blushes furiously. "It's fine. I was done."

"What were you working on?" I sit down in the chair next to the couch instead of heading for my bedroom to change.

"Nothing." She's fidgeting with her hands.

"Really." I arch my brow at her and wait. "Nothing?" Her blush deepens. Interesting... "Sadie. What were you doing?" I don't honestly know why I'm pushing this, but now I really fucking want to know what she was doing.

"Promise you won't laugh?"

"Well, now I'm not promising anything."

If she could shoot daggers from her eyes, she would be right now. "Maverick."

"Specs."

Letting out a little huff, she opens her computer up again. "Fine. But if you start to judge me, I'll..." she trails off.

"You'll what?" I can't hide my growing grin; this is too much fun.

"I don't know. So don't judge me."

I lift my hands up. "Fine. No judging."

The computer comes to life with some random couple on the screen. "Reality TV? That's your dirty little secret?"

"No judging." She narrows her gaze at me. "And yes. I like to watch these ridiculous dating shows to unwind sometimes."

I move to the couch, sitting down on the other side of Cat. "Okay, show me."

The incredulous look Sadie gives me is honestly funny as shit. "You're joking."

"Nope. But can we eat at the same time? Something smells amazing."

Sadie jumps up off the couch. "Oh! I made dinner."

I follow her into the kitchen and watch her bustle around the space as if she's been here for years, not less than a day. She plates some pasta with a red sauce that is clearly the source of that aroma I noticed when I got home. Then she pulls out two small bowls of salad from the fridge and sets them on the counter. Taking a step back, she looks at me. "I'm hoping you like pasta."

"I do." Closing the distance, I pick up a fork and take a bite. Flavours explode on my tongue, and I quickly swallow only so I can take another, larger bite. "This is really fucking good, Specs."

She stands up straighter, her head ducked, but I can see the smile my praise brings. "I'm glad you like it. I called Willow to see what kind of food you might like; I wasn't sure if there was a diet plan or something during the season. But she said anything was fine as long as it was high protein. So I thought my mom's Bolognese would be a good option. I remember my brother eating tons of it when he was on the track team in high school."

God, she's so fucking cute when she rambles. But I can't let myself think that for too long. Especially when it's clear I need to make damn sure she knows her staying here doesn't come with strings attached.

"I appreciate the food, but you know you don't have to cook for me. I have premade meals in the freezer." It's clearly the wrong thing to say, as her face falls slightly, and I scramble to recover. "Not that I don't like it. I do. I just don't want you feeling like you have to." Good fucking God, now I'm the one being awkward. What is it about her that makes me all mushy and shit? I know if I don't get it together, she's gonna realize I like her more than I should. And that...can't happen.

"You're giving me a place to stay, the least I can do is cook. Besides, I like feeling useful. I like doing things for other people."

"When's the last time you let someone do something for you?" The question is out there before I can overthink it. But goddamn it, I want to know. And I want *her* to know it's okay to just let someone else take care of things for once.

She bites her lower lip, and it takes all of my restraint not to reach over and free it. But after a few seconds, her answer is exactly what I was hoping to hear.

"When I let you bring me here."

"Good answer," I say gruffly. Then I set the bowls of salad on the plates and pick both up, needing to do something before I get stupid and kiss her. "Now let's go watch this show of yours."

CHAPTER EIGHTEEN

Sadie

"Tell me again, what's an RBI?" I ask Willow as she leads me through a maze of hallways in the depths of the stadium complex. My head is brimming with baseball facts and statistics that, hopefully, I don't get mixed up. When I asked Maverick to teach me the basics so I didn't look like a fool at the game today, he initially tried to tell me it didn't matter. But I disagreed. If the world thinks we've been dating for a while now, it stands to reason that I should know something about the sport.

So last night, we ordered pizza, and he walked me through the basics of the game.

But now that I'm here without him since he's spending the game in the dugout with his team, I'm wishing I had started learning this stuff a long time ago. Even without him by my side, I know everyone will be watching me closely. My reactions, my enthusiasm, all of it on display.

"RBI stands for run batted in. It's when a player makes it home from another player's hit."

"Okay, and —"

"Sadie, girl, you need to relax! No one will be quizzing you on baseball facts, I promise."

Her gentle smile is probably meant to be reassuring, but all I can do is worry that she's questioning my freak-out.

"Right. Of course. I know." I force a smile that seems to do the trick as we resume walking to our seats. When she first invited me to attend, I assumed she meant we'd sit in the stands like everyone else. Then she explained she was taking the day off to watch the game with her boyfriend's family. Which, apparently, means sitting in a reserved area right beside the dugout.

My pulse speeds up when I see the packed stadium full of Tridents fans and the cameras everywhere, from their internal marketing team and the local media covering the game. Then my heart races when my gaze lands on the men out on the field. I find number 17 in an instant, the same number emblazoned across my back. This is the first game where Maverick's out on the field for warm-up, even though he won't be playing. There was no mistaking his outright joy when he came home last night and told me he'd be out there today.

For a brief second, I thought he might hug me, he was so excited. Over the last while that I've been staying at his place, it's been impossible not to notice how the small touches have increased. The graze of his fingers against mine when I pass him something, shoulders bumping together in the kitchen when we're both in there. And it's not just that. He's started making me coffee every morning, somehow getting the cream and sugar ratio absolutely perfect every time. When I'm working, he'll bring me over a fresh glass of water without asking. My shampoo was running low, but before I could get out to buy some more, a brand-new bottle appeared. Those moments, when I can almost fool myself into thinking his actions could mean something *more*, are becoming harder to ignore.

I know it's crazy, and impossible, and a terrible idea. But God, I wish it was real. That I had a man treat me the way he does, not because of an arrangement, or appearances, but because they truly cared about me. Wanted me.

But he didn't hug me.

And it's not real. My feelings might be, but they will never go anywhere.

We reach our seats, and Willow introduces me to Ronan's mother and his daughter. As their conversation flows around me, I let myself watch Maverick. He looks good, too good, in that uniform. The pants cupping his butt, the jersey looking like he was born to wear it. He seems relaxed, too. The most relaxed I think I've ever seen him. It's obvious, to me at least, that this is where he belongs. Out there, playing ball. Empathy floods me as I realize how difficult it must have been for him these last several weeks, not playing.

Whoever it is he's throwing the ball back and forth with says something, and his head turns, his gaze meeting mine. I tentatively lift my hand in a small wave, then snatch it down immediately, feeling silly. Until he lifts his and gives me a rare smile.

"No freaking way, did Mav just smile at you?" Willow gasps, grabbing my arm. "Good Lord, I didn't think he knew how to do that."

She's teasing. I know this. But a burst of protectiveness shoots through me anyway.

"Just because he's not the most outgoing guy doesn't mean he doesn't smile."

Willow's eyebrows raise nearly to her hairline. "Okay, down girl. I didn't mean any offense." Her head tilts to the side. "I know there's a good guy underneath the bad boy exterior. The whole team does. It's why he's still here. Because even when his reckless choices land him in trouble, we believe in him and want nothing more than to help him. It's why my uncle is so happy you're in the picture."

"What does that mean?" I ask, even though I'm not sure I really want the answer.

Willow waves at Ronan on the field, a huge grin on her face before she turns to me to reply. "I don't know exactly. But I think it's because he wanted Mav to have something, or someone, to ground him, and help him remember that good things exist in life. I don't know the details of his past, but I'm assuming it wasn't great. And when you don't have a great past, you need something really great to keep you moving forward. You're that something great for Mav."

My heart is cracking in two at Willow's words. She's right, I know she's right, even though I also don't know the details of who Maverick King is and where he came from. But I can tell there are broken parts of him, damaged pieces from his childhood that he hides from everyone. And I can tell, despite all that, he's a man worthy of love and happiness if he could just believe that for himself.

But Willow's wrong if she thinks I'm the person to help him understand. Because I don't mean anything to him, not really. I'm not "something great" as she put it. I'm just a girl he bailed out of a crappy situation and ended up in an even more complicated one as a result.

I look across the diamond and find him again, this broken man whose name is on the back of my shirt. And as he turns to jog off the field with the rest of his teammates, his eyes find mine, and his lips tip up ever so slightly again.

There's no more denying it for me. I want to be the woman to put Maverick King's heart back together again.

I don't see him the rest of the game, as he's in the dugout with his teammates, and I'm in the stands with Willow and her family. I'm unsure what I should do when the game ends. Do I just go home, or am I meant to wait for him? Willow takes the decision out of my hands after the Tridents make an easy win and she stands up, takes Ronan's daughter's hand, and gestures to me.

"Come on, let's go find our boys."

Ronan's lovely mother, Pam, waves us off. "I'll head home, see you later, girls."

Then I'm following Willow and Peyton down the few steps to the gate that opens onto the field. It's crowded with players, staff, media personnel, and grounds crew all bustling around. But I find Maverick quickly, leaning against the railing of the dugout, staring out at the field.

I'm not sure I'm allowed in there, so I make my way over to the other side of the railing until I'm close to him. He turns to face me, and I'm graced with another small smile.

"Hey, Specs. What did you think of your first game?"

Apparently, I've become quite skilled at figuring out what Maverick *isn't* saying when he talks, because I easily detect the wistfulness in his tone. He's wishing he had been out there playing today.

"It was good. Fun. I don't know that I understood everything that happened, though."

He reaches a hand out, and tentatively, I place mine in his. He laces our fingers together as I glance around, certain there must be a camera on us. But there isn't. They're all paying attention to the other players.

"We can do some more lessons at home."

"Okay," I whisper back, not letting him see how that word, *home,* got to me. How can one word, one single word, make my entire body warm while making me feel empty at the same time?

Willow calls my name, and I look to the side to see her gesturing for me to follow her. "I think I have to go," I say, looking back to Maverick. He gives me a nod and lets go of my hand. I turn to leave, but I haven't taken more than two steps before he speaks again. And this time, what he says doesn't just make me feel warm. This time, he makes the very air I breathe feel ten degrees hotter.

"You look good wearing my name, Specs."

CHAPTER NINETEEN

Sadie

When Maverick walks out of the bathroom after his shower, there's a strange expression on his face.

"Are you okay?" I ask, making my way over to him, concern mounting that his injury is acting up or something.

He won't meet my gaze but gives a sharp nod. "You...you left something in there." His clipped words are followed by him walking swiftly into the bedroom and closing the door.

Baffled, I peer in the bathroom. "Oh crap!" I hastily snatch the bra off the towel rack. Oh my God. My face is aflame with mortification. How could I have forgotten that? I've only just started to come to grips with admitting my full-blown attraction to the man. To myself, that is. Every night since the baseball game, where I finally saw him in his element, I've lain awake, tossing and turning, unable to stop my mind from fantasizing about the beautifully broken man sleeping out on the couch.

I guess it makes sense that with the lack of sleep, I'd eventually do something stupid, like forget my bra in the bathroom when I showered after finishing work earlier today. I'd changed into

my workout wear and done some yoga in the living room while
Maverick finished whatever he was doing at the stadium.

He came home as I was starting to prepare dinner, and after
a grunt hello, he headed straight into the bathroom. He was in
there a long time, long enough for me to finish prepping dinner
with the exception of adding some sliced avocado to the salad.

Now I'm stuck standing in the hallway with a ma-
roon-coloured lace bra in hand, anxiously waiting for him to
come out of the bedroom so I can put it away. And possibly
suffocate some screams of embarrassment in the pillows.

He opens the door, and his gaze lands on the bra I'm clutching to my chest. Then, slowly, he drags it up to my face. We face
off. Right there, in the hallway outside the bedroom. I can hear
my pulse pounding in my ears, feel the heat rising within me,
and the urge to kiss him growing. What would he do, I wonder?
Would he push me away, or would he hold me in those strong
arms. Would he plunder my mouth, taking it further than we
have so far, with our chaste kisses just for show.

When he opens his mouth, I lean forward. Only to have a
metaphorical bucket of cold water dumped over my head.

"Colin's coming over to talk about your gala this weekend
and what happens after that."

"Oh."

Yeah, that's all I manage to say. *Oh.* Then he's brushing past
me and heading toward the kitchen. Apparently, we're ignoring
the bra incident.

I hurry to put the offending item away and take several slow,
deep breaths. He's not interested in me that way, clearly. Everyone says Maverick is reckless and impulsive. And by everyone, I

mean the media, Willow, and, well, him. I know there's more to it than that, but if he were even the slightest bit attracted to me, wouldn't his reckless and impulsive nature have him acting on it by now?

Clearly, whatever I feel is one-sided. And any actions I think of as him reciprocating is not that at all. Maybe I'm just so starved for affection and attention after having my heart battered by Dirk, I'm seeing things. That must be it.

By the time I walk back out to the kitchen, Maverick's on the couch with Cat in his lap, purring loudly. Ignoring him, I go to the kitchen to finish dishing out dinner. It's weird he's not standing here, insisting on helping like he has every other night, but I guess bra-gate has him needing some space.

Heck, maybe he took one look at my bra and lost his appetite. It might be lacy, but it's also not exactly small. It can't be to contain my generous breasts. Maybe the stark evidence that I'm not a size two was enough to make him need space.

Except he's not like that. I don't know how I know that, but I do. Maverick's not the kind of man to judge on appearances, or size, or anything like that. Not when he himself has been judged unfairly for so long.

"Ouch!" I cry out, so lost in thought I managed to slip while slicing the avocado and cut myself instead. Blood is welling up as I move to the sink to rinse my hand, and then he's there.

"What happened?" His voice sounds worried as his arms wrap around me from behind, crowding me against the sink as he gently takes my hand out from under the cold water to inspect it. "Shit, Specs. What did you do?"

I want to push back against him, move him away from me. But I also want to sink into the protective, caring hold. This is why I can't focus. Because, for the life of me, I can't make sense of this man's actions.

"I wasn't paying attention. The knife slipped. I'll be fine," I say as Maverick tears off some paper towel and wraps it around my finger. He's still gently clasping it in his hand as he turns off the tap and moves to my side.

"Let's go get it cleaned up and make sure you don't need stitches."

I try to protest as he holds my hand in his, wrapping his free arm around my waist as if he's worried I might faint or something, and walks slowly to the bathroom.

"Maverick, it's just a little cut, honestly. It doesn't need stitches."

But my attempts at reassuring him that I'm fine are ignored as he sits me down on the closed toilet seat and lifts my hand in the air, giving me a look that tells me I'm to keep it there. I heave a sigh and prop my elbow on the counter.

He crouches down, removing a first aid kit from under the sink, opening it with a fierce concentration. I can't help but stare in amazement at his gentle caregiving as he pulls out gauze, bandages, and some plastic vials of liquid.

"Okay. Let's take off the paper towel and see what we're dealing with," he says softly. When he glances up, there's nothing but concern and compassion in his eyes, and it floors me to see this side of him. All I can do is nod.

He's incredibly careful, unwinding the paper towel to reveal the small cut. An adorable furrow appears between his brows as he turns my finger, prodding lightly. "Good. It's small, doesn't seem too deep. We can just clean it and bandage it here. No stitches necessary."

I resist the urge to tell him *I told you so.* Because this man, this sweet, kind man who is painstakingly gentle as he breaks the tip off one of the vials and squeezes what I assume is sterile water over the cut, is making it hard for me to formulate a clear thought, let alone talk.

He dabs it dry with gauze before wrapping a bandage around my finger. Then he takes away my ability to breathe.

Lifting my finger, his eyes trained on mine, Maverick presses the lightest of kisses over the bandage. "All good." His voice is nothing more than a hoarse whisper, but I feel it vibrate through my entire body.

"Thank you," I whisper back.

He shifts away, the space between us making me want to whimper in disappointment. But I let him take a step back, and another. Then I stand up, and with one more little smile, I walk past him, hoping he can't see just how deep I am in all of my feelings.

Back in the kitchen, I make sure I didn't drip blood onto any of the food before finishing the salad and dishing everything up. Setting the plates on the counter, I busy myself by pouring glasses of water and setting out cutlery. "Is Colin coming for dinner?"

"No. He just texted that it'll be an hour before he's here."

I can't bring myself to look at him, instead sitting on the very edge of my seat.

"Sadie."

My food goes down my throat in a solid lump.

"Yes?"

"Can you look at me?"

I set my fork down and force myself to turn in my seat to face him.

"I'm sorry if I crossed a line. When I…you know."

"Oh, you didn't," I reply breezily, even though I feel anything but. "It's fine. You were just being kind. Thanks for that, by the way."

His blue eyes bore into me, and I fight not to squirm under the scrutiny.

"Yeah. No problem."

It feels like time stands still as I wait to see if he'll say anything more. But he doesn't, turning instead to his meal. We eat in silence. In fact, the next hour passes in silence. But it's charged, somehow. I want so badly to just blurt out the words *I like you, I wish this wasn't fake*. But I'm terrified.

When the knock on the door comes, it's a relief. Maverick opens it with a frown. "Why didn't you use your key?" he asks as Colin comes into the room.

"Because it's not just you here, asshole." He gives me a nod. "Hey Sadie, how's it going?"

"Fine," I manage to squeak out. I stand, my hands clasped in front of me. "Can I get you something? Tea, beer, water?"

Maverick looks at me strangely. "He can get his own drink, Specs."

My face flushes red again. "I know. I was just being polite."

"Yeah. Polite. It's a novel concept for you, isn't it?" Colin shoves Maverick gently, in his good shoulder, at least. "Thanks,

Sadie, I'm good. Let's get down to business. We need to make sure everything's good for the fundraiser next week."

"Right," I say, the word sounding hollow. How has the time passed by so quickly?

"Oh, but I wanted to say, good work on that dinner with the guys from Velocity. They loved meeting Sadie, and I got an email today that they're sending some sort of package for you." Colin gives me a wry smile. "If you need representation, you know how to find me."

"Oh my God," I murmur. "I swear, I didn't mean to hijack the conversation or anything, I don't know why they're sending anything."

"Because they think making you happy is the key to keeping Mav happy." The no-nonsense way in which he says it, and the complete lack of reaction from Maverick, makes Colin's statement land flat for me.

"It means this is working. Everyone is buying into the idea of Maverick settling down now that he's with you, and if we can continue to avoid drama, we can secure that contract you want, Mav." He gives his brother a meaningful look. "Which means not letting Eli suck you into anything."

Maverick's gaze darts to me, then back to Colin before hardening. "Got it."

I want to ask who Eli is, but Maverick's body language couldn't be any more clear in saying "don't go there" so I don't. I bite my tongue again and add Eli to the long list of things I don't know about the man I'm living with.

The conversation shifts to the fundraiser itself, with Colin wanting to make sure it's clear what I'll have to do that night, and how we can maximize exposure of Maverick playing the doting boyfriend.

Eventually, Colin leaves, and I curl up in the corner of the couch, petting Cat, who comes to sit beside me.

"I'll be back in a bit."

I lift my head to see Maverick opening the door, but he's gone before I can ask where he's going. Not that it's any of my business, I know. My head drops back down to the couch, and I let my eyes close, listening to the sound of Cat's loud purr.

The next thing I know, strong arms are lifting me from the sofa. "Wh-what?" I say sleepily, trying to get my bearings.

"Shh. Go back to sleep." The deep rumble of Maverick's voice washes over me, and I feel my body relax. I'm barely conscious when he lays me down on the bed, covering me with a blanket. Then soft lips graze my forehead, and gentle fingers stroke through my hair.

I must be dreaming. That's the only thing that makes sense, and the only explanation for why I reach for those fingers, pulling on them, mumbling *stay*.

It's a good dream. In it, he crawls into the bed beside me, gathers me in his arms, and holds me close. And I sleep deeper than I have in weeks.

But when I slowly blink my eyes open the next morning, feeling more rested than I have in a long time, there's an indent in the pillow beside me. And the ghost of his arms around my waist still lingers. Leaving me wondering exactly how much of it was a dream...

CHAPTER TWENTY

Maverick

I shouldn't have done that. That's all I can think as I pound out the miles on the treadmill at the stadium.

When I woke up, it was still dark out. And I was wrapped around Sadie's warm, luscious body, touching every part of her I could. She was holding my hand tightly to her chest, and I could feel the soft exhale of her breath on my skin.

It was the same exquisite torture as when I woke up in bed with her after the wedding, only this time she had no fucking idea I was there.

I'm a goddamn asshole. She was mostly asleep when I laid her in bed and she didn't know what she was doing, grabbing my hand and murmuring *stay* in that sleepy, sexy voice of hers. I had no fucking business climbing in behind her and letting my arm drape over her body. It doesn't matter that she wouldn't let go of my hand, or that even asleep, she shifted backward until her ass was tucked up into my pelvis, making things instantly hard under my pants.

Fucking hell. I should've waited until she was fully asleep and then left. No, I should've let go of her hand in the first place and never laid down. Because the second my body came into contact with hers, it was like a shot of calm straight into my veins. Everything from the day melted away, the bolt of desire I felt seeing her lace bra in the bathroom, the panic when she cut herself, the overwhelming sense of rightness when I bandaged her up. All the mixed-up feelings I've no business having disappeared, and I wanted to stay wrapped around her forever.

It's why I snuck out in the early morning hours, long before anyone else would reasonably be up, and came to the stadium. Thank fuck we've all got twenty-four-hour access. I took a plunge in one of the ice baths that are always ready, then hit the gym. I know I pushed my luck carrying Sadie last night, and fuck if my shoulder isn't mad at me today. But even if it sets me back, I can't bring myself to say I regret it. Feeling her sweet, sleepy surrender into my arms was heaven. She trusts me to protect her, to take care of her. And that's the most heady feeling in the goddamn world.

The swish of the gym doors opening reaches me, and I know my solitude is over. Damn, guess I've been here longer than I realized. Punching the buttons on the treadmill, I slow my pace down to a fast walk and start cooling down, returning my heartrate to normal.

"Hey Mav, you're here early."

Glancing to my side, I see Rhett, or Darling as we call him, stepping onto the machine next to me. He's a solid player in the outfield, with an accuracy to his throws that's impressive, even here in the major leagues.

I give him a grunt of acknowledgment. The guys know I don't talk a lot, so there's no expectation for more. Except a part of me wants more. I can't explain it, but part of me is sick and tired of holding everyone at arm's length. I see the other guys and their friendships, the camaraderie going deeper than just teammates, the way it is with me. I've never had that kind of connection with anyone except Colin.

And I can't help but wonder what I'm missing.

Clearing my throat, I slow down my pace even more. "Yeah, couldn't sleep so I figured I'd come in and get an early start."

Darling's head whips over to me, shock registering on his face. I get it, that's probably the first time I've just engaged in casual conversation with him, despite our playing together for years. When I talk to the guys, it's always about baseball. Never anything personal.

"Are they gonna let you play in a game soon?"

"Fuck, I hope so." My words come out sharper than I intended. "Sorry. Just, y'know."

"Yeah, man. I get it. Being on the IL as long as you have must have been tough." Darling glances over at me before increasing to a run. "We've missed you on the field."

Six words. Six fucking words, and that unfamiliar part of me that suddenly wants more of a relationship with these guys that I spend so much of my time with over half of the year cracks wide open.

"Thanks," I reply gruffly, punching the stop button on the machine. I don't know how to respond. I want to, but I don't know how. And that makes me feel like a fucking dumbass with the emotional intelligence of an ant.

"See you soon," Darling calls out as I walk away.

"Yeah."

There I go with those fucking one-word answers again. If I'm gonna try this whole connecting with people thing, maybe I need *How to Have a Conversation for Dummies* or something. Jesus.

The building is busier now as players and staff arrive for the day. I'm due in to see Lark for a PT session, then if all goes well, I'm headed out to the field for practice in a couple of hours.

"Hey, Mav." Lark's bright voice reaches me as soon as I enter the therapy area. The short blonde is bouncing up to me with way too much peppy energy to handle right now. "I saw you on the treadmill when I arrived. Did you already go through a set of weights?"

"Yeah. And an ice bath."

She nods and leads me into her treatment room. "Okay, well, let's check your range and see how things are going. What did you do for upper body?"

We go through the stretching program, testing my range of motion and strength in my injured side. I can't tell from her expression if Lark is pleased with my progress or not, leaving me hoping like hell I haven't set myself back between last night and this morning.

Exercise is the best way to chase away my demons, but between carrying Sadie to bed, and pushing it in the gym, I'm now realizing I could have fucked everything up. But just as my panic is starting to climb, Lark steps back with a beaming smile.

"This is incredible, Mav. You're healing really well. Like, better than expected. Your range is almost back to normal, and I think you're good to increase the load on that arm. Still not quite game-play level, but definitely back to daily practice and warm-ups with the team. If things keep going this well, my guess is you'll be back to full capacity in the next couple of weeks."

I exhale a loud curse. "Thank fuck."

Lark just laughs. "I know it hasn't been easy being off for so long, but really, you're lucky your injuries weren't more serious."

The unspoken message is received. I got lucky this time, in a lot of ways. The accident could have injured me worse than it did, and not only that, it could have hurt someone else. I know I can't let myself get in a situation like that again.

Which means Colin's right, the fucker. I have to talk to Eli. And make it clear I won't be roped into his bullshit any longer.

"Alright, let me tape your shoulder for practice today. We'll continue with that for a few more weeks, probably even when you're back in the game. It's good to give that injured joint some added support."

Lark's efficient movements have my shoulder covered in athletic tape in no time, and she makes me go through a few more movements to make sure the tape isn't impeding anything.

"You're good to go. But I want another ice bath session after practice, and let's get Jorge to review your weight training program tomorrow to make sure that's all in good shape."

After finishing up with Lark, I make my way to the executive offices in response to an email from Willow.

I knock on her door, and her head lifts to greet me with a smile. "Mav, hey! How are you doing? Come on in."

Willow Lawson is a force of nature. She's someone I respect and she's friends with Sadie, making me just a touch nervous, seeing as I have no idea what this meeting is about.

"Doing good," I reply, sitting down in a chair. "Lark thinks I'll be cleared to play in a couple weeks, depending on what Doc says."

Willow's smile is genuine and stretches wider. "That's fantastic to hear. But I wanted to talk about something else." Her smile falls ever so slightly. "I probably shouldn't be saying any of this here since it's not work-Willow talking right now. But I wanted to touch base with you about Sadie."

My spine stiffens. "What about her?"

Willow drops her gaze to her hands for a minute before looking at me again.

"She's a really good person. Amazing, really. Has a heart of gold and would give you the shirt off her own back if you asked. She loves her work, and her family, and puts all of that first, every single day. In the few years I've known her, I've never once seen her be cared for the way she takes care of everyone around her. She's the girl that insists on covering the tab, even when she only has one drink. She makes sure everyone else is happy, that their needs are met, and she leaves nothing for herself. It's why she put up with her asshole of an ex for so long. And it'll be the reason she'll stay with you unless you give her a different one. She'll want to make you happy, make your life easier, do whatever she thinks you need her to do. And she won't stop unless you make her see that her worth isn't in what she can do for others, but simply in who she is. That you want *her*, not what she does for you." Willow pauses and drops her forehead in her hand. "I don't know if I'm making sense, and I'm probably overstepping my boundary as her friend and your coworker. But I keep seeing photos of you two, and she looks at you with such hope in her eyes. Like you could be the one to finally give her what she wants — her own happiness, and actual love. And if that's not you, if that's not what you see yourself doing with her, then I'm just saying, break it off now. If you're only in this because she makes you happy, or because it's easy, and not because you could love her the way she deserves, then do the right thing and let her go."

Willow falls silent, and all I can hear is the roaring sound of my heart racing. Everything she said is so accurate, so eerily on the nose, it sends me into a moment of panic that she might know Sadie and I are just pretending.

But fast on the heels of that panic comes something else. Willow just confirmed what I was already figuring out about my Specs. That she's the type to sacrifice herself, her own happiness, for everyone else. And isn't that exactly what she's done? She's put my needs, my career, my future, first. And in doing so, she's made my cold heart warm up for the first time. She's made me realize I don't have to keep everyone out, because not everyone is against me. Her loyalty, her commitment to helping me, it's changing me.

"She does make me happy," I start slowly, feeling the words out. "And she does make everything better. Easier. But there's a hell of a lot more to it than just that."

I push back my chair and stand up, suddenly filled with an impulsive need to find Sadie. Except I can't. I have to go to practice. *Fuck.* I finally wrap my head around the idea of telling her that something's changed, that I don't want to pretend to have feelings for her, that I actually *do* have feelings for her, and now I can't do a goddamn thing about it.

Staring Willow straight in the eyes, I finally say it out loud. "I care about her. A fucking lot. And letting her go is the last goddamn thing I plan to do."

CHAPTER TWENTY-ONE

Sadie

"I should've hired someone to do my makeup," I lament to Ali who's on a video call with me as I try once again to get my eyeliner on straight. "I look like a clown."

"You do not. Just stop fiddling with it, it's fine."

I take a step away from the mirror and look down at her image on my phone. "Are you sure this dress isn't too much?" I turn to the right, smoothing the soft fabric that drapes over my stomach and gathers to one side. The tulip hem splits on a diagonal, showing a lot more leg than I'm used to and saying nothing of how bare my shoulders feel in the thin straps.

"That dress is just the right amount of too much. You look like a freaking goddess. It was made for your curves, and that shade of green is stunning with your hair. I'm so glad you decided to style it that way."

Ali's compliments float over me as I run a hand over my wavy hair, swept over one shoulder. Simple gold earrings glint in my ears, understated, but elegant.

"What would I do without you?" I ask, smiling down at my best friend. "You have me looking gorgeous and actually *feeling* gorgeous. It's a miracle."

"Knock 'em dead, babe. And by *them*, I mean dirtbag Dirk. He's going to literally keel over and die when he sees you looking like this with your hot baseball god on your arm."

I blush instantly. "Ali, quiet," I hiss. "He might hear you."

"So? I'll put money on his jaw dropping to the floor when he sees you. Trust me. There might even be drool."

I giggle. I can't help it. But the picture of Maverick King drooling is too good. A girl can dream... "Okay, okay, I better go. I'll call you tomorrow. Thanks again, love you."

"Love you, girly. Have fun."

After ending the call, I stand in front of the mirror for another minute or two. "I can do this," I whisper to the girl in the mirror. No, the beautiful woman in the mirror.

Turning on my heel, I open the bathroom door and walk out into the living room. Maverick instantly looks up from his phone, and I have to bite back another giggle, because Ali nailed it.

His mouth falls open as he lifts one hand to scrub along his jaw. "Damn, Sadie. You look stunning."

There's a rawness to his voice I haven't heard before. And something in his eyes that almost makes me falter.

"Thank you," I whisper back, clutching my small evening bag. "You look nice, too."

Nice is an understatement. I'm at a loss for words. The only ink showing is the tattoos on his hand and knuckles, the rest covered by a crisp black shirt under a tux with a subtle sheen to

its midnight colour. He looks like the most sinful of tempta-
tions, someone that promises wicked pleasure if you dare to get
close.

And I desperately want to.

When I reach his side, he lifts my hand and tucks it carefully
into his arm. "Ready?"

All I can do is nod. He walks me out the door and to the
elevator, not letting go of my arm the entire ride down to the
lobby and out to the waiting town car Colin organized for us.

Only then does he release his hold on me so I can carefully
slide into the car. He rounds the back and opens the other door,
sitting next to me. So close his intoxicating scent surrounds me.

I startle when he picks up my hand, my gaze shooting to his
face, where I see a small smile. His thumb starts to stroke back
and forth over my knuckles as we simply stare at each other as
the car pulls away.

The drive to the hotel where the gala is being held isn't a
long one, not even long enough for me to try and gather some
composure.

Our car pulls up and Maverick is out and rounding the back
to open my door in an instant. He takes my hand and tucks it
securely in the crook of his arm, drawing me in close to his side.
If this is the last opportunity I'm going to have to soak in his
affection, fake as it may be, I'm going to enjoy it as much as I
can. I lean into him slightly, bringing his upper arm in contact
with my torso. I feel more than see him glance down at me as we
walk into the ballroom.

I might have been here earlier today to help make sure everything was set up and decorated properly, but I'm still stunned

by how elegant and beautiful the space looks. Along one wall are tables filled with silent auction items, a band is in the corner playing soft background music, and scattered throughout are promotional images that will hopefully encourage everyone to open their wallets and give generously.

"Sadie, there you are." Gus approaches us, looking at Maverick. "And Mr. King. Thank you for joining us and for your donation. It was extremely generous."

I'm immediately confused. As the head of fundraising, I'm normally aware of all major donations to the foundation, but I certainly don't remember seeing one come through from Maverick.

"I believe my agent stated it was to be anonymous." Maverick's words are clipped, his spine ramrod straight as he stares at my boss.

Gus's mouth opens and then closes, and I watch him turn red. "Of course, it is, I just assumed since you and Sadie... I'm so sorry, Mr. King. Please, enjoy your evening. I had better go and check on the food."

I watch, bewildered as Gus hurries away, before turning to stand in front of Maverick. "What was that about?"

Maverick lifts a hand to rub the back of his neck, still not meeting my gaze. "Nothing. He shouldn't have said anything."

Just then, the pieces click.

"Wait. Two weeks ago, there was an anonymous donation of fifty thousand dollars." I grab his arm. "That was you?"

Slowly, he brings his gaze to meet mine. "Yeah. But I didn't want you to know it was me."

My initial shock softens into something else. "Why not?"

"Because I didn't want you to think it was me paying you for, you know. Being with me. I honestly just wanted to donate. I give that amount and more to various charities every year, and this year it felt right to make a gift to the hospital. I swear, it had nothing to do with us."

He sounds so worried that I might be offended by his generosity, when in reality, I'm touched. Not for a second do I feel like he was trying to compensate me for pretending to date him, because instinctively, I know he respects me too much to do that.

My hand lifts to cup his cheek, pulling his gaze up from the floor again. "Maverick. Thank you." I slide my hand around to the back of his neck and tug gently.

He brings his face down and turns it to the side, likely anticipating I was going to kiss him but wanting to respect my boundaries.

Joke's on him. Because right now, I don't care if he doesn't return my feelings. I want to kiss the man who has found his way into my heart.

His head jerks slightly when my lips land on his, but he recovers immediately, moving to grip my hip in one hand and cup the back of my neck in his other. He takes control of our kiss, pressing firmly into mine.

It would be easy to get swept away, to forget where we are, but the obnoxious sound of my ex's voice coming from somewhere nearby penetrates this perfect moment and we break apart.

"Sadie," Maverick starts to say, but I give my head a tiny shake.

"Later. Dirk."

His eyes widen at my whisper, then lift to look behind me. I can tell the moment he sees my ex. His hold on me tightens as he draws me into his arms. From the outside, it probably looks like a simple hug. But his head dips down, and then his lips are on my neck before traveling up to my ear, leaving goosebumps in their wake.

"Leave this to me, Specs."

"Sadie?" Dirk's arrogant tone has me clenching my jaw as we turn slightly to see him approaching, with none other than his paralegal, Gina, on his arm. Or as I like to call her, the woman I walked in on him in bed with. As I look at her, wearing a bright red bodycon dress that I could never, and would never, wear, I don't feel the pang of embarrassment, of self-criticism, that I expected. There is no automatic comparison of myself to her, only a detached sense of pity that she's now stuck with a man like Dirk.

"Derek. Didn't realize we'd be seeing you here," Maverick says calmly. Wait. He knows what Dirk's name is...doesn't he?

"It's Dirk. And Maverick fucking King. Gotta say, this is a surprise." Dirk sticks out his hand, completely ignoring me.

But Maverick ignores his hand in return. "Why would it be a surprise? I'm pretty sure everyone in the city knows I'm the luckiest bastard around to be dating this amazing woman." Maverick's voice is hard, but his words still manage to worm their way inside of me, sparking something warm deep within.

Dirk's eyes narrow, then widen, and it's almost comical to see him trying to make sense of the situation. Then Maverick's hand is on my chin, tipping my face up so he can press a gentle kiss to my lips.

"Specs, how about we go and get you a glass of champagne to celebrate tonight. I'm sure Darren and his date have other people they'd like to see."

Dirk's blustering is audible as Maverick propels me away from them. As soon as we're far enough away, I let loose the giggle I've been fighting down. "Oh my God, that was incredible. How was that so effective at pissing him off?"

I'm treated to one of Maverick's rare smiles. "Because men like that asshole think they're the center of the universe and everyone should revolve around them. It throws them wildly off course when they encounter someone unwilling to give them that."

I hug his arm a little tighter. "Well, thank you. Highlight of my entire evening. I'll never forget it."

Maverick's eyes darken. "Not if I have anything to say about it. He doesn't deserve any mental space when you think about tonight. I plan on you having much more pleasurable memories."

Just like that, everything and everyone around us fades away. Maverick toys with the ends of my hair, his fingers dangerously close to the top of my breast. If I inhale deeply, he'll graze the bare skin.

It's as if he figures that out the same moment I do, because his eyes drop to my cleavage for the briefest of seconds before returning to my eyes.

"How long were you with him?" he rasps.

"Just over two years," I whisper. He lets out a rumbling sound.

"So it's been over two years since a real man made you come."

My mouth falls open in shock. Never has a man said something like that to me.

"Tell me I'm right, Specs. I know I am."

His confidence is warranted. I nod.

He stares at me for another second, before growling, "Fuck it."

This time when his hand lifts up, it isn't to the back of my neck but the front, cupping my throat gently, holding me possessively as he kisses me again.

And there's absolutely nothing fake about this kiss.

He keeps it short, chaste, and audience appropriate given where we are. But when my eyes flutter open after his lips leave mine, there's no mistaking the intent in his eyes.

"Tonight, Specs. When we get home. We're gonna talk about this thing between us."

His words are a promise. And despite months of planning and all the hard work I put into this event, I suddenly can't wait for it all to be over.

Chapter Twenty-Two

Maverick

I didn't mean to go that far tonight. Not this early on, at least. But somewhere between seeing Sadie in that dress and then putting her ex firmly in his place, I lost any self-control. I had to let her know my intentions. And judging by her reaction, I'm not the only one counting down the minutes until we're home.

It's no small relief to see her desire mirroring my own when she looks at me with that small smile, or when she tucks herself into my arms. I might not have the first clue what to do with a normal relationship, but at least I know I'm not alone in my attraction, in my feelings.

When we finally get to escape the event, we find ourselves in the town car, riding back to my apartment. I lift her hand to mine, kissing her knuckles. "You were incredible tonight. That was one hell of an event." I turn her hand over and kiss her wrist. "You look stunning." Another kiss.

"Maverick," she murmurs, and I lower her arm to look at her. Lust is mixing with hesitation in her eyes, and I cup her cheek with my free hand.

"What are we doing?"

I give her a wry smirk. "Hopefully, admitting there's more to this than just an act for the media. Beyond that, it's up to you, but I have ideas."

Her sharp intake of breath is coupled with all the hesitation being replaced with wonder. "You...really?"

Staring straight into her deep green eyes, I reply, "Yeah. You're doing something to me, Specs. Changing everything. Making me want more. Only from you."

She doesn't say anything right away, but I'll wait her out. The car pulls up outside my building, and I kiss her hand one more time before sliding out and walking around to open her door.

I take her hand and start to move toward my apartment, only for Sadie to pull me to a stop.

"You say you want more, but does that mean only tonight, or..."

Ah. Now I see where the hesitation came from. She's right to ask, I just hope I can answer in a way that won't end this before it has a chance to start.

"I told you I've never been in a relationship. I don't know how to do that. But with you, I find myself wanting to try."

It's as real an answer as I can give, and inside, I squirm at the vulnerability I've shown. Sadie still holds the power to hurt me, to hurt my career. Giving in to these feelings could still come back to bite me in the ass. But I can't seem to stop this runaway train now that it's picking up steam.

"I want to show you how you deserve to be treated by the man you're with." My voice drops lower as I take in her full lips, slightly parted, and her blown pupils. "I know this is crossing a line. I know this is more than we agreed to. But I want you. I want you to let me have you tonight. But if you don't want that, then just say the word, and I'll walk away. I'll go and stay with Colin tonight, and every night, for as long as you need to stay here."

It's nearly impossible, but I force myself to take a step back. To let some space come between us. And when I see her suck in a gasp, I know it's the right call. I've overwhelmed her, thrown a curveball straight at her, and now she needs to decide whether she's going to swing at it or not.

But waiting for her decision is torture.

When she turns and takes a step toward my building, my shoulders sag in disappointment. Until she looks over her shoulder, a coy expression on her face, and reaches a hand back. "You have me, Maverick."

I take her hand and everything she's offering me. This time, our kiss is even deeper than the ones at the event. I don't give a fuck if anyone sees me devour her lips. Let them. Let them see this perfect woman come undone for me.

But when a car honks, Sadie pulls back, her hair mussed from my hands raking through it. Just like I imagined that very first time I saw her in the hospital stairwell. She licks her lips, her cheeks pink. "Let's go inside," she murmurs, drawing her fingers down my chest.

The elevator ride up to my floor is interminably slow. But the doors eventually slide open and I drag her down the hall to my apartment. My usually steady hands are shaking as I turn the key and open the door. The second it closes behind us, something comes over Sadie.

I watch her hips sway as she walks over to the couch, stopping to stroke Cat's back before balancing on one leg and lifting the other.

"Let me," I say hoarsely, coming to her side. Heat is simmering in her eyes as she nods. I drop to the floor, taking her foot in my hand, drawing my fingers up the soft skin of her ankle. Undoing the strap of her heel, I slowly slide it off before lifting her foot slightly to press a kiss where it meets her shin.

"Maverick," she whines quietly, and I just smirk against her skin.

Then I move to the other one and do the same. Lifting it reverently, removing her shoe, then kissing the silky-smooth skin.

I'm on my knees in front of her, this goddess deserving my worship. Tilting my head to look up at her, my hands start to roam up her legs, under the hem of the dress that's been driving me wild all evening. When I reach her thighs, I feel her quiver. Now the wrap hem of her dress comes in handy as I part it slightly to press featherlight kisses to the tops of her knees.

"Oh my God."

Hands land on my head, fingers gripping my hair. I continue to rain soft kisses all over her legs. Those luscious thighs I've spent far too long picturing wrapped around my head, shaking under my touch.

My hands snake farther underneath her dress, dragging up her outer thighs until I meet the curve of her hips. But instead of finding what I'm looking for, I'm met with bare skin.

"Specs," I rumble low, staring up at her. "Were you bare this whole time?"

She tugs her lower lip in between her teeth and nods, and that is my undoing.

I surge up, capturing her trapped lip with my own teeth and tugging it free before bruising her lips with my kiss. The very idea that she was walking around the event, holding my hand, allowing me to touch her, all with nothing on underneath has my mind going fuzzy with pure lust.

My hands find the zipper on the side of her dress and I start to slide it down, incrementally slow. She whines against my lips. Good. Let her be as crazed for me as I am for her.

When it finally hits the end, I slide my fingers under the thin straps that are all that stand between me and seeing my girl naked. That's when her hands come up to cover mine, stopping me.

"You first."

I lean back slightly and realize the nerves are back. "Whatever you say, Specs." I dart back in to press a swift kiss to her lips before removing my hands from her body and making quick work of shucking off my jacket and unbuttoning my shirt. I'm already toeing off my shoes when Sadie giggles.

"There's no rush, Maverick. We have all night."

Her fingers go to my belt and she slides it out of the loops. I shrug off my shirt and she freezes, her tongue darting out to lick her lips.

"Like what you see?" I ask with a heated smirk.

"Oh yeah," comes her breathy reply. I take over undoing my pants, pushing them down over my dick that's already hard and straining to be free. Then my socks come off and I stand there, nothing but my boxer briefs covering me. And the raw appreciation in Sadie's expression, the desire emanating from her, is hotter than anything I've ever experienced.

"Specs," I growl, drawing her gaze up to mine. "Let me see you."

This time she doesn't stop me when I move to pull the straps down her shoulders. The fabric slides over her generous tits, revealing a black strapless bra that's cupping them the way I want my hands to as soon as fucking possible. I push the dress down her hips, somehow not letting myself look down at what I'm guessing is a fucking gorgeous, glistening pussy, keeping my eyes trained on her face. It doesn't take an idiot to recognize she's still a little nervous. But I'll do whatever it takes to get her to believe her soft curves, every fucking inch of them, make her the most stunning woman in the goddamn world to me.

I let her reach around to unclasp her bra, knowing that removing the last barrier is powerful for her. But when it falls to the floor, and those tits are revealed to me, there's no holding back my groan.

"Jesus fucking Christ. You...you're... fuck, Sadie. Specs. You're gorgeous." I stumble over my words, my brain completely fried by this woman.

"Touch me?" she asks, and those two words are all I need.

My hands cover her tits, squeezing the flesh before thumbing her nipples into stiff peaks. I dip my head down and cover one with my mouth, teasing it with my tongue as she grips my shoulders.

"Oh God, yes!"

I move to the other one, lavishing it the same way. Her hands start to roam across my back, over my shoulders, and down my arms. And everywhere she touches, heat follows.

"I need to taste you," I mumble, kissing my way down the soft slope of her stomach. I crouch down again, bringing me perfectly in line with her glistening sex. It's all I can do not to dive right in, but I make myself look up at her, checking in. There's no trace of hesitation, just need.

Using my thumbs, I part her folds, then lean in and swipe my tongue up her slit, groaning as the taste of her explodes on my tongue, sweet and musky. "Fuck," I moan, licking her again and again, my fingers slipping and sliding around her sex as I feast on her like a starving man given his first meal. I suck her clit into my mouth, letting my teeth graze the hood just lightly, but enough to make her shriek and grip my hair tight enough to hurt. I lean into her, shoving my entire fucking face into her pussy, letting her cover me in her juices. I could die here a happy man. Her hips start to grind against me, and it's a damn good thing the couch is behind her because I can feel her shaking as I lick and suck.

"Oh God, I'm gonna... Oh God!"

That's all the warning I get before her body trembles into her orgasm. My only regret is that a part of me wasn't inside of her to feel it.

"I want another, Specs. I want you to come all over me again and fucking again."

"Maverick, I can't," she gasps, her hands grabbing at me. I lift myself up to stand and grip her chin.

"Yeah. You can. And you will."

Not giving a fuck about the fact that my face is covered in her, I kiss her and swallow down her moan. Then I'm back on my knees, this time lifting one leg over my shoulder before dragging my fingers through her dripping sex.

"You're gonna squeeze me so goddamn tight, Specs. We're not stopping until I've felt you come on my fingers and my cock."

I slide one digit in, then draw it out and put it in my mouth, sucking deeply, my eyes trained on hers.

"Holy crap," she breathes, and I give her a wicked grin.

The next time it's two fingers, and I slide them in and out a few times, twisting one way, then the other, watching her reactions to figure out what she likes. When I stroke against the walls of her pussy, her back arches, those lush tits pushing out, begging for my touch. But my hands are busy.

"Cup your tits, Specs. Squeeze those nipples for me."

She complies instantly, her head thrown back as her hands tease and pluck at her breasts. "That's a good fucking girl."

I time my words for exactly when I plunge my fingers back in, curling them over to stroke that spot I've found and covering her clit with my mouth at the same damn time.

And that's all it takes.

Her cries echo around the room as she lets go of her tits to grip the back of the couch, her entire body trembling as I pull every last bit of her orgasm out of her, licking up every drop of her release.

Pressing one final kiss to her clit, I slowly withdraw my fingers. I straighten to standing, my knees protesting how long I was down there, but it was fucking worth it.

There's a dreamy expression on Sadie's face as she leans against the couch, a soft sheen of sweat covering her skin.

"You're beautiful," I say, gripping the back of her neck and pulling her face to mine. "Fucking beautiful. And you'll be even more beautiful bent over this couch. Wait here, Specs."

Chapter Twenty-Three

Sadie

He really didn't have to tell me to stay here; I'm not sure I could move even if I wanted to.

My bones are like liquid, the only thing holding me up is the couch.

Never. Not ever. Not with a partner or with my toys have I had two powerful orgasms back-to-back like that. And Maverick's promising more? Good grief, I may not survive.

But there's no time to worry about that because he's back, foil packet in hand. He cups the bulge in his underwear, squeezing it as he smirks at me, and maybe I'm possessed by some sex goddess because all I can think about is tearing away that fabric and pouncing on that cock.

"Keep staring at me like that and I might be tempted to let you do something about those wicked thoughts I'm guessing are running through your brilliant mind."

I drag my gaze up to meet his. "You had a taste of me, I want one of you."

Maverick barks out a laugh before gripping my throat in that gently possessive way he did at the event earlier this evening.

God, was that really only a couple of hours ago? It feels like so much has happened. "I had more than a taste, Specs. And you'll get one. But first, I promised you would come on my cock."

Oh my God, the dirty words coming out of his mouth have me biting back a whine. A *whine*!

He places the condom packet on the back of the couch next to me and never drops his stare as he pushes down his underwear. But I can't contain my gasp when his cock is free. It's long, and thick, and curved just a bit at the tip. I reach my hand out, wrapping it around his length, and Maverick groans as he shifts closer, stepping out of his boxers.

"Fucking hell."

His voice is tight, as if he's barely holding back. And I want that. I want him on the edge just as much as I am, desperate for more. I experiment with sliding my hand up and down, twisting my wrist slightly. He's hot and hard, and when he presses his chest into mine, tipping my chin up for a kiss, trapping my hand and his dick between us, I swear, I can feel it throb.

Maverick manages to tear himself away, taking a step back, making me drop him. "Turn around," he growls and I find myself moving, leaning over the back of the couch, pushing my ass out toward him. Gone are any thoughts of self-consciousness, any hesitations about my curves or whether he wants me. There's no question of that anymore.

"Fuck. Look at you, babe. Fucking hottest woman in the goddamn world, all of this for me." His tone is almost reverent as he drags his hand down my spine, making me arch into his touch. His other hand joins the first when he reaches my ass, those strong fingers kneading into my flesh, gripping it tightly.

I sense him bending over me, and his lips follow the line of his fingers, kissing his way down my back. "Are you ready, Specs?" he asks when he reaches the base of my spine.

"Mm-hmm." I nod against the couch, my eyes closed. And I am. Oh God, am I ever ready for him.

The telltale crinkle of the condom wrapper opening is followed shortly after by his hand pressing on my upper back. "Arch for me. Give me that pussy."

I tip my hips up, and his fingers dip down between my legs, spreading my arousal. "Good girl. So fucking ready for me."

His fingers are replaced by the blunt head of his cock as he swipes it back and forth against my folds. But I need more.

"Maverick, please." I open my eyes and twist my head to look at him. "Please."

"I've got you, Specs."

His cock sliding into me stretches me in ways I've never experienced before, delicious pain mixing with pleasure. He rocks back and forth a few times and my body eagerly follows, desperate to take all of him.

"More," I gasp, reaching back, trying to feel him. I don't get his body, I get his hand as he leans forward to place our linked hands on the couch beside my head, and with one more thrust of his hips, he's in. "Oh God, yes," I sigh as his lips kiss my shoulder.

"You feel like heaven," he whispers. "Better than heaven."

Slowly, he starts to move, our moans and sighs mingling together as he slides in and out, reaching deeper into me. The softness only lasts a few moments before he lets go of my hand and wraps his arm around me, drawing me up and against his chest. He grips the front of my throat again, and I turn my head, helpless in his hold as he plunges in and out of me, sending me careening toward an orgasm that I know will shatter me.

But he'll hold me together.

"Mine."

I don't have time to think about what he means before his fingers find my clit, rolling over it, teasing it, until I'm screaming out his name, my body giving in to the extreme pleasure he promised me.

And just as I expected, as my orgasm rolls through me, leaving me weak and so thoroughly satisfied, Maverick holds me up, never letting me go until I feel him stutter and shoot off inside of me as he shouts out his release.

We stay there, draped over his couch, both of us panting and exhausted for several minutes before he slowly withdraws. I feel the loss of him, leaving me empty and drained. But he kisses my back and once again he whispers, softly this time, "Wait here."

He's back quickly, and his hands trail all over my body before lifting me up from the couch and turning me in his arms. Warm blue eyes search my face, and I know he's seeing my dopey smile when his lips curve up in response. He kisses my forehead before gathering me in against his chest.

"That was spectacular."

I can feel the rumble of his voice with my head pressed against him the way it is. And my arms squeeze him tighter in response.

"Can I take you to bed and make you scream my name again?"

My entire body shudders, and he just chuckles. "I'll take that as a yes."

But when he goes to scoop me up, I find my voice. "No, don't. You have to protect your shoulder."

The smirk he gives me, combined with the raised eyebrow, shouldn't be nearly as sexy as it is. Then again, maybe it's his hand squeezing my ass that's turning me on.

"Specs. We're gonna pretend you aren't insulting my strength right now. If I want to carry you to bed and fuck you until my name and my cock are the only two things you remember in the morning, then I'm goddamn well gonna do that."

My mouth falls open as I feel him hardening between us. "O-okay," I stutter, then shriek as he bends down again and picks me up as if I way nothing, tossing me over his shoulder. "Oh my God, Maverick!"

His hand lands on my ass in a light smack, and I feel his rumble of laughter. "That's right, Specs. That's what you're gonna be saying all night long."

I tumble down onto the bed, bouncing in a way that probably isn't very flattering. But the hungry look in his eyes says otherwise.

I can't look away, I don't want to, as he climbs on the bed and crawls over my body, kissing his way up my stomach, pausing at my breasts to tease the already sensitized flesh, before continuing upward. His lips capture mine in a kiss I could lose myself in. This entire evening has been like a fantasy, a dream come true. When he lifts his head and looks at me, the smoldering heat that's lit his eyes on fire all night has been replaced with something I can only describe as total awe. As if he, too, can't quite believe this is happening.

"You're gorgeous. And tonight, you're mine."

CHAPTER TWENTY-FOUR

Sadie

I wake up feeling deliciously sore and exhausted in the best possible way. There's no erasing the smile on my face, or the residual tingle between my legs from Maverick's scruff as he made me come on his mouth over and over again. I lost count after round three...

But then I roll over, and instead of the sexy, sinful man who made me hoarse from screaming his name last night, there are only tangled sheets and an empty pillow.

I sit up, clutching the sheet to my chest, listening carefully, but hearing only silence.

It wasn't all a dream. I know that, my body tells me that, and the faint musky scent of a night filled with sex hangs in the air.

So where is he?

My brain is starting to fire with all kinds of scenarios, none of them good. Then, I hear the sound of a door opening. I grab the first piece of clothing I can find, which happens to be one of Maverick's shirts. Ignoring how it catches over my breasts and barely covers my ass, I cautiously open the bedroom door, trying to determine whether it's him or not.

You dummy, who else would it be? Drawing in a deep breath, I pad softly down the hall to the open living space, and there he is.

His back is to me, but the gray tank he's wearing still makes me want to bite my lip. The way it clings to his muscular back and displays his ink and strong arms is making me wish I'd put on my panties with the slippery situation happening between my legs.

He turns, seeing me, and the tiny smile on his face morphs into something else when he takes in my outfit.

"Holy hell," he grounds out, crossing the space that separates us in just a few steps. His hand catches the hem of his shirt, and using it, he tugs me closer. "Morning, Specs."

His reaction to seeing me goes a long way to dispelling the insidious thoughts I had when I woke up alone. Feeling bold, I loop my arms around his neck, making the shirt ride even higher. And of course, that drags his hand that's still clutching the shirt up my bare legs.

"Morning," I whisper, going to lean in for a kiss when I suddenly remember something. "Oh crap. Morning breath." I clap my hand over my mouth and snap my head back. But Maverick's free hand lands on my throat and he's then he's kissing me, his tongue plunging into my mouth, without a care for fuzzy teeth or stinky breath.

When we finally break apart, I'm panting heavily, and that tiny smile is a full-on satisfied smirk.

"If you're gonna worry about something stupid like morning breath, don't go walking around in nothing but my shirt."

His hand squeezes my bare ass to emphasize his point and I let out an undignified squeak.

"It was the first thing I could find to put on!"

"Did I say I was complaining?"

I can feel the heat turning my cheeks red. And against my better judgment, I blurt out, "Dirk wouldn't let me kiss him until I'd brushed my teeth. I guess old habits and all that."

His smirk is gone, replaced by a scowl. "Don't mention that shitstain's name when you're wearing my clothes and looking well fucked."

Did my knees just wobble? They might have. Because that was hands down the hottest thing anyone has said to me. Ever.

"You want breakfast? I just had omelets with my neighbor, it's what we do every Saturday. But I can make you one."

The abrupt change in both subject and tone has me giving my head a slight shake.

"Wait. You have omelets with your neighbor every Saturday?" I ask.

Maverick shifts to lean against the counter, letting his hands fall from my body. "Yeah. He's in his seventies, doesn't get out much. But he looks after Cat when I travel. We have a standing breakfast date every weekend I'm in town."

He sounds almost bashful admitting this to me, and I feel like I've been given an exclusive peek behind the heavy curtain of privacy Maverick keeps wrapped around his entire personal life.

"That's lovely," I say, smiling. "And I would love an omelet." That earns me another small smile before he turns and starts doing something with the items I am only just realizing are on the counter beside him.

"Coffee?" he asks over his shoulder as he chops up a green pepper. "I've already had one with Ralph but could use another if you wanted some."

"I'm on it," I reply, moving to grab the coffee pot. The sink is right next to where he's working, and when I come up beside him to fill the carafe with water, his lips land on the top of my head. It's so sweet, so domestic, so *unexpected*, I have to hide my grin of surprise. Is this another side of Maverick no one else gets to see? The side that has breakfast with an elderly neighbor, takes in stray cats, and kisses the top of my head just because I'm near him?

Because if it is, I'm here for it. All of it.

I get the coffee going, then quickly go to pull on some underwear. While I'm in the bedroom, I have a brief debate with myself. Should I get dressed, or should I stay in just his shirt? In the end, the way he responded to seeing me in his clothes has me feeling so good, I decide to stay like this with the only addition being a pair of panties. There's something about eating breakfast bare-assed that I can't quite make myself do.

Ducking into the bathroom, I muffle my shriek of dismay at what I see in the mirror. How in the hell did he not run for the hills when he saw me?

My makeup from last night is smeared under my eyes, my hair is a rat's nest. Good Lord. I brush my teeth, scrub my face clean, and attempt to run a brush through my hair. As I'm working the last tangle free, Maverick appears in the reflection, leaning against the door frame of the bathroom.

"Breakfast is ready," he says, not even bothering to hide the way he drags his gaze up and down my body. I stare at him through the mirror until his eyes meet mine. He breaks first, turning without another word and walking back to the kitchen. With one final check that I no longer look like the worst morning after possible, I follow after him into the kitchen that now boasts the aroma of fresh coffee and a savoury breakfast.

My stomach lets out a loud rumble and my arms immediately wrap around it, as if I could muffle the sound.

But Maverick just chuckles. "Guess you worked up an appetite last night." He shoots me a wink, then gestures to the bar-height counter where two plates of food sit.

"I thought you already ate?" I ask as I lift myself onto one of the stools. He takes the other.

"Yeah, but I'm always hungry. Figured I'd keep you company."

Yet again, it's such a simple, sweet gesture, my heart melts.

We eat breakfast quickly. Maverick's an incredible cook; my omelet is full of flavour and perfectly fluffy.

My plate has just a few bites left, and I want to savour them slowly when I hear my phone vibrating somewhere. I've got zero intention of answering it until I'm done eating, but Maverick says, "It's been going off for a while, ever since you went to brush your teeth."

My stomach falls. The last time my phone went crazy was when the news broke about our fake relationship. What could it be this time?

I climb off my stool and locate my evening bag quickly, removing my phone. And I breathe a sigh of relief.

"It's just my mom."

I walk back to the counter and hop up on my stool before opening her text messages.

> **MOM: Alright Sadie, your dad says I shouldn't bug you but how long must I wait?**

> **MOM: When do we get to meet this new man of yours?**

> **MOM: The photos of the two of you at the gala last night are wonderful.**

> **MOM: You look radiant.**

> **MOM: I'm just so happy for you.**

> **MOM: But I want to meet this man!**

> **MOM: Dinner. Tonight. Non negotiable.**

> **MOM: Love you**

"That's a lot of messages."

I look up at Maverick, placing my phone face down on the counter so he can't read them. "Yeah, Mom hasn't quite figured out that you don't need to send a separate message for every sentence. In her mind, there's a word limit or something."

He chuckles. "So are we going?"

"Going where?" *Crap.* So much for him not reading the messages.

"To dinner. With your parents."

I gulp. "Do you really want to do that?"

Spinning toward me in his seat, Maverick folds his arms across his chest and studies me. "Do you want to?"

My heart starts to pound. This feels like more than just a conversation about dinner with my parents.

"I...I do, I mean, my mom wants to meet you, and I've been dodging her requests for a while, so..." I trail off, my mouth suddenly dry. "But only if you really want to. We don't have to. The gala was meant to be the end."

There. I said it. Hopefully, Maverick can also see there's more at stake than dinner with my parents. Hopefully, last night meant something to him. Hopefully...he doesn't want our arrangement to end, but rather to change.

Because I don't want to be in a fake relationship with Maverick King anymore.

I want to be in a real one.

His answer comes swiftly. In one move, I'm lifted off my stool and brought onto his lap, my legs spreading wide to straddle his. One hand goes to the back of my neck, tangling in my hair, while the other lands on my lower back, pushing me in closer to him.

He draws close, then pauses, his lips hovering over mine. Our foreheads meet, and my eyes flutter closed as I wait.

"I'm not ready for us to end."

CHAPTER TWENTY-FIVE

Maverick

I don't do families.

Never have. Not since my mom died when I was three.

That's gotta be why, walking up the path to Sadie's childhood home, my palms are sweaty and my heart's racing.

But I'm not the only nervous one.

Sadie hasn't stopped fidgeting since we left my apartment. She'd been worrying at her lower lip until I finally kissed her at a stoplight. Then she switched to twisting her hands in her lap until I covered them with mine.

Focusing on her nerves surprisingly helped me to ignore my own until right now.

Her parents' house is well-kept, fitting right in the suburban neighborhood that's a far cry from the ones I grew up in, in Northern British Columbia. Bouncing around from foster home to foster home, a couple of them were decent, but most of them were not.

Just then, the front door opens, and an older woman who is most definitely Sadie's mom, judging by the red hair and wide smile, steps out, her arms already open.

Sadie drops my hand and picks up her pace, walking up the steps to the front porch and straight into her mother's arms.

By the time I reach them, they've broken apart, and Sadie looks back at me with a nervous expression. "Mom, this is Maverick. Maverick, this is my mother Doreen."

I'm reaching my hand out to shake her mother's when I'm caught off guard by her stepping forward, ignoring my outstretched hand, and wrapping her arms around my waist instead.

"Save the handshake for Henry, I'm a hugger."

"Mom! You could at least make sure he's okay with that first," Sadie protests, but as her mom steps back, she simply arches a brow at her daughter.

"Listen. If he's your new beau, then he'll have to get used to me hugging him hello."

"What about consent," Sadie grumbles, flashing me an apologetic look as she takes my hand. "Sorry," she whispers, but I just give her a tight smile.

"It's fine," I whisper back. And it is. Am I used to strangers hugging me? Fuck, no. But did it feel kind of nice, for just a moment, to be greeted warmly by someone with no expectations of me? Yeah.

We walk into the house, and it's just as homey on the inside as I suspected it would be. The entry hall is lined with family photos, and as it opens into the living room, you can tell it's a much-used space. The couch is draped in what looks like hand-knitted blankets and a dozen throw pillows. More photos adorn the walls here, most of them of two younger kids, I'm guessing Sadie's siblings. It's strange there aren't more of my

Specs, and I file that away as something to ask her about. There's a recliner pointed toward the television, and the entire space screams *a happy family lives here.*

I let Sadie lead me into the kitchen, her mom still going on about something to do with her sister, I think. Honestly, this all feels like an out-of-body experience. Like I'm a spectator, watching a show from the sidelines, praying I'm not called on to perform.

Then the sliding door that leads to the backyard opens and Sadie's dad walks in. He heads my way, and I feel my spine stiffen. My experience with father figures can be described as mixed, at best.

"Maverick King. Can't say I ever thought I'd have you for dinner," he says, and I relax slightly at his seemingly welcome tone. We shake hands, his grip firm. "Henry LeDuc. Can I get you a beer?"

"No thanks, I don't drink, actually."

That earns me a raised eyebrow. "Ah. Athlete diet rules or something? Hope you can eat some potato salad. Doreen makes it taste so good, you'll want seconds."

"Nah, not a diet thing, just a personal choice," I answer, and his expression morphs to one of respect.

"Got it. How about a sparkling water? We keep them for when the girls visit."

"Sounds great."

He hands me a can from the fridge before turning to Sadie. "Where's my hug, young lady?"

I watch her face stretch into a wide smile. "Hi, Daddy."

It's obvious Sadie grew up very differently from me. I watch her move around the kitchen with her parents, the three of them so comfortable and at ease with each other.

After a few minutes, Henry taps my shoulder. "Come on outside with me to finish the grilling? We'll be eating soon."

Well, this is a first. I've never, not once, had to deal with a girl's dad. But I've seen enough movies, heard enough stories, to know what I'm in for.

And I hope like hell I don't mess this up.

"I haven't seen my daughter smile like that in a while," he starts, opening the lid to a massive barbecue lined with some delicious-smelling steaks. "That idiot she was with before, her smile wasn't nearly as big. Thanks for that."

"No thanks needed. Sadie's a wonderful woman." I lean against a post at the edge of the covered deck area and look at her father. "Her ex didn't deserve her."

Henry looks at me, respect clear on his face. "No. He didn't. The question I have to ask is, do you?"

It's a fight not to shift on my feet. He's not pulling any punches. But while whatever I have with Sadie might have started off unconventionally, and with zero feelings involved, I'm not shying away from the fact that things have changed.

"I like to think I do."

"I've heard about you. About some of the things that land you in the media."

Ah, shit. I knew this was a possibility. That he'd bring up my past actions. The fact that I've never bothered to explain myself to the media before could bite me in the ass now. What proof do I have for her dad that I'm not the reckless asshole the press makes me out to be?

"But I also know better than to take what I see in the media at face value."

Thank fuck.

"I appreciate that. There's truth to some of it, but there's also more to each story," I say calmly, hoping my tone belies the tension I feel. I keep my gaze steady, not wavering from Henry as he studies me.

"It's not my business what actions you've taken in the past, as long as they don't negatively impact my daughter. But it will become my business should you choose to act in a way that puts her at risk now or in the future."

"Understood."

Henry nods. "Good. Now, let's get these steaks off the grill and go eat."

Pushing off the post, I follow him inside. Sadie makes her way over to me and wraps an arm around my waist. "Everything good out there? He didn't give you a hard time, did he?"

I lean down and kiss her forehead. "Nothing I wasn't expecting." She still looks worried, so I rub my hand up and down her back. "It's all good, Specs." The lines on her face smooth out for the most part, just in time for her mom to bustle past with plates of food.

"Here, let me take some of that," I say, reaching out to lift one of the dishes from her hands.

"Oh, thank you, Mav. We'll set it all on the table and dig in."

Soon we're all seated around a wooden table that reminds me of one owned by a foster family I lived with. I can remember loud chaotic meals seated in these light wood chairs, fighting over who would get the last bread roll. There were good moments in my childhood, interspersed throughout a lot of bad. And being here with Sadie's parents is bringing up those good memories again.

Doreen makes sure we're all well-fed, and the conversation is surprisingly easy. Her parents don't pester me with questions about baseball or my injury, and I find myself relaxing more and more as the evening goes on.

When it's finally time for us to leave, I'm not surprised by Doreen's hug this time. It's longer and tighter than the first one she gave me.

"You two come back next weekend when Sienna's in town, and I'll make lasagna." She pats my chest. "I make the best garlic bread you've ever had."

"Thanks, Doreen." I give her a genuine smile. Then a larger hand lands on my shoulder, not my injured one, thankfully, and I turn to face Henry. We shake hands again, and then I *am* surprised when he, too, pulls me in for a brief backslapping hug.

"Take care, Mav."

"Will do."

Goodbyes said, I take Sadie's hand, and we walk to my car. I open her door, and once she's in, I move around to my side and climb in.

The first part of the drive home is quiet; Sadie just looks out the window at the city going by. But at a stoplight, I sense her shift in her seat, and glance over to find her looking at me.

"Everything okay?" I ask, gripping the steering wheel.

"Yeah," she replies, reaching out to take one of my hands, bringing it to her lap. "Are you okay? I sort of got the feeling you were a little uncomfortable at first. I'm guessing you're not used to the whole meet-the-parents thing."

I squeeze her hand gently. "Can't say I've ever done it, seeing as you're the first girl I've ever wanted to be with for more than a few hours of fun."

She makes a happy sound at that statement, and my lips turn up in a smile. "But your parents are great. You're lucky to have them."

"Will you tell me about your parents?"

My jaw clenches tight. "That's not exactly a pleasant conversation. Let's not ruin tonight with it."

I'm hoping like fuck she'll drop it. And thankfully, after a long few seconds of silence where I can feel her gaze on me, she does.

If I had it my way, I'd never let Sadie know the full depths of the shit I went through as a child.

Her light doesn't need to touch that darkness.

Which means I need to deal with Eli, and soon. Before he becomes a problem — and not just a secret — between me and Sadie.

Chapter Twenty-Six

Maverick

I'm out on the turf, shagging balls with some guys in the outfield during a low-key practice the team is having on a rare day off between games. With the season drawing to an end, and playoffs in sight, they're all tired.

Not me. I'm ready to fucking go. The sun is shining, my shoulder feels good, and I made Sadie come three times in a row last night.

For once, I feel like shit is going my way.

"What's this? You comin' for my position, Mav?" Darling shouts as he ambles up to the group of us in the outfield. The guy I was tossing back and forth with jogs over, slapping Darling's held-up hand as he passes by to take his place at batting practice. "Maybe I'll try taking over the hot corner and let you handle all the shit that gets by you infielders for a change."

Rhett's smiling, and his tone is obviously teasing. And instead of scowling like I normally would, my good mood has me firing back at him.

"Sure. Consider this my tryout. I mean, how hard can it fucking be when you shitheads have all the time in the world to make a catch out here."

Darling throws his head back and laughs. "Damn, man. Don't hold back!"

I smirk and whip the ball at him. "I won't."

We fall into an easy rhythm, increasing the distance between us every few throws. Until he throws one that looks like it's going to veer left and I lunge to make the catch. The ball hits the tip of my glove, bouncing right back out. And momentum carries me forward and down, making me land on my bad shoulder with a loud *oomph*.

"Mav!" Rhett's shout registers as I roll onto my back, cradling my arm.

Fuck. White-hot pain lashes my shoulder as I struggle to contain my rage and agony. One stupid move. One fucking idiotic moment of needing to prove myself, and I've just fucked everything up.

My teammates reach me and try to help me get up, but I push them away with a growl. Staggering to my feet, I see Coach and Lark hurrying over.

"What the hell happened?" Coach barks.

Darling answers for me as Lark takes my arm and supports it gently, probing her way up my bicep.

"My throw went wide; he went for it but landed wrong."

"Jesus Christ, Mav. Go with Lark and get everything looked at." Coach pulls his hat off his bald head, then shoves it back on. I don't want to see the pity in his eyes, but he can't hide it. He thinks I'm done for.

I shrug off Lark's touch. "Fine." I abandon my glove and hat that fell off at some point and storm off the field, every step shooting daggers of pain through my body. I can't fucking believe this is happening.

I hit the dugout, ignoring everyone's concerned questions about what happened and go into the locker room where I start to pace. I know I'm meant to go straight to the trainer's area for an assessment, Doc might even be waiting for me if Lark's texted him. But I can't face them. Not yet.

"Fuck!" I shout. "Goddamn it!" I kick over the empty container waiting for all of our dirty practice gear. There's a pounding in my ears as I move to the wall, lifting my good arm, ready to put a fucking hole in the cement.

"Maverick!"

Somehow, Sadie's voice reaches down through the tunnel I feel like I'm in, pulling me out of the darkness. When the rage lifts, my vision clears, and I see her standing in front of me, arm outstretched. I let her take my hand and pull me into her soft body.

"Oh, Maverick," she murmurs as my head falls to her shoulder. "Are you okay? I saw you go down. Willow got me in here as quickly as she could."

I didn't even realize she was watching us practice. Humiliation that she saw me fall mixes with overwhelming relief that she's here.

We stay like that for several minutes, my good arm holding her to me, my head on her shoulder, her hand stroking up and down my back, and her voice whispering softly in my ear. Saying what? I don't know. But it somehow soothes me.

"Mav, we need to get your arm looked at."

I lift my head at Lark's voice. When Sadie goes to step away from me, I pull her back. "Come with me. Please," I say in a hoarse whisper. Lifting her hand to stroke my hair away from my face, she nods.

Together we follow Lark down the long hallways in the belly of the stadium until we reach the assessment area. We head straight for one of the treatment tables just as Doc walks in.

"Okay, Mav, let's do some quick range tests, then we'll get an X-ray to make sure everything's good. I hear you came down pretty hard on that shoulder."

Doc's tone doesn't reveal anything, which doesn't help my anxiety. Only Sadie's presence at my side is stopping me from spiraling even further than I did in the locker room.

She stopped my impulsive rage in its tracks. I would have done something stupid, trashed the locker room or punched the goddamn wall, if it weren't for her.

I let Lark move my arm through a series of positions, wincing only once.

"Good. Let's get those images and see what we're dealing with."

Sadie stays behind, her arms wrapped around her middle as I follow Doc and Lark into another room. Thankfully, the X-ray is done quickly and then I'm back at her side. She takes my hand in both of hers, lacing our fingers together. I don't hesitate to accept any and all comfort she's offering.

We're silent as we wait for Doc.

He doesn't take long, and this time when he walks in, he's smiling. "Good news. No damage to your clavicle. It still looks well-healed. I think you jarred things, and there's no question that would hurt, but nothing looks amiss. I'd say call it for today, ice that shoulder, and you're still on track to play next week."

I exhale loudly. "Thank fuck." My head falls forward as I hear Sadie asking some questions. I can't focus on what they're saying because my head is spinning with relief.

"Come on, let's get you home." Sadie tugs on my hand, and I lift my head to realize we're alone. She's standing in front of me, and I pull her in between my legs. With me still seated, my head hits her at chest level and I don't think twice about laying it down against her soft body, carefully wrapping both arms around her, and sinking into her warmth.

I feel her gently playing with my hair and all the emotion of the past hour seeps out of me, leaving me completely exhausted.

She steps back and this time I let her pull me up to stand. We walk to the locker room where I notice someone has already cleaned up the shit I kicked over. Sadie goes to my locker, grabs my backpack, and looks over her shoulder at me. "Do you need anything else?"

I shake my head no.

We leave the stadium. I still haven't said anything since Doc told me I didn't reinjure my shoulder. I should probably say something to the woman beside me whose calm comfort has settled me and stopped me from doing something stupid.

But I don't. Instead, I let her lead me over to her car and open the passenger door. I sink down and stare out the front window at the stadium.

It's only when Sadie turns on the engine that I turn to face her.

"Thank you," I say quietly. "For being there." It's a pitiful statement, barely scratching the surface of what I'm feeling, but with her, I know it'll be enough. I know she'll get what I'm not saying.

Because somehow, Sadie LeDuc knows me. Better than anyone. Better than I know myself.

And today, she showed me that I'm not alone. I have a person now. Someone in my life, just for me, who's not there to benefit from me, but is there just because they want to be.

Someone who makes me feel like it's okay to relax and let go. Because she'll be there, by my side.

Chapter Twenty-Seven

Sadie

"We're goin' out, Specs."

I look up from my computer to see Maverick leaning against the wall, arms folded over his chest. "We are?"

He pushes off the wall and nods as he walks over to me. Slowly, his eyes locked on mine, he pushes my laptop shut as he leans forward, one hand landing on the back of the couch, next to my head. "Yeah. So go put on that purple dress from the wedding. The one that drove me crazy wanting to touch you in ways I couldn't back then." He drops his head even closer to my ear, his whisper hot against my skin. "Because tonight, I can."

I hold back a whimper as he pulls away, a smirk on his face. The jerk knows how he's affecting me right now, all dirty promises and barely-there touches that make me want to pant for more.

Since admitting to each other we wanted to stay together for real, we've been insatiable. Every moment we're both at the apartment is spent naked, except for when I manage to be strong enough to deny him so I can get some work done.

I could go back to the office. Gus wants me back there. But I kind of like working from here, enjoying stolen moments with Maverick when he's not at the stadium for practice or a rehab session.

Every time I make him smile, it feels like a little victory. Especially since those smiles are becoming more and more frequent. When he puts his arms around me, I feel safe. Cared for. And the rare moments he lets his guard down, resting his head on my stomach and letting me play with his hair, it's all I can do not to melt. Slowly, he's softening. Opening to me. To us. And it's incredible to see the change. Willow commented on it the other day over a glass of wine. He's been smiling at practice and even joined some of the guys for lunch at Maura's diner.

I won't take credit for the changes in him, though. That's all his doing, his choosing to let go of his demons and find a way forward that comes from a healthier, happier place.

Setting my computer down, I stand up and walk to find him in the bathroom, running his fingers through his hair, making sure the curls sit just right. I wrap my arms around him from behind, laying my head on his back.

"Will you tell me where we're going?" I ask pertly, grateful he can't see my excited smile. But of course, the darn man senses my excitement, judging by his chuckle.

"Do you really want to know?"

He spins around, his hands coming under my arms to lift me up. My legs wrap around his waist as I let him carry me into the bedroom, where he sets me down on top of his dresser.

I'm wearing just a thin pair of leggings and he's in jeans. The press of his pelvis against mine makes me want to grind into him. He's turning me into...I don't know what. A wanton, desire-driven, pleasure-seeking woman who is so different from how I was just a few weeks ago. She's unfamiliar, yet exciting. A welcome change.

"Keep doing that and we'll never leave," he growls, and I just give him an impish smirk.

"Maybe that's my plan."

His lips press against mine, bruisingly hard. But he lifts away before I can even get my arms around his neck, and this time I don't hold back my sound of protest.

"Get. Dressed." He squeezes my thighs before stepping away, going to the closet and grabbing the hanger that holds the lavender dress from Heidi and Max's wedding. I watch him lay it out on the bed before he strides over to the drawer where I finally unpacked some of my clothes.

I let out a small *eeep* when he pulls out a cream-coloured set of panties and strapless bra, and he smirks at me as he puts it on top of the dress.

"You have five minutes, Specs."

I wait until the door closes behind him before letting my upper body sag against the wall, a delirious grin on my face. *That man...*

But after only a few seconds, I hop off the dresser and do as I've been asked. I don't have any desire to disappoint Maverick or mess up whatever plans he has for tonight. Especially since I have a feeling those plans are going to involve a lot of orgasms.

With likely only seconds to spare, I give myself one final look in the mirror before grabbing a pair of sandals and opening the bedroom door. "Ready!" I announce as I walk out into the living room, coming to an abrupt stop.

Standing in front of me is Maverick King.

Holding flowers.

"Are those for me?" I ask stupidly, taking a slow step toward him. He chuffs out a laugh and closes the distance between us, cupping my chin and kissing me softly.

"Of course they are. Cat would just eat them."

I smile against his lips, kissing him a few more times, short and sweet pecks that are just enough to make his grip tighten before I step back. Holding out my hands, I make a *gimme, gimme* motion. He passes the bouquet and I lift it to my face, inhaling deeply.

"They're beautiful, thank you."

I lift a hand to brush down his cheek, and he turns to press a kiss to my palm.

He's a man of few words, but what he doesn't say with his voice, he conveys with his actions. And as I learn his language, I find myself falling deeper and deeper.

To my surprise, when we walk out of the apartment and enter the elevator, Maverick doesn't push the button for the lobby. Rather, he presses the one for the very top floor. But when I look at him, his face is unreadable.

We exit the elevator into a hallway much like the one on Maverick's floor. I let him guide me to the end where he opens a door that leads to a stairwell. My confusion is replaced by absolute wonder when he holds open the door at the top of the stairs and I step out onto the rooftop.

"Oh my goodness," I murmur, hardly knowing where to look first. Candles are flickering all around me. There must be hundreds of them: tall pillars and shorter votives in glass holders. Maverick laces his hand with mine and draws me forward, along a path through the candles to the center of the space. There's what looks to be a set of outdoor furniture, a low table and small two-seater couch. And on the table is a silver bucket with a bottle chilling on ice, two glasses, and two covered plates.

I sit down, my gaze still darting all around. There's small lights strung up around the perimeter, adding to the candlelight, so the entire space is bathed in soft, warm light. From up here, the sounds of the city are muffled, and when Maverick clicks on something behind me, the gentle radiating warmth of the outdoor heater adds to the feeling of being in our own little world, away from everyone and everything else.

"This is incredible." I take his hand when he finally sits next to me and lean over to kiss him. "Thank you."

He gives me a bashful smile before pouring two glasses of wine. Handing me one, he lifts his to me in a cheer. "To us."

The simple toast has me fighting back tears. His transformation from a reclusive, misunderstood man into a romantic one is so dramatic it still takes me aback.

I sip my wine to save me from saying anything and to buy some time to control my emotions. For all that he's put into this amazing night, I somehow know he's not ready for me to say the words of how I feel about him.

When I lower my wine glass back to the table, I'm more composed. Until, that is, he lifts the cover off the plates in front of us. Then I can't contain my delighted laugh.

"How did you know?" I ask, already lifting my fork, eager to dig into the somehow still-steaming hot dish of what appears to be my absolute favourite meal.

"Willow asked your friend Ali." He looks at me with such satisfaction and pride as I lift a forkful of gooey macaroni and cheese to my lips. "It's from a local place that does southern cooking. Darling told me it was good."

I let out an embarrassing moan when the flavours explode on my tongue. "Oh my God, it's *so* good." I take another bite, and another, before looking over to him, realizing he hasn't touched his food. "Okay, you need to eat, too, or this is going to get awkward really fast."

Instead of answering, Maverick leans over and kisses me. Then his tongue darts out and licks the corner of my mouth. "You had a little sauce..." He sits back and smirks. "But you're right. It is good."

He picks up his fork and starts to eat, staring at me with such heated intensity I don't know if it's the patio heater or him making me feel like I'm about to combust. I turn my attention to my food, trying to distract myself from the desire building inside of me. Then his hand lands on my thigh, stilling me with slow strokes of his thumb. He's no longer staring at me, now seemingly focused on his own meal. But his thumb is inching higher and higher until my food is forgotten as I try not to pant and gasp, not to shift and squirm to get his touch where I want it the most.

He brushes across my damp panties and my teeth sink into my lip.

"How's your food, Specs?" His smirk tells me he knows exactly where my focus is right now.

"Maverick," I whisper as his thumb slips under the edge of my panties.

All I hear is the clatter of a fork hitting the ground, and then he's on his knees in front of me, shoving up the hem of my dress and spreading my legs.

"Fuck, Sadie. I thought I could do it. I thought I could give you this perfect night, woo you, be all romantic and shit. But I can't keep my hands off you. I need you. *Now.*"

He doesn't wait for me to say anything before dipping his head down and kissing me right over the top of my panties. My hips lift off the couch to meet him, and he uses that second to pull the scrap of lace down, tossing them over his shoulder, thankfully missing the hundreds of still-burning candles.

His gaze returns to mine. And I lean forward, dragging my fingers through his curls.

"You have me."

CHAPTER TWENTY-EIGHT

Sadie

I woke up this morning to Maverick's head between my legs, stirring me from dirty dreams to an even better reality. He didn't let me out of bed until I had screamed his name.

Having already made the decision to go into the hospital to work from my office today, I had to fend him off the entire time I was trying to get ready and eat breakfast. For a man who claims to not know how to be in a relationship, he certainly is beating out any and all of my past boyfriends.

I've been at work for several hours now, and to my immense relief, aside from a few curious looks, no one has said anything about my absence. Or my relationship. I've managed to stay on top of things from Maverick's apartment, so the workday flies by, and before I know it, I'm driving home.

Home.

When did his apartment start to feel like home?

I'm still musing over that when I let myself in, bending down to scratch Cat behind the ears, then toeing off my shoes. I take a quick shower, wrap myself up in a towel, and wander into the bedroom. Traces of the two of us are everywhere, intermingled.

My necklace sits beside his watch in a dish on the dresser. My clothes hang next to his. Glasses of water sit on each table on both sides of the bed.

What started as a publicity stunt has become something very, very real. And very wonderful.

I dress in one of his shirts and a pair of shorts and go to the kitchen to heat up some leftovers from last night. How he pulled it off, I still don't know, he wouldn't explain anything. But the entire evening was magical.

Once I'm settled on the couch with reheated macaroni and cheese in hand, I turn on the television. Maverick's at the game tonight, and while he said it was doubtful he'd play, I'm eager to see if I can catch a glimpse of him in the dugout. Thanks to his lessons, I now know enough about the sport to follow along, cheering when his teammate Rhett makes it around the bases to home. The camera follows him off the field, and there's Mav, leaning against the railing, looking every bit the superstar athlete.

And then he looks to the camera and winks, and I let out a little squeak. *Was that seriously for me?* I giggle and eat my dinner, my eyes glued to the screen, watching for any more peeks at my tattooed hottie.

A couple of hours later, the game has been over for a while and I'm trying to keep myself distracted while waiting for Maverick to come home. I want to ask him about that wink... I want to tell him his butt looks good in those baseball pants... I want to do all kinds of things to him and with him.

When a knock on the door comes, I hurry over to it with a wide smile, expecting it to be Maverick. Although, why he wouldn't use his key makes that assumption a silly one, which I realize the second I swing the door open.

My smile falls as I take in the man before me. His hair is unkempt, his clothes too big for his thin frame. A fuzzy, scraggly beard covers half his face, and his eyes are wild, pupils dilated.

"Where's Mav?" he demands, lifting one hand up to chew on very dirty nails.

Before I joined the hospital foundation, I spent several years working various jobs at a homeless shelter. Starting as frontline staff to get through university, I eventually moved into an administrative role, managing their budget and writing grants for funding. My years spent there, along with the extensive training I went through, has given me an awareness for when I'm facing someone with an addiction problem.

And looking at this man, it's clear he's a substance user in need of a fix. I start to slowly edge back into the apartment, preparing to close the door. He doesn't seem overly agitated or violent, but I'm alert, nonetheless. And I definitely don't want to tell him I'm alone.

Unfortunately for me, he figures it out.

"Fuck, he had a game. Fuck! *Fuck*." He mumbles the last bit under his breath, raking his hand through his hair as he shakes his head. "Fine. I'll wait." He starts to pace up and down the hallway. Part of me is glad he's not forcing his way in, but I also can't help but worry about Maverick's neighbours if any of them were to come out of their apartments.

My gaze darts over to my phone, still sitting on the couch. If there was only a way to get it and text Maverick without escalating anything.

"How do you know Maverick?" I ask instead, hoping to find out who he is. Maybe I should be more focused on closing the door and staying safe, but something's niggling at me, driving my need to know who this man is.

"Brothers," he mumbles.

That brings me up short. *Maverick has another brother?* I rack my brain, quickly trying to think if I've ever heard mention of this. But the only thing I can think of is the name Eli.

Just then, the elevator doors open, and Maverick walks out. He looks at me, then at the man who is now standing quite close. Rushing forward, he places himself between me and the man, his fists clenched.

"What are you doing here, Eli," he growls, confirming that this man, who calls himself Maverick's brother, and the mysterious Eli are one and the same.

"You weren't answering my texts." Eli's eyes bounce all around, looking anywhere but at his brother. "I need —"

"I know what you need. But I'm done giving it to you. I ended up in the fucking hospital last time I helped you."

Pieces of the puzzle start to click into place but I know I'm still missing a lot. And judging by Eli's expression, he can't hear the obvious pain lacing Maverick's words. Then again, I'm not sure Maverick catches the flash of hurt on Eli's face, either.

"Mav. Brother. C'mon. Don't do this." His voice turns pleading, desperate. But Maverick is a wall of stone.

"Get out."

Eli stares at him for another minute. His devastation is plain to me. Which makes me wonder, is this the first time Maverick has said no to him? My heart breaks for both of them in that moment. Eli storms over to the door to the stairwell, opens it, and slams it shut behind him without another word.

Maverick whirls around and grabs me, his eyes scanning my body, looking for something. "Are you okay? Did he touch you? Fuck. I'm so sorry I wasn't here. Shit, Specs. Tell me you're okay."

He sounds panicked, more than I've ever heard in his voice, and I grab his wrists, bringing his hands to my heart as I step toward him. "I'm fine. Maverick, breathe. I'm okay, he didn't do anything."

Slowly, I see Maverick calm, but there's still an edge of tension thrumming through him. I lead him to the couch, and when he's sat down, I lower myself next to him. When he immediately gathers me into his arms, pulling me into his lap, I let him. He needs this right now.

But he also needs to hear something.

"Eli said he was your brother?" I start, and after a few seconds, Maverick exhales and nods. "And he wanted money from you, for drugs, I'm guessing?"

Maverick's head falls forward to rest on my shoulder. "Yeah."

I consider my next words carefully. "How many times have you given him money?"

"Too many."

"Can I ask why?" I say softly, stroking his hair.

"Because he's the closest thing I have to a brother, just like Colin. Because we were older than him, so we got out first, and we left him there. Which means he believes it's our fault he turned to drugs, and we weren't around to keep him away from it." As he blurts all of this out, his voice is full of despair, and anger, and grief. And my heart breaks for him.

"But that's over. I'm not going to give him anything. He doesn't get to come here, scare you, put you in danger." He lifts his head now and looks at me with anger written all over his face. "It'll never happen again. I'm so sorry, Specs. You should never have to be around him."

"Maverick, no." I cup his face in my hands. "He didn't threaten me or hurt me or even scare me. I've worked with people who use drugs before, I know the signs of escalation to watch for and how to keep myself safe. He surprised me, that's all."

"Still. I'm done with him, I swear."

"You can't push him away, not like this. He needs help and based on how he reacted to you kicking him out, he came to you hoping you'd give him that support."

"He came to me for money to buy drugs, that's all," Maverick growls, shifting me off his lap. "And I'm done with that."

"You don't have to give him money to help him," I urge, trying to get him to understand. "But abandoning him isn't necessarily the right answer, either."

Maverick moves abruptly, standing and walking over to the kitchen. I get up to follow him but freeze when I see him standing with his hands on the counter, his head hanging low. Making my way over to him slowly, I reach out a hand and place it on his back.

"I can't... Can we talk about this later?" he says in a low voice.

"Yeah, sure," I reply softly. "Whenever you want. I'm here."

He pushes off the counter, turns, and takes me in his arms, his head coming to rest on top of mine. I can feel his heart racing under my cheek as he holds me tightly to him, and I hug him back just as close.

And I hope that someday, he'll let me in. All the way. And show me every part of himself that he still keeps hidden. If I didn't know about Eli, what else don't I know?

CHAPTER TWENTY-NINE

Maverick

Finally.

The end of the national anthem dies off and the crowd roars. I'm back. After almost ten weeks, I'm finally jogging out onto the field, taking my position at third base, ready to fucking play ball.

For the next three hours, nothing else matters except the game. Coach said I'll only be in for three innings, and as much as I wanted to complain about that, I bit my tongue. I know it's so I don't overdo it, and in light of what happened last week during practice, it makes sense.

That just means I'm going fucking hard while I'm out here.

Our opponents, the Boston Revs, are solid competition, and the first batter gets a single off Kai's pitch. Tension vibrates through me as I watch the play. And when the ball flies my way, muscle memory kicks in, sending me back to catch the pop, then whipping it to second for the double play.

The home crowd erupts, and my teammates swarm me with back slaps and shouts.

I'm fucking back.

The next half, I'm not up to bat. I let Lark check my arm, my attention only half on her questions. Because Ronan's up to bat.

The crack of wood contacting with the ball has me leaping forward to join the other guys at the rail. "Fuck yeah, Sin!" I shout as he rounds the base for an easy double.

From there, everything moves quickly. Two more hits make for two runs in, and we're in the lead. When I jog back out to the field, my blood is pumping. This is what I live for. This game, this is everything to me.

Even though we end up taking the loss against the Revs, it's a good game. And my shoulder's fine, which I keep having to tell everyone, from Coach, to Lark, to the fucking press that Colin made me promise I'd talk to if they approached me postgame. Which, of course, they did.

"Yeah, it felt great to get back out there." *Of course it fucking did, what a stupid question.*

"I'm grateful to be here, all healed." *I wouldn't be playing if I wasn't healed enough, dumbass.*

"No comment." I glare at the reporter who actually fucking thought he could ask me about the accident. Turning away, I head into the locker room. I just want to get home and see Sadie.

Most of the team is already there in various stages of undress. I head straight to the showers, cranking the water as hot as I can before stepping in. I let the water wash away the annoyance of having to actually interact with the press.

Wrapping a towel around my waist, I head for my locker.

"Maverick fucking King is *back*, baby!"

My head turns at Monty's shout. He's got a wide grin as he starts a slow clap that everyone else gradually joins in. There's no use fighting the discomfort that comes when I'm the focus of so much direct attention, and I can feel my cheeks heat.

"Cut it out." I try to scowl, but Monty points at my face, his smile somehow growing wider.

"Holy shit, he's smiling! Someone get a camera, it's history in the making, boys!"

I shove him away, but he's right, I am smiling. Tonight was fucking awesome, and I'm happy.

Smiling is the obvious reaction.

"My dude, this is a good look for you." Monty ignores any sort of personal space boundary and the fact that we're both still wearing nothing but towels around our hips as he drapes his arm over my shoulder. "That's a panty-melting smile, my friend. Good thing you don't do it often, or we might start feeling inadequate around you."

"Fuck off, Monty," I mockingly growl. "It's not just my face that makes me better than you."

A chorus of laughter and good-natured jeers go up and Monty steps away, bringing his fist to his chest and twisting the imaginary knife. "You wound me, Mav."

I smirk. "It only hurts because it's true."

Monty tosses his head back and laughs. "Damn, bro! What did I ever do to you?"

"Still glad I'm back?" I say archly, fighting to school my grin into my usual scowl.

"Fuck, yeah," he says, his tone shifting on a dime to completely serious. "Really glad."

"Thanks," I reply quietly, grateful everyone else has moved on and isn't paying attention anymore. "Me too."

Monty gives me one more nod before winking at me. "And the personality change they gave you when they fixed your shoulder is pretty great. Make sure you thank the surgeon for that on my behalf, okay?"

My bark of laughter breaks free as he saunters over to his locker. "Fuck you, Monty."

"Why would you do him when you've got Sadie waiting at home?" Kai shouts from across the locker room.

I point at him. "You're right. Why am I still here talking to you fuckers?" I finish getting dressed and grab my bag. "'Night, boys."

My smile remains the entire time I'm walking out of the stadium and into my car, and only starts to fade as I drive home. My mind feels like it's playing a game of fucking ping-pong, bouncing between wondering what kind of reception I'll get from Sadie and analyzing the interactions with the guys tonight. I can count on one hand the number of times I've felt like I belonged in a social situation. Sure, I play ball with these guys and see them almost every fucking day. But I used to do the bare minimum. Leaving as soon as I could, talking just enough to get by. Hanging out after a game, giving each other shit, just having fun, that's always been the stuff I avoid.

Until tonight. And fuck if I didn't actually enjoy it, even if my laugh felt a little rusty.

But Sadie. We didn't talk anymore about Eli last night, and when we finally climbed into bed, I could tell Sadie was keeping herself apart. I fucking hated it. But there's parts of me I don't know if I'll ever be ready to show her.

Last night, my past decided to show up and fuck with my present. And I wasn't even there to stop it from happening. For fuck's sake, what was Sadie thinking? She should've slammed the door in Eli's goddamn face. Except she would never do that. She's too good of a person to push someone away like that. But I also don't need her getting involved in my shit.

I'll handle Eli. Don't fucking know how, but I will.

Unlocking the door to my apartment, I mentally push thoughts of Eli, and of baseball, aside. Compartmentalizing. That's what my social worker when I was a kid called it. She also said I was really good at it, and someday that strength could bite me in the ass if I never figured out how to integrate the different parts of my life.

Yeah. Got it.

The living room is dark, so after petting Cat and setting down my bag, I toe off my shoes and walk softly to the bedroom. Sadie's curled on her side, her red hair spread across her pillow. And for a couple of minutes, I just stare at her. Even in sleep, she somehow radiates peace and calm, and settles something inside of me.

I head to the bathroom to get ready for bed and strip down to my boxers. Then, carefully, I climb into the bed behind her and gather her into my arms. She lets out the cutest little snuffle before turning over, her eyes blinking awake.

"Hey," she murmurs before nestling closer into my arms.

I kiss her forehead, letting my lips linger there for a second. "Hey."

She tips her head up, her eye lashes fluttering against her cheeks. I dip down to cover her lips, keeping it soft, letting her lead, even though my dick is already starting to tent my boxers.

A leg drapes over mine, and Sadie brings her hand to my chest, pushing on me. I brush the hair away from her face. "Thought you were asleep?" I ask before kissing her again, gently biting her lower lip.

"Mmm. I was. And I was having a really good dream." She wiggles around on top of me, pressing her pelvis down on my growing cock. Then she lifts herself off my chest, her hands going to the hem of her shirt, stripping it off.

"And then I realized it didn't have to be just a dream."

Chapter Thirty

Sadie

Maverick's gaze devours me as I settle my hands back down on his bare chest.

"You gonna tell me what that dream was about, Specs?" he growls, lifting his large hands up to cup my breasts. "Or can I try and guess."

I swivel my hips, letting the impressive bulge under his boxers hit me in all the right places. "You can try and guess, or I could show you."

His eyebrows lift as a wicked grin covers his handsome face. "Okay, show me." He moves his hands, folding them behind his head, looking every inch the arrogant asshole so many assume he is.

Only I know different. I know that beneath his tough exterior lies a good man with a protective instinct for everyone he cares about, and a heart that deserves to be loved.

He just needs to believe that about himself.

Leaning down, I kiss along his scruff-covered jawline, avoiding his lips even as he growls at me. I make my way down his neck, bringing my hands into the mix, running featherlight touches all over his body. Tonight is about him, not me. I want to tease him, torment him, and bring him to the point where he lets go and trusts me to take care of him the way he always does for me.

My lips land on his chest, pressing lightly over the area where his fracture was. My hands start to knead his upper arms, feeling the ridges of muscle, of pure power. When he starts to bring his arms out from under his head, I stop and shake my head.

"Keep them there."

He grunts but does as I say. Resuming my path, my hands draw down the underside of his arms, along his upper ribs. I kiss my way down to his nipples, letting my tongue circle the flat disks, listening to his sounds of pleasure.

"I need to touch you." His voice is gravelly, and I can't deny the pleasure I feel, knowing my plan is working.

"You can touch, but you can't stop me. I'm in charge right now," I say primly, lifting my head to meet his gaze. "Understood?"

The look of pure desire he shoots at me makes me want to shiver and melt into him, but I won't be distracted from my mission.

"You're in charge." His hands land on my upper thighs, squeezing tightly.

The thrill of victory runs through me. I know just how much trust he's giving me, even by saying those words. Shifting back slightly, my hands come to the top of his boxers.

"These need to go." I move off his lap, and Maverick wordlessly pushes them down, then kicks them off with his feet.

But as I move to return to my position straddling him, he stops me. "So do yours."

Even though I was already planning on getting naked very soon, I arch my brow at him. "Have you already forgotten who's in charge?"

He surges upward, his hand cupping my throat, catching me by surprise and forcing me to stare at him. "Baby, you can be in charge all you want. But that doesn't mean I'm gonna lie here and do nothing." His lips steal my breath with a punishing kiss that leaves me whimpering when he pulls back.

With a smirk, he lies back down. "Get naked, Specs."

Fine. I'll let him have this one. I hurry to strip off my pajama shorts, my sex already feeling hot and needy. When I swing my leg over his hips again, his hands shoot out, cupping my head, tangling in my hair, and tugging me down for another kiss.

"Your lips are addictive," he rumbles against me, and I moan in response. He's trying to take control again. However, I'm determined not to let that happen.

Not yet, at least.

Pulling free, I wiggle my way down his body, once again trailing kisses over his hot skin. This time, he doesn't stop me. I reach his cock lying heavy and long against his thigh.

Wrapping my hand around the base, I squeeze experimentally, watching his face. His eyes droop closed, his mouth falling open slightly. I squeeze tighter, and his hand clenches the sheet at his side. My tongue darts out to lick a stripe up the underside and his eyes fly open, his other hand coming down to push my hair back from my face.

"Fucking addictive," he murmurs, echoing his earlier words.

I suck him into my mouth, running my tongue along his crown before slowly sliding down, taking as much as I can without choking. When I pull back, releasing him with a pop, I glance up to see that look of pure wonder on his face. The expression that tells me he can't quite believe this is happening. It's a look I both love and hate.

I love that he feels this way with me. That I make him feel so good, he can't believe it's real. And I hate that he doesn't simply believe it is, and that he deserves whatever I give him and so much more.

I take him in again, letting some saliva drip down to lubricate the rest of him so I can use my hand as well. Squeezing, twisting, licking, and sucking. My eyes flutter closed. His fingers are in my hair, holding it back. He keeps muttering dirty, sweet words to me, driving me on, making me hotter and wetter, and all the more determined to have him fall apart.

"Shit, Sadie." He starts to lift his upper body, curling up. "Baby. I'm gonna come."

I smile around his cock and keep going, pushing him as far into my mouth as I can, swallowing and pulling back before doing it all over again. I can feel him swell in my mouth and feel his hands tighten their grip in my hair, and then he's cursing and shouting my name. I swallow everything down that I can. Licking him clean like a freaking lollipop.

Never in my life have I enjoyed giving a man a blow job. Until this very moment. I feel like a goddess as I rise, taking in Maverick's chest heaving with every breath, and the look of absolute ecstasy on his face.

I did that. Me. Sadie LeDuc, whose ex said she was *boring*.

Straddling his upper legs, I keep my hands still, resting on his lower abdomen. When he opens his eyes to look at me, the fire burning inside of me turns into an inferno at his expression. I shriek when he grabs my hips and pulls, making me fall forward.

He kisses me, then slaps my ass with one hand. "Give me that fucking pussy."

Digging his fingers in, he pulls again, and I shuffle forward, lifting my hands up to brace on the headboard. The first time he wanted to do this, I thought he was insane, and I tried to refuse. Dirk never wanted to go down on me, and this position? Yeah, right. But Maverick insisted, and the way he devoured me led to one of the most intense orgasms of my life.

I can feel his fingertips digging into my flesh, that possessive hold making my pulse speed up.

A light tap on my ass has me looking down to see Maverick's face between my legs.

"Just so we're clear. I'm in charge now."

That's all he says before latching his mouth around my clit and sucking hard.

I shriek out his name, the wave of sensation from that one action hitting me everywhere. He releases me, only to drag his tongue up and down my sex, lapping at me before giving my clit a few flicks, every single one sending sparks through me. My grip tightens on the headboard as I start to rock back and forth, chasing my orgasm that's building and building. Maverick rumbles out a sound, the vibrations making my thighs clench around his head.

"Oh my God," I moan, my head dropping forward as I grind down onto him. Somehow, he manages to get a hand in between my legs and slides two fingers inside me. At first, he simply glides them in and out as he kisses and licks. But my needy whimpers betray me, and with a low chuckle, he finally gives me what I desperately want.

His fingers curl in again and press against my G-spot. At the same second, he flicks my clit with his tongue so rapidly it almost rivals my favourite vibrator. And that's all it takes.

When I eventually manage to shimmy my way down his body, feeling boneless and happy, but still wanting more, he kisses me. And the taste of me on his lips only drives that insatiable need higher.

Maverick shifts us so we're on our sides, facing each other. I let him lift my leg to drape it over his, opening me to him. We stay like that, making out, for several long, luxurious minutes, hands and mouths tracing pleasure all over each other.

Then he rolls us over so he's hovering over me, his lips never leaving mine as he reaches out blindly, pawing at the bedside table until something falls to the floor and we break apart.

He grabs the condoms he was searching for and drops them on the bed beside us, then moves back in to kiss me again, but I stop him with a giggle and my hand on his chest. "Wait! What fell off the table?"

He shifts over and glances down, then shakes his head. "My phone. Don't care. Want you."

We both fumble for one of the condoms, but he gets it open and rolled down his cock. Then he lowers onto his elbows and kisses me sweetly. I lift my legs up, wrapping them around his back, reaching between us, and notching him to my entrance.

He pushes in slowly, never letting up on our kiss until he's all the way seated inside me. Only then does he break away, letting our foreheads touch instead.

"Heaven," he murmurs. And that one word says so much more.

Our hips start to rock. Slowly at first. As if we have all the time in the world and nothing else to do but be here together.

Then something else takes over. Some deep-seated need. A primal desire. And when he grabs my hip, holding it tightly as he starts to rock faster and harder, I moan out my encouragement.

"Yes, oh God, yes. More. Maverick. *More.*"

He dips down and captures my breast in his mouth, grazing over my nipple before releasing it and doing the same to the other side.

I grip his hair, tangling my fingers through the curls, holding him to me as I writhe underneath his unrelenting thrusts. Until he rears back, forcing my hands to drop as he comes up over me, never stopping the push-pull of his hips. He grabs my legs and lifts them up to his shoulders.

"Fuck, Specs. Look at you. Look at your perfect fucking pussy taking me like this. Like you were made for my dick." His growly dirty talk makes my back arch up off the bed. One large hand covers my breast again, squeezing almost painfully but stopping just this side of pleasure. Then he drags his hand down over the slope of my stomach to play with my clit, palming it, pinching it, then flicking it with his thumb until the combined sensations overwhelm me and I come undone, crying out his name.

His own orgasm follows right after, his ragged shouts echoing the thrusts of his cock driving into me. He collapses down on me, his lips kissing whatever skin he lands on. His heavy weight is welcome and I run my hands up and down his back, loving the feel of his surrender.

He rolls off after a minute, going to the bathroom to deal with the condom. Climbing back into the bed, he moves in beside me, rolling me onto my side before wrapping his large body around mine and kissing the top of my head once it's pillowed on his arm.

"You're changing me, Specs. In a really good way." His soft statement fills me with indescribable feelings of happiness. And cocooned in his embrace, everything feels right. I'm exactly where I want to be.

My last thought as I drift off to sleep, safe and satisfied and deliriously happy in his arms, is a simple one. Yet it holds the power to change everything.

I'm in love with Maverick King.

Chapter Thirty-One

Sadie

Maverick left today for a stretch of away games, and I already miss him. So much so that I texted Ali on my way home from work, asking if she wanted a night of takeout and trashy television. She agreed, and we ended up gorging on Chinese food and cheap wine at her place.

In between bites of ginger beef, checking in on the game, and yelling at the dating show we're sort of watching, I brought her up to speed on everything going on between me and Maverick.

Everything except the fact that I'm in love with him. That's something I feel like I should tell him first.

It's late by the time we turn off the TV, and after so much wine, I'm easily convinced to just sleep here. When we're in her bed, Ali shifts onto her side and says, "I'm really happy for you, Sadie."

I smile at my best friend, the woman who has been with me through so much for so long. "Thanks."

Ali yawns and rolls over. "And if any of the other Tridents are looking for a lady, you know where to find me."

As per always, she falls asleep instantly, soft snores coming from her side of the bed. It doesn't bother me, not after almost twenty years of friendship and more sleepovers than I can count.

I roll onto my side and pick up my phone. There's two messages from Maverick, and judging by the time, he must have sent them right before his game started.

MAVERICK: Hey Specs. Hope you're doing okay. If you need anything just call Colin.

I smile in the dark. Always looking out for me in his own gruff way. And his second message, sent a few hours after the first, makes me silently swoon.

MAVERICK: Wish I could kiss you goodnight.

The team is down in Denver playing the Bandits tonight and tomorrow, and it's only one hour ahead. If he's asleep, that's fine, but I can't go without responding to him.

SADIE: XOXO. I know it's not the same. I miss your kisses too. Good game tonight!

To my surprise, I see the three dots pop up immediately.

MAVERICK: Can I call you?

I quietly slide out of Ali's bed and move to the living room, closing her door behind me. Then I reply.

SADIE: Yes

An incoming video call lights up the screen and I nervously pat at my hair before answering.

"Hi."

One gruff word from him and I'm biting my lower lip, wishing he was here. That he was walking in the door of his apartment instead of being miles away.

"Hi," I reply quietly, sitting down on the couch and tugging a blanket over my lap.

"Where are you?" he says with a small frown.

"Ali's. But I fed Cat before I left and I'll go back early tomorrow."

"Specs, it's fine. Cat's used to me being gone. I can call Ralph tomorrow and ask him to go over if you want to stay with Ali."

I'm already shaking my head because I don't want to stay here. It doesn't feel right, even though I know his apartment will feel so empty without him.

"No. I'm going back there tomorrow; I was going to make omelets with Ralph."

Surprise crosses his face, followed quickly by a slow smile. "You're gonna do omelets?"

I nod. "If you think he'd like that."

"I know he would. He's been bugging me to bring you over."

"Then I'll do it. Just cheese, right?"

"Yeah. Don't even try to sneak in vegetables." Maverick's grinning now. "And Specs?"

"Yeah?"

"Thank you."

MAVERICK: That photo of you and Cat made my day, Specs. Talk tonight?

SADIE: Sorry about last night, can't believe I fell asleep! Good luck today!

SADIE: That was rough. Hope your shoulder is okay.

MAVERICK: This is fucking ridiculous. I miss you. Fucking time zones.

SADIE: Hey! I'm here, just saw you called. Call me back?

MAVERICK: Hey. Shit, I'm just heading out with the guys for some BP before the game. Call you in a couple hours?

SADIE: Darn I'll be in a meeting.

SADIE: This sucks.

MAVERICK: I know. I'll be home soon thank fuck.

SADIE: Miss you.

MAVERICK: Same.

The reality check of dating a professional athlete has hit hard these last few days. I guess I was spoiled when Maverick was still on the injured list; he was home all the time instead of traveling with the team.

But now, he's back playing, and we're five days into a week-long stretch of away games, and I'm hating it. The first couple days were fine between the night at Ali's place and breakfast with Ralph, who has to be the sweetest old curmudgeon I've ever met. Honestly, he reminds me a lot of Maverick. Not that I'd ever tell either of them that. But they have the same caring, protective, giving nature hidden under a layer of gruff, grumpy vibes.

But coming home from work to an empty apartment and cooking for one, night after night, doesn't feel the same. Even if only a few weeks ago that was my reality. I miss Maverick.

And these stinking time zones are making it impossible for us to connect. Taking out my phone, I mentally calculate what time it is for him in Minnesota, where they're playing tonight. He'll be on the field, but maybe we can connect when he's back at the hotel.

> **SADIE: Good luck tonight. I just got home, going to turn on the game and try to find you. Call me later? XOXO.**

I set my phone down, go to the bedroom to get changed out of my work clothes, and come back to the living room in time to hear my phone vibrating. Dashing over, hope flaring that maybe he's not on the field yet, I answer without looking at the screen.

"Maverick?"

A derisive snort meets my breathless greeting. "Not likely. What the hell are you doing, Sadie? How long do you plan on playing this game?"

"Dirk." My stomach fills with lead. "Why are you calling me?"

I knew I should have blocked his number. What the hell does he want? I sit down on the couch, and Cat hops into my lap, circling a few times before settling in, his weight a small comfort.

"I just told you. I want to know when you're gonna realize a guy like Maverick King will never be with someone like you for long. Cut your losses and we can talk about trying again."

My mouth falls open at his arrogance, to say nothing of the cruelty of his words. I stand up, dislodging Cat. I'll make it up to him with some treats later, but right now I need to move, do something to expel the rage building inside of me.

"Listen to me carefully. You are an asshole," I hiss, hearing Dirk's intake of breath at my curse. "You're a sniveling, whiny, greedy, rude bastard who's terrible in bed. The only reason you're calling is because you can't stand the fact that I'm not broken up over you cheating on me. Well, guess what? I'm grateful you did that. Because who knows how long I would have stayed with you, suffering through mediocre sex with no orgasms. You did me a favour. Now I'm with a real man who knows exactly how to take care of me, in and out of the bedroom. So get this in your little head. I am *never* coming back to you. I *never* want to speak with you again. Goodbye and good riddance."

I push the end button, probably a little too hard, and immediately block his number. My heart is pounding, but God, it feels good to have done that.

Turning on the television, I see the game has just started. Maverick's not on the field, so I hurry to the kitchen to reheat some food for dinner and feed Cat. Just as I'm about to return to the couch, there's a knock on the door. Checking first, I see Ralph standing in the hall with a container of something in his hands.

I open the door with a smile. "Hello, neighbour, what can I do for you?"

"You watchin' the game?" he says by way of greeting, and I step aside with a nod.

"Of course, I am. Would you like to join me?"

He stomps inside, and Cat immediately trots over with a *meow*. Ralph bends down slowly to pet his head before straightening. Yeah, just like Maverick. *A total softie.*

Ralph looks at me. "Got a fork? I forgot one."

Hiding my smile, I go to the kitchen and retrieve one, as well as my own dinner, before joining him in the living room. He's sitting down in the large chair and accepts the fork with a grunt of thanks.

And that's how I end up watching the Tridents play the Toronto Wolverines with Ralph providing colourful commentary throughout.

He leaves shortly after the game, and once I've tidied up from dinner, I wander around aimlessly, staring at my phone more often than necessary, hoping for a call. Finally, an hour after Ralph goes home, it rings.

"Hi!" I say, probably sounding way too excited, but I don't care.

"Hey." He chuckles, confirming that, yes, I did sound like an eager beaver. "Did you actually watch the game?"

I pull back the covers and climb into bed with a smile. "Sure did. Ralph came over and we watched together."

"Oh, really?"

"Yup. He taught me a lot."

Maverick laughs. "How many times did he shake his fist at the ump's calls?"

"Every time."

"Sounds about right."

I hear sounds of sheets rustling and can't hide my wistful sigh.

"Two more days, Specs."

I'm nodding, even though he can't see me. "I know. Oh, you'll never guess who called me today."

"Who?"

"Dirtbag Dirk."

Immediately, my phone vibrates with a notification to switch to video. I click the accept button, and when Maverick's face fills the screen, he looks furious.

"Why the fuck is that asshole calling you?" he growls. His anger on my behalf is a turn-on. Or maybe it's him being shirt-less, all those muscles and tattoos on display.

"Hmm?" I try to subtly check I'm not drooling, but I'm busted when Maverick raises an eyebrow at me. "Oh. He was just being his usual gross self. Trying to tell me you'd never want me long-term and I should go back to him."

As I say the words myself, I'm pleasantly surprised at how easily I dismiss them. The truth is, even if Maverick and I don't last, I would never ever go back to Dirk. Because the man on the other end of the phone line has made me realize I deserve so much better than Dirk ever gave me.

"Specs. Don't fucking listen to him. Don't answer his calls. He's a lying sack of shit who's a goddamn baby throwing a tantrum because he lost his favourite toy." Maverick's words drip with contempt. "What happens between us is none of his fucking business. I swear to God, he does not deserve to even breathe the same air as you. And if he comes near you again, I'm gonna make it so he never can."

"Easy, tiger," I say, smiling at his glowering face. "I already told him to get stuffed and blocked his number. I don't believe a word he said."

I watch him sag back against the headboard of his hotel room bed.

"Good. Fuck, I wish I'd been there with you when he called." He runs his hand through his hair in frustration, and I wish it was my fingers tangling in the strands, not his.

"You can't fight all my battles," I say quietly. "But thank you for wanting to."

"I'm not some knight in shining armor," he says gruffly.

"I know. But you are a good man."

He drops his gaze for a second before looking back up at me through the screen. "I want to be. For you."

It takes a monumental feat of strength not to blurt out that I love him in that moment. But somehow, I resist.

For now.

CHAPTER THIRTY-TWO

Maverick

There's a reason I prefer traveling overnight when everyone is sleeping. And when Monty sinks down in the seat next to me on the bus, it reinforces why. I want to keep my AirPods in and ignore him, but he's like a fucking puppy dog sometimes, all smiles and laughs, and no sense of when to let shit go.

"So," he says expectantly. I smother my sigh of frustration and press pause on my music.

"Yeah?"

"You and Sadie. That's still a thing?"

He's grinning and swear to fucking God, if I didn't know he means no harm, I'd slap the smile off his face.

"Yeah."

His shoulder shoves into mine. "C'mon, Mav, we're past the whole single-word-answer shit, aren't we? We're buddies now!"

I guess my face says it all because Monty winces. "Okay, maybe not buddies, but…"

Ah, shit, I can't. I shove him right back, harder. "Shut up and stop pouting, *buddy*. What do you want to know? I'm not talking about my sex life, just so we're fucking clear."

Swear to God, his face lights up like a kid on Christmas morning. Not that I've experienced that myself, but I've seen it on TV enough times.

"Really? Okay. Well, she's awesome, and funny, and nice. And it seems she's making you more funny and more nice. So, like, that's cool. Are you guys happy? Is it serious?"

"Slow your goddamn roll there, Monty. He doesn't have to tell you shit." Ronan shifts in his seat across the aisle and shakes his head with amusement at our catcher. Guess he thinks the same as me about Monty's resemblance to a golden retriever. Can't help but love 'em, even when they drive you nuts.

Leaning forward, he meets my gaze. "Honestly, it's none of our business how things are with you and Sadie. But I will agree with one thing. Even though we haven't known each other that long, I can see you're different since you've been back on the field. In a good way. And if it's because of Sadie, then that's awesome."

Now I've got both of them looking at me, waiting for some sort of answer. But what the fuck am I meant to say that won't reveal too much of my past or be too fucking sappy?

"Yeah. She's a great woman and we're happy. I'm also glad to be back on the field." I shrug. "Are the two related? Maybe. I don't know. I'm just gonna keep playing ball and making her happy."

"Aww, man, I love that." Monty lifts his hand up for a high five, and I just stare at him. "C'mon. That was good! We're bonding."

"I think that's enough bonding for today," I reply dryly, turning to face forward again. He gets the message and doesn't bug me again, leaving me alone to play my music.

And as soon as I close my eyes, she's there. Red hair, glasses, and a smile that's just for me. She makes me feel hopeful, for once in my life. Hopeful for a future that involves more than just baseball.

The problem is, my life has taught me not to hope for anything. Because as soon as I do, it gets ripped away from me.

But just this once, I want to believe it'll be different. That Sadie will make everything okay, the way she always has.

The next day's game goes well, and now we've only got one more in this series before we can head home. Thank fuck. I want my own bed, and I want Sadie in it.

For years, I didn't care about traveling. I didn't have a home I was attached to or someone waiting for me. Aside from Colin, Ralph and Cat are the only two living creatures who even know when I go out of town. Even Eli doesn't know my schedule.

But now there's someone else. Sadie's there to get my text messages or phone calls, and she's waiting for me to come home.

The locker room postgame is loud. We won, bringing us that much closer to making the playoffs. I'm not sure if I deserve to be here, what with missing ten weeks of the season, but the excitement is still contagious. And the guys don't seem to share my reservations about my involvement. When I caught a pop fly that came straight to me at third, closing the seventh inning without our opponents getting any runs in, my teammates went wild.

I slowly rotate my shoulder, remembering the pull when I jumped to make the catch. Lark has already instructed me to find her before I leave for the hotel so she can check things over. I want to ignore her, not risk her saying I need to ease off or not play as many innings. But all it takes is picturing Sadie's worried face if she found out somehow, and I know I'll go and find the trainer.

"Championship, here we fucking come! I can taste the win, baby," Kai shouts, and is immediately met with protests.

"Shut up, Yami!"

"Fuck, now we're jinxed."

"Goddamn pitcher's getting ahead of shit."

I keep my head down, saying nothing, but a smirk crosses my face. I'm not that superstitious, yet even I know you shouldn't say anything about winning a game that's still several weeks away. Especially when our spot in the playoffs isn't totally secure yet.

"Holy *fuck*!" A shaking, angry voice roars over the room. It takes a second for me to place it, then my eyes land on Ricky Orson. The center fielder's face is bright red as he glares at his phone. Even from across the room, I can tell his knuckles are white from gripping the device and his shoulders are rising and falling rapidly. Then he yells again, another loud *fuck*, and throws his phone to the ground before storming out of the locker room.

"What the hell was that all about?" Sin asks after a few seconds of stunned silence. No one moves at first, then Darling goes over and picks up the cracked phone, tapping on it carefully to wake the screen.

"Oh, shit." He sounds shocked, and coming from the laid-back southern boy, that's telling. Whatever's on that phone, it's not good.

A bunch of other guys crowd around him, staring at the phone. I hang back. I might be starting to get closer with some of the guys on the team, but I don't belong over there. I barely know Orson. And I don't do emotional bonding shit, no matter what Monty said on the bus last night.

"No fucking way." Kai's eyes are wide. "They were solid, man. She came to the last home game and they looked so fucking happy together."

Slowly, everyone disperses from huddling around Darling. He sets Orson's phone down in his locker and goes back to his own to continue dressing. The somber mood is weird, considering how everyone was hyped not that long ago. And while I have suspicions about what was on Orson's phone, not knowing what set him off has me on edge.

When Sin drops down beside me, letting his head fall back against the divider between his locker and mine, his eyes are troubled.

"What happened?" I ask in a low voice.

"His wife wants a divorce. She sent him a fucking text message, telling him she'd be gone when he gets home and that the papers would be on the kitchen counter."

Shit. No wonder the guy walked out of here looking like his world was ending. Now Kai's comment makes sense.

"They were married eight years. She's been there for him his entire career. He was gonna retire soon because he wanted to spend more time with her. And now it's over. Who the hell does that? Who ends a marriage over a text? And right at the end of the season too."

The fact that Ronan Sinclair has only been with the team for one season and already knows all these details about a teammate I've played with for a hell of a lot longer isn't lost on me. It drives home just how distant I've been from everyone. So hell-bent on not letting anyone in, I'm on the outside, unaware of anything important in their lives, like marriages and retirement plans. And these are guys I spend more than half the fucking year with, day in and day out.

But what's happening to Orson is also a reminder of *why* I don't let anyone get close to me.

Because as soon as they're close, they can hurt you. And you never know when it's going to happen. Everything can be going great for years and then your parent can die, your partner can leave you, or your team can drop you.

And you're left alone.

I'm so tired of being alone.

CHAPTER THIRTY-THREE

Sadie

Tonight. He'll be home tonight.

There was a strange energy coming from Maverick when we talked yesterday. I assumed it was because they lost their game and probably won't make the playoffs, but it seemed like more than just that. A wall was between us, a wall I didn't even notice until I hung up and realized there was none of the usual softness in his words. No *I miss you*. Nothing.

But finally, in just a few hours, I can see him in person and figure out if I'm making a bigger deal out of this than I should.

Honestly, I didn't expect him being away for so long to be this hard. But Maverick is someone who says so much without words that having to rely *only* on words was incredibly challenging. And as much as I don't want to think too hard about the future, not when it feels so uncertain, I can't help but worry about how we would manage an entire season of this, of him traveling half the time and me staying at home.

But that's a future problem, and I have no desire to face it now. Not when I'd much rather be getting ready for his return.

The apartment is clean and the fridge is stocked with everything I need to make him a delicious dinner later tonight. Ali invited me over for dinner yesterday, but I declined, not wanting to put my nervous energy on her.

Why I'm nervous is another thing I have no desire to face.

When a knock comes at the door, it makes me jump. Going to it, I look through the peephole, and am shocked to see Eli standing there. His head is hanging down, but his clothes look clean. Still, I'm acutely aware that Maverick isn't on his way home from the stadium just yet. I'm here alone and will be for several more hours.

I open the door a crack. "Hi, Eli," I say cautiously.

"Sadie. Hey." He looks at me then, and his eyes are clear, although tired-looking. Dark circles ring them and his cheeks seem hollow. "Is Mav around?" he asks hopefully, his face falling when I shake my head. Something seems different with him this time.

"Okay. Thanks." He turns to leave and I open the door more. "Wait."

He looks over his shoulder at me, confusion clear in his expression.

"Do you want to go get a coffee?"

I don't know why I'm asking this. Well, part of me doesn't. The other part knows exactly what I'm doing. I see a man hurting, in need of something. And if I can help, I will. Just not here.

"Sure?" he replies, half question, half statement.

I give him a sharp nod. "Okay. Give me two minutes." I close the door and lock it quietly before hurrying to grab a sweater, my keys, and phone, stuffing them in my bag. Slipping into my shoes, I open the door again, half expecting to find an empty hallway. But Eli's still there, twisting his hands together.

"Are you sure my brother will be okay with this?" he blurts out, and that one question, asked with so much genuine concern — not for himself, but for me — gives me the confirmation this is the right thing to do. He needs someone to hear him out right now.

"Yes. It's just coffee. I'm buying."

We silently make our way to the coffee shop next to Maverick's apartment, and after ordering and paying for our drinks, we sit down at a small table.

I wait. One thing I know from my previous work is not to push things. He came to Maverick's apartment for a reason, just as he agreed to have coffee with me for a reason. And I'm not scared. He's not behaving as if he's under the influence of anything. All I see is a man calling out for help.

His hands shake slightly when he sets down his coffee cup, finally lifting his head to look at me. "How much has Mav told you about me?"

I answer honestly. "Not much. I'd heard your name once or twice, but it wasn't until the last time you came around that he told me who you were."

Sadness plays across his face. "Yeah. Brothers from another mother. That's what we called ourselves when we were younger. Young and stupid, I guess. Promised to always be there for each other and shit." He barks out a harsh laugh. "You don't go through the shit we did, with parents who'd rather drink and hit us, and not bond somehow. Mav, he...well, yeah. It was shit. I was the youngest. So he and Colin aged out of the system before me. Funny how that promise to be there for each other didn't hold up in the real world."

He's hurting. Angry and hurting. And it's so achingly familiar to the sense I get from Maverick sometimes. Two boys who were abandoned so young, who grew up in a broken system that never gave them a sense of belonging. Two young men thrust into a world where they had no one to depend on but themselves. It makes me wonder if Colin is the same, or if he somehow found his way to something better. And it breaks my heart to hear even these small crumbs of information about Maverick's childhood. I suspected it was bad, and Eli's harsh summary confirms it.

"I know Colin thinks I'm a piece of shit who just takes Mav's money. And I do. I'm not gonna lie about that. But they left me. They walked out without looking back and they left me in that fucking place with no one."

"And you've spent years blaming them for whatever happened? Whatever bad choices you made were because they aged out before you?" I try to control the sharpness of my voice, to stay calm and compassionate, but I'll be damned if I'll let Eli blame Maverick for any of this.

His eyes widen in surprise, then narrow, but only for a second before he drops his gaze to the table. Seizing the moment, I push on.

"Your brother cares about you deeply. Why else would he keep stepping up every time you ask for something? Why would he keep giving you money, even though he knew you weren't using it for anything good? Why would he keep bailing you out of whatever situation you ended up in if he didn't care about you? But you've been taking advantage of that. Of him. And I think you know that."

Eli slumps even farther in his chair, mumbling, "Yeah."

I, on the other hand, sit up straighter, hand wrapped tightly around my coffee mug. The warmth seeps into my hands, strengthening my resolve. Maybe it's not my place. After all, Maverick and I are still new, despite what it seems like to the rest of the world. But I feel compelled to try and help.

"You know Maverick would do anything for you. So why not ask him for what you truly need?"

Sorrowful brown eyes lift to meet mine, hope flaring in them. "How do you know what I need?"

"Because I've worked with people struggling with addiction before. And I know you can hit a point where you're on a precipice. You either ask for the right kind of help, and commit yourself to that path, or you go the other way. Alone. And from what I can guess, you don't want to go it alone."

I watch him swallow, his jaw clenching. It's up to him now. If I'm right and he wants help for his addiction, I'll do whatever I can to assist him. I'll get Maverick on board any way I can, and together we can support Eli the right way.

"You're a good person," he says hoarsely after a few silent moments. "My brother's lucky to have you." He stands up from the table and pauses, his hand resting on top of his coffee cup. "Thank you."

I watch him leave the café before slowly exhaling. I have no idea what he'll do now. But I hope he makes the right decision. And I hope Maverick listens to him when he does.

As I make my way back home, my phone rings. I answer, already smiling.

"Hey, you. I was just thinking about you."

"You were?" Maverick's rumbly voice sounds surprised, which simultaneously makes my heart ache and melt. Some day I want him to realize he deserves love and affection. To be important to someone.

"Yeah. You'll never guess what just happened." I reach his building and walk inside, feeling light and happy. "Eli came over."

Chapter Thirty-Four

Maverick

"Eli came over..."

There's a ringing in my ears because that's all I hear. Sure, I know she's still talking, but I can't focus on what the fuck she's saying; my mind is fixated on the fact that my drug-addicted little brother was around my girl again.

"...and I think he might actually be serious. If you want, I can help you research some options, so if he does ask, we're prepared."

"What?" I manage to say, the word sounding like it's someone else talking, not me. "What the fuck did you say?"

She falls silent for a second. "I said, Eli came looking for you, and we went for coffee and talked. And I think he wants to consider treatment for his drug addiction. To get better."

"I... Jesus, Specs. I don't want you talking to him. Just, *fuck*. I'll be home later. We'll talk about it then." Our team manager calls us over for boarding. "Gotta go."

I hang up without giving her a chance to respond, which is a dick move, but I'm so fucking overwhelmed right now. I know she was trying to help, but my head is a goddamn mess.

Shame about how long I enabled Eli's habit under the guise of "helping him" is warring with the protective instinct that wants to keep Sadie far away from the dark parts of my past. Then the overwhelming guilt that I'm calling my brother a dark part of my past hits, and I feel like I'm drowning from it all.

Fuck. Who the hell knows what he told her about me, about my childhood. For all I know, she's discovered just how fucked-up my life was and is busy planning her escape.

I could kill Eli for doing this.

Apparently, my fuck off vibes are strong because no one bothers me the entire flight home. I should be glad of that. I know I'd snap the head off anyone who tried to ask me about Sadie right now. But at the same time, a distraction from my fucking thoughts might have helped. Instead, I spent three hours stewing over what the hell I'm gonna do when I get home.

As soon as the plane lands and we're free to go, I head to my car without so much as a wave at the guys. Once I'm inside, I open my phone.

> **MAV: Where are you.**

> **ELI: 10th street grill. Why?**

> **MAV: Stay there.**

I reach the dive bar in less than half an hour. The air is rank with stale smoke, sweat, and alcohol. I fucking hate places like this. My foster brother is seated at the bar, a glass full of light amber liquid in front of him.

"Why the fuck did you go see Sadie?" I bark at him, not bothering to sit down. He looks up at me with clear eyes for a change, and for just a second, I see a glimpse of the boy I once knew. Before Colin and I moved out. Before everything went to shit for Eli.

"I was lookin' for you," he mumbles, looking back at his drink.

I grab his shoulder and push him roughly, forcing him to look at me. "You don't go near her ever again. Fucking hear me? If I find out you talked to her, you're dead to me."

"Jesus, Mav." His wounded look does nothing to affect me. "What do you think I did, fucking attack her? We talked. I wasn't planning on it, trust me. I would never..." He shakes his head. "Fuck. I would never do anything to a woman, especially not one who means something to you. I can't believe you'd even think for a second —"

"Don't tell me what I think." My jaw is starting to ache from clenching it while he was attempting to defend himself. "All that matters is that you stay the fuck away from her."

Eli stands abruptly, his stool scraping along the bar floor. He's as tall as me now, unlike when we were teenagers and he was a scrawny little thing. He's still skinny, but now we meet eye to eye.

"Did she tell you what we talked about?" he fires back. Part of me is relieved to see this side of him. This strength I haven't seen in a long time. It sure as shit beats the dead-eyed junkie I normally see.

"She said something about you getting clean," I say gruffly, willing to give him that. "And if you're fucking serious, then we'll talk."

Eli shakes his head, and there's no mistaking the pain on his face. "You don't believe it. I get it."

I wave a hand around at the dive bar. "Well, when I find you in places like this, where I know damn well your dealer is just waiting for you, what am I supposed to think?"

That pain I saw a second ago morphs to anger. "You know what, Mav. Fuck you. Fuck you and your goddamn moral high ground. You think you're better than me? I might have fucked up in the past, but at least I'm trying to do better. At least I'm open to doing better. To being a better man. You're so fucking trapped in the past, in who you think you are, you can't let yourself be happy for even a second. I'm betting you got mad at Sadie for talking to me, didn't you?"

His accurate assumption hits just the way he planned. My hands ball into fists as I step forward. He notices and scoffs.

"What? You gonna punch me, like you do any other guy you think is fucking around with a woman? You really think I'm like them? Fuck off. I thought we were brothers. Brothers don't turn on each other. Brothers don't walk away. But that's what you're good at, isn't it? Shutting people out and walking away. You did it ten years ago, and you're gonna do it again now."

My heart stops. At least that's what it feels like. "Is that what you think?" I say hoarsely, unable to comprehend how the fuck Eli thinks I ever abandoned him. "After everything I've done? All the times I've looked the other way or bailed you out of shit? You think I walked away from you?"

I can't stay here looking at his angry face any longer. Turning on my heel, I do exactly what he's accusing me of. I walk away. But a hand grabs my shoulder. My bad one. And I turn to see a fist flying at me out of nowhere.

I take the punch. It's not a hard one, and I know Eli didn't put his full strength behind it, but it still snaps my head back when it connects with my cheek. Lifting my hand to check for blood, I stare at him. "Feel better now?"

The bar around us is silent. Guess they're used to the occasional fight because no one is coming to kick us out.

"Fuck you, Mav," Eli says hoarsely, his voice thick with emotion. "Fuck you."

I nod once, then turn away from him again. This time, he doesn't stop me from walking out.

When I get back to the apartment, my cheek is throbbing and my mood is as black as the night sky. After leaving the bar, I didn't go straight home, even though I knew Sadie was waiting. At some point, I turned off my phone to silence the notifications coming through. The truth is, I don't know what to say to her. Hell, I don't even know if I can face her. In the back of my mind, I know she doesn't deserve this. But that's overshadowed by this unwavering need to protect myself. To put an end to us before she gets any further under my skin. Before she gets close enough to hurt me.

Except I'm almost certain it's too late for that.

Pushing my front door open, I take in the silent apartment, the only light coming from a lamp next to the couch.

"Thank God you're back!" Sadie comes flying out of the bedroom and straight into my arms, which band around her automatically. My mind might know I need to put distance between us, but my body hasn't caught up.

"Where were you? I thought your flight landed hours ago." She lifts her head and her eyes widen. "Oh my God, your face! What happened?"

Fingertips lightly brush my bruised cheek and I pull back. "I went to see Eli."

"And he punched you?" She tries to step toward me, but I step back, making her freeze. "Maverick, what's going on?"

"You shouldn't have talked to him. I didn't ask you to get involved in his shit."

"What? Maverick, I was just trying to help." She gives me a confused look, and it just about breaks me. But Eli was right. I'm good at walking away. I can do this.

"I didn't ask you to help. I actually remember telling you not to. Telling you to leave it alone."

"You never said that. I asked about your family, about Eli, and you said you didn't want to talk about it. That's it. That's all you said." Her voice is starting to shake.

"Doesn't matter," I growl. "It's not your responsibility to deal with my brother, it's mine."

"I care about you, Maverick," she cries. "That means I care about your family. And I'm not going to just sit back and not do anything when I think I can help!"

"I didn't ask you to help," I repeat, grinding out the words between clenched teeth.

When Sadie speaks again, she sounds so fucking sad, it's like a dagger to my heart. "Oh, Maverick. What happened to you?

Why can't you let someone be by your side to support you and help you with the hard things?"

"Because no one has ever been there. My entire life, no one has ever supported me." The confession falls out of me, and if anything, it fuels my anger. How dare she pull these truths from me? I've never told a fucking soul how alone I've always felt. How hard I fight, day in and day out, to carry shit by myself, not even letting Colin get too close.

"I'm here. I'm trying to be here for you."

"Maybe you shouldn't. You can't fix things for everybody else, Sadie. Go and fix your own shit instead. Why are you spending your life always trying to make everyone else happy and never yourself? Jesus. Focus on that and not my brother. Not my life."

"Wow," she says bitterly. "That's harsh. Even for you." Her arms are wrapped around her stomach now. "You know what, I'm going to go. You need to figure out what you're really mad about. Because it isn't about me talking to Eli, is it?" She shakes her head. "I thought we were past this and you weren't that guy anymore, the one who reacts first and thinks last. Guess I was wrong."

I want to shout at her and tell her she's not wrong. That I *have* changed because of her. But I can't make myself say it. I can't tell her how fucking terrified I am that she'll see all of me, all of the mistakes I've made in the past, and just like everyone else — my mom, my dad, every foster parent, every so-called friend — she'll leave.

It's better this way. Better I make her go while I can still convince myself she was nothing to me. That I'm fine alone, the way it used to be.

My silence sends a message. I watch her turn and walk into the bedroom, emerging a few minutes later with her suitcase.

"I'm going to go now." Her voice is hollow as she comes to a stop in front of me. "I hope you find a way forward, even if it's not with me. You're a good man, Maverick. But if you don't find a way to let go of this misbelief that you need to go through life alone, then I worry the good that's inside of you will never be seen by the world. And you deserve to be seen. All of you."

I don't turn to watch her leave, knowing that part of me would want to stop her, to get on my knees and beg her to forgive me and to help pull me back to her light. But I can't do that. I won't do that.

So I stay there, staring at the wall, until I hear the door softly close.

And then I sink to the floor and let my head hang heavy with the weight of what I've done.

CHAPTER THIRTY-FIVE

Sadie

I have to give Ali credit. As far as best friends go, she's a keeper. All it took was one incoherent sob through the phone line, and she knew just what to do. Within half an hour of me arriving back at my crappy old rental, she showed up with a bottle of tequila and a giant bag of chocolate covered almonds.

She made me take two shots before I told her anything. Even with the alcohol warming me, loosening the choke hold around my heart, I couldn't bring myself to share certain details that felt too private for anyone to know.

But I told her about Eli and Maverick's reaction to me talking to him. When I finish explaining how he told me to focus on my own issues instead of his, I feel hollow inside. Like saying it somehow makes it real and steals everything good and warm and happy from me.

"Oh, Sadie. You know he didn't mean it, right?" Ali wraps her arms around me, pulling me in for a hug I'm not sure I really want.

I do want a hug, just from someone else. But the man I want one from has pushed me away, so I guess I'll take what I can get. I reluctantly hug her back and let her take some of the emotional weight from me.

"I know he didn't mean it to be hurtful, but he meant what he said. And he's right. I did get caught up in helping him with his image. And then I fell for him. I did forget about my own mess for a while, but that didn't make it go away. I hid from it, staying at his apartment and getting wrapped up in his world. But that's not where I belong." I push back against her hold, turning to grab the tequila, pouring another shot, and tossing it back before continuing. "If anything, he did me a favour, showing me where I stood with him before I told him how I felt. I don't know that I could have handled seeing his face when he heard me say I'm falling in love with him." My shudder isn't feigned, and I shake my head. "No. This is better. I had to walk away. I already stayed too long in a relationship where I wasn't actually loved. I won't do it again."

Ali doesn't say a word, just fills our shot glasses again and hands me mine, clinking the two together before throwing hers back. Four shots in and I'm feeling no pain. In fact, the room is spinning a bit, to be honest.

I slump back against the couch and shift around, trying to get comfortable.

"I will miss his apartment, though. And the sex. Definitely gonna miss the sex."

"Okay, you're cut off." Ali giggles, rolling her head to the side to look at me. "But I bet it was good. He looks like he'd be good with his bat and balls."

We both dissolve into laughter at that, and it takes a while to calm down. But once I have a little bit of control, I look at her, feeling morose. "It was really good. Like, home run every time good." Ali snorts, but I'm on a roll. "He hit it out of the park. Rounded all the bases. Handled his wood really well."

"Oh my God!" Ali starts cackling and I let myself go, joining her. It feels better to laugh instead of cry, which is the only other option right now.

Thanks, tequila.

I wake up the next morning confused. This isn't Maverick's bed, with pillows soft as clouds yet somehow still supportive. And it definitely isn't him beside me.

"Ali?" I mumble, cringing when I get a whiff of my hangover breath. "Oh man. I hate tequila."

With a groan, I drag myself out of bed as Ali starts to stir. Stumbling into my dingy bathroom, I brush my teeth and try to run a comb through my hair, giving up half way through and pulling it back into a messy bun. By the time I stagger back into the bedroom, Ali's sitting up blinking at me with bleary eyes.

"That's the last time we drink that much tequila," I say, pointing a finger at her and frowning.

"Whatever. You needed some oblivion last night." She rolls out of bed, somehow shaking off the effects of last night a lot easier than me.

I make my way into the tiny kitchen and turn on the coffee maker. Looking around the sad apartment, a wave of sorrow hits me. Wrapping my arms around my stomach, I lean against the counter, remembering the last time I was here. The night Maverick insisted I was moving in with him.

When Ali reappears, I stare at her. "I want to move out of here."

She simply nods. "I don't blame you, this place is gross."

"It was the best I could do when everything went bad with Dirk," I say defensively. But apparently, Ali's not going easy on me today.

"No, it wasn't. You could have stayed with your parents or with me, but you wanted to get into a place of your own. You settled. Just like you did with Dirk, and with so many other things. You don't think you deserve nice things, to be happy, to live the life *you want to live*. That's why you keep ending up in crappy apartments and crappy relationships. Because you get so focused on keeping everyone else happy, and then you settle for less yourself. You forget how long I've known you. And I know Sienna and Simon took a lot of the attention when you were kids, and you were happy to let them. But somewhere along the way, you turned that into a reason to believe you weren't as important as them. You deserve happiness just as much as anyone else."

The beep of the coffee maker gives me an excuse to turn away from her harsh truth, so similar to what Maverick said last night. But once I have a steaming mug in my hand and have passed another to her, I've come up with a reply. One that doesn't exactly address everything she's saying, but it's a start.

"What's so wrong with wanting everyone around me to be happy?" I blow across the steam coming from my mug. "I like taking care of people."

"Yeah, but you forget rule number one. Put your own oxygen mask on first. You use up all your energy on everyone else and leave nothing for yourself. That's not healthy, Sadie. And that's not going to change until you figure out what you want and you go get it."

I take a sip of coffee. "The problem is, I want a man who doesn't want me back." My heart physically hurts saying it. "I can't put my needs first. Because all I'll get is heartbreak."

Ali comes up beside me and rests her head on my shoulder. I let mine fall on top of hers and we stand like that for a minute.

"I'm sorry, Sadie."

"I know."

Straightening, I push off the counter and look around the crappy apartment. "But if I can't have him, I can at least have a better apartment." Turning to look at her, I raise my eyebrows. "Want to help me find somewhere to live?"

Ali's face breaks into a grin. "I've got an even better idea." She drains her coffee cup and sets it down before continuing. "Wanna be roomies?"

"Your place is tiny, Ali," I protest.

"I know it is. And my lease is up next month. You can move into my place until then and we can find a two bedroom to share. Who needs men? Chicks before dicks."

I let out a laugh as I consider her idea. Part of me rebels. Just like the hug last night, she's ultimately not who I want to be with. But it's a smart plan. Together we can afford something a hell of a lot nicer than this. And having her around all the time will help me get over Maverick a lot faster.

"Let's do it."

Against my better judgment, we end up at an upscale wine bar with Willow and Lark that night. I had no desire to go out, but when Willow's message came through, Ali saw it and insisted we go.

Which is how I landed here, sitting at a high-top table with my best friend and two women who work with my ex...whatever Maverick was to me.

Willow, being remarkably perceptive, figured out something was wrong as soon as we walked into the bar.

"What did he do?" she asks, pulling me into a hug. "And do I need to hide a body or write a press release?"

"I like her," Ali comments, nodding at Willow. She lifts her hand and waves at the two other women. "I'm the best friend. And if there's ever a body to deal with, I'll help."

Once our glasses are full of a delicious-looking pinot, I take a deep breath.

"Maverick and I aren't together anymore."

That's all I say, and all I plan to divulge. There's no way I'm revealing details about Eli or Maverick to Willow and Lark. I won't betray him by sharing anything he wouldn't want them to know.

"Something tells me there's a hell of a lot more to that story, but I won't pry. I *will* say, he's more of an idiot than I expected if he's pushing you away." Willow covers my hand with hers. "I'm sorry, babe."

I sniff back a tear, dashing away the one that actually does fall. "I'd say I'm fine, but I'm not." I blink at the other girls. "And I don't want to talk about it. Honestly. So someone else say something, please."

"Baron asked me to marry him and I said yes." Lark looks like she might be sick, which seems odd, considering what she just said. That is, until she goes on to say, "But I think I made a big mistake."

Silence falls over the table as we all stare at her in shock. Willow recovers first, giving her head a slight shake. "Okay, one thing at a time. What's the big mistake?" she asks cautiously.

Lark turns a morose look her way. "I don't really want to marry him."

"Oh, thank fuck." Willow relaxes into her seat. "That's not a mistake, that's the smartest thing you've said about that idiot in a long time."

She's pulling no punches, and it's clear how Willow feels about Lark's partner. I'm just happy to have the attention off me and my relationship woes, though I feel for Lark. She looks miserable.

"You're not the one who has to tell him and his mother," Lark says miserably, staring into her glass of wine. "It's going to be awful."

"Maybe, but you can do so much better than him."

I raise my glass, tilting it toward Lark. "To doing better than the men we're with."

She lets our glasses touch but frowns at me. "Mav's a good man. I really am sorry it didn't work out."

"I know he's a good man. I'm just not right for him." I shrug, trying not to let it show how much that statement stings. "Besides, I was talking about my ex. He wasn't even half the man Maverick is. And now that I've been with someone like him, I know I'll never settle for less again."

"I can drink to that," Lark says with a watery smile. "To never settling for less."

The four of us raise our glasses and drink together. And while it still hurts, and I know I'll be missing Maverick for a while, I feel a little bit better having my friends around me.

The pain feels more manageable with their support.

Chapter Thirty-Six

Maverick

I slam my glove down on the bench, barely holding back a curse. What a fucking shit show of a game. Any hopes of us making the playoffs might as well be dead in the water now, and I'm to blame.

I'm playing like a goddamn rookie out there. Fumbling everything and swinging at trash pitches. It's a fucking miracle I'm still in the game. Coach is either an idiot or he's enjoying making me suffer.

"Get it together, Mav," the man in question snaps. "You're off your game this week and we can't have that, son. So figure your shit out because I need my guy back by the time you get out on that field again. You hear me?"

I nod without meeting his stare. He storms away from the corner of the dugout I've sequestered myself and my bad mood in. The game continues, everyone giving me a wide berth.

I don't need to figure my shit out. I know exactly what's wrong. It's been four days since Sadie walked out. And my performance has steadily gotten worse over the last three games, and today it's at an all-time low.

The connection couldn't be more obvious.

But the fix? Impossible.

I jog back out onto the field for the next inning and thank fuck the ball doesn't come my way. Kai manages to strike out two players in quick succession, and then Darling and Sin field a hit like a dream team, giving us the third out.

Even so, we take a loss.

The locker room is subdued. Thankfully, no one comes at me for my shit performance. Guess they heard Coach yelling at me earlier and figured that was enough. It's not; I deserve all their anger and disappointment.

As I'm walking out to my car, Ronan jogs up beside me. "Mav. Hold up."

I don't slow my steps. "Not interested, Sin."

He grabs my arm and I spin around, fists clenched. "Seriously. I don't wanna talk."

He folds his arms across his chest and stares at me. "Too fucking bad. You're lucky it's just me out here and not everyone else."

Great. Here it comes. I knew it was too good to be true that no one yelled at me in the locker room. Guess they were saving it for now.

"I played like shit. I know. It's the yips. I'll figure it out," I bark.

"It's not the yips. The others can think it is, but you and I know it's not that." His voice is deadly calm. "Willow told me about you and Sadie. I'm sorry, man, I know you really liked her."

My heart stops. Fucking grinds to a halt right there in the parking lot as I wait to see what else *Willow told him.* Because there's only one person she would have heard anything from. And it's the woman I thought would never betray me by spilling my secrets.

Was I really that wrong?

"She asked me if I knew what happened because Sadie's keeping quiet about it. Guess all she said was that things didn't work out, and she refused to say more. So I'm asking. Is there more? Do you need anything from me, from us? Because no matter what you fucking think, you're not alone. The guys, we've got your back, Mav."

Well, fuck.

That's not what I was expecting him to say. "I'll be fine," I reply gruffly, unable to think of any other response. "Gotta go." I push past him, reaching my car and climbing in without looking back.

But the entire drive back to my cold, dark, lonely-as-fuck apartment, I can't stop thinking...

What have I done?

Rolling over in bed the next morning, my hand lands on the pillow next to me just as it has every morning since I last slept with Sadie. The smell of her shampoo has faded, but I can't bring myself to wash it.

When it became clear last night that Sadie hadn't betrayed my trust, hadn't told anyone anything about what really went down between us, something cracked inside of me.

She didn't spill my secrets, but I didn't trust her not to. If anything, that one fact has me tied up in knots.

It doesn't take a genius, or even someone experienced in relationships, to know that without trust, you've got fuck all. So maybe this is the proof I need that I did the right thing by pushing her away before we got any deeper.

I don't have to be at the stadium until the afternoon, leaving me aimless and with too much time and space to get caught up in my thoughts this morning.

Grabbing a few items from the fridge, I cross the hall and knock, then open Ralph's door. "Hey, old man, you up for some breakfast?" I call out when I don't see him in the living room.

I head to the kitchen and start chopping ingredients for an omelet.

"What are you doing here, it's not Saturday," he grumbles as he shuffles down the hall. "Where's that girl of yours? She makes good coffee."

I hide my wince. "She's not coming, man. We're not seeing each other anymore."

I can feel the weight of his stare. "You screwed up, boy."

All I can do is nod. Then I turn to the stove and start cooking. "Make yourself useful and get the coffee going."

"Won't be as good as hers," Ralph mutters under his breath as he slowly makes his way around the kitchen, pulling down two mugs and the instant coffee from a shelf and putting water on to boil.

Soon we're sitting down and eating. The food is tasteless in my mouth. I make myself finish and clean up the dishes. "I gotta go get ready for practice. See you later," I say woodenly. Ralph stares at me, and I know he can see right through me, but thankfully, he doesn't say anything.

Back at my apartment, I change into some workout clothes before heading out for a run around the city. But once I get back, I'm no more settled than I was before. After a shower and a protein shake, I lean against the counter and stare at my couch, where Sadie spent so many days working. Trapped here because of me and the dumb as fuck idea Colin had, to make her pretend to date me.

This is all my fault. Any pain she's feeling and all the misery I'm feeling is because I was the fucking idiot who couldn't stop myself from protecting her from that asshole of an ex.

The fucked-up thing is, even now, knowing how it all worked out, I'd do it again in a heartbeat.

An hour later, I haven't moved from the spot on the couch I slumped into. And I wouldn't be moving, if not for the knock on my door. I suppose I shouldn't be surprised when I open it and see Eli standing there. And truthfully, it's not him that is the surprise, it's what he looks like. For the first time in a long time, his clothes are clean and well-fitting. His eyes are clear, and his hair looks washed. He looks like a regular guy, not an addict.

"Hey, man," he says nervously. "I know you told me not to come around or be near Sadie. I know I'm taking my life in my hands by being here. But I had to risk it so I could thank her."

Of all the shit I thought he'd say, that wasn't even on the list.

"Thank her?" I croak.

He nods. "Yeah. I dunno how to explain it, Mav, talking to her was like a fucking wake-up call or something. I knew I was in deep shit. Too deep. But she got me to see how I was pulling you in, too. And that's...it's not okay, bro. I never wanted to do that, I swear. I was mad at you and Colin, but that wasn't fair. Fuck —" He rakes his fingers through his hair, trembling slightly. "None of this is fair. Our goddamn lives haven't been fair. And I made it worse. For myself and for you. I've blamed you two for not being the brothers you said you were, but really, I was the one that pushed us apart."

I stand there, slack-jawed, staring at him. What the hell happened? But no sooner do I think that, I have my answer.

Sadie. Sadie happened. I step back and wave him inside. I see him glance around, no doubt looking for her. If he notices the lack of any sign of her being here, he doesn't comment. Instead, we go to the couch, and then he continues to blow my goddamn mind.

"After she and I talked, that same fucking day, I went to a local shelter and made an appointment with an addictions counselor. When you saw me at the bar, I'd just filled out a form to apply for residential treatment. The publicly-funded ones have long waits, but the counselor got me on the list. And I've been clean. Well, aside from smoking some joints to make it through." He lets out a harsh laugh. "The counselor said it was impressive I could manage on just that. But I can't do it forever. I need help. Real help. Just gotta hope a bed comes available soon."

"I'll pay." The words are out before I can think about them. But I don't need to. This is the help he needs. This is what I can do for him. Better than anything else I've ever done by far. "Find a private one. The best available. I don't give a fuck what the cost, I'll pay."

Eli's eyes widen as he shakes his head. "No way, Mav, I can't let you do that. You've already done so much."

"Yeah, all the wrong shit," I bite out. "I've failed you so many times, Eli. Every time I gave you money, knowing it was going to drugs, I failed you. Don't let me fail you this time. Let me pay. Please."

We stare at each other for a second. Then Eli's eyes fill with tears. "Fuck, man," he whispers. "Thank you."

I don't know which one of us moves first, but then we're hugging, hands slapping each other's backs, both of us crying. And at some point, my tears become less about him, and more about me.

I guess Eli senses the shift and pulls back. "Hey. Mav. What's goin' on?"

"I fucked up."

"Shit."

I nod, swiping away the moisture on my cheeks.

"What did you do?" he asks cautiously.

"Pushed her away before she could leave me." One simple sentence that somehow sums up all the ways I'm fucked-up inside. All the broken pieces of me, captured in just a few words.

"Do you know why you did it?"

Reluctantly, I nod. "Because good shit never lasts. So why drag it out if I know it's gonna end soon anyway."

Eli snorts, making my head whip up to glare at him. He holds his hands up in defense. "Look, I love you, and I know you can beat my ass, but I'm gonna say it anyway. That's the biggest pile of bullshit I've ever heard."

"Fuck you," I start angrily, but he gives his head a sharp shake to stop me.

"No, fuck *you*. Listen to me, Mav. We were dealt a shit hand. All of us. Our families were piles of shit and we grew up in a broken system with everything stacked against us. But look at what you did. Look at what Colin did. You guys left our fucked-up childhoods behind and rose so far above it all. He's a goddamn lawyer-agent-whatever, with a girl he loves and a life that looks nothing like the one he left. You're a fucking superstar baseball player, making more money than any of us could have dreamed of as kids. And you have a girl who makes you happy. That's all good shit, and it's worth having even if it doesn't last forever. Wouldn't you rather be happy for a short time than never at all? I know I would." His voice turns bitter at the end. "I'd take what you have for even a day if I could, just to know what it feels like to be happy and loved."

I want to tell him he's wrong, that it hurts to see what could be and know you can't have it, but I know he'd tell me to get my head out of my ass. The only thing telling me I can't have it — have Sadie — is me.

Somehow, Eli's words and his wish to live my life for a day breaks down whatever resistance was left in my heart. I already knew I fucked up pushing Sadie away, but I had accepted there was no way to fix it. That I didn't deserve to make things right.

But seeing him like this, knowing she's responsible for my brother finally wanting to get his shit together, knowing she did that because of her feelings for me, something shifts.

I might not fully believe I deserve her, and she sure as hell deserves better than a fuckup like me, but I don't want to go back to the half life I was living before she came along. Or stay in the hell I'm living in, now that I've had a taste of what my life could be like with her.

Looking at my brother, I say the words I've never told anyone but Sadie.

"Eli, I need your help."

CHAPTER THIRTY-SEVEN

Sadie

The best thing about renting a furnished apartment is that there's not much to pack up when you leave. It didn't take me long to decide sleeping on Ali's couch or even sharing her bed would be better than staying here. Thank God for month-to-month lease agreements. I don't even care that I have to pay for the next thirty days, I want out of this crappy place. All I see when I look around is sadness.

My sadness from before Maverick and my sadness now, after him. Missing the man I fell in love with, the man who, somehow, without me even realizing it, helped me become a better, more authentic version of myself.

I've realized he was right. I was hiding from my own discontent by putting all of my energy into him and our relationship. First, by wanting to make sure our ruse did what it needed to do, which was selling him as a changed man and helping him establish a new image. Then, in wanting to see what was growing between us and whether it could be something real.

For weeks, I convinced myself that I was fine. That I was over Dirk and the hurtful things he said, and that I was happy with who I was. But Maverick was the one to show me how much more I could be. How free I could feel if I let myself be open to showing the world my true self instead of just the pieces of me I thought everyone wanted. It was more than just wearing a bold dress or choosing something new to eat or drink.

It was about discovering what I want in life, instead of always going along with what I thought was expected of me. He showed me that, in ways I don't even fully understand.

And in the week since I last saw him, I've tried desperately to hold onto that. I'm doing things I never would have done before, like eating dinner alone at a restaurant I'd always wanted to try. And buying a new green blouse that is so different from anything in my closet. Of course, it wasn't lost on me that the restaurant was one Maverick had talked about, and the blouse was one I knew he would love. He's still in my heart and my mind. I still love him.

I fold a shirt into my suitcase, then stand to get another armful of clothes from my closet when a knock at the door makes me pause. It can't be Ali, she's at work for the day. And my parents don't know exactly where I'm living. It was easier that way rather than dealing with their worries over me living in such an unsavoury neighbourhood.

When I open the door, my heart leaps out of my chest and into his. At least that's what it feels like when I greedily drink in the sight of Maverick. He's wearing jeans that are molded to his perfect butt and strong legs, and a gray T-shirt that hugs those biceps that can hold me so tightly. It's hard not to fling myself into his arms, following my heart.

"Hey, Specs." His voice sounds gravelly and raw with unfiltered emotion. His expression is drawn, and the dark circles under his eyes mirror my own. There's still some faint bruising on one cheekbone from his altercation with Eli, and it's a forceful reminder of the day everything fell apart.

"What are you doing here?" I whisper, trying desperately to suppress the flare of hope filling my body.

"Can I come in to talk?" he says by way of answer, and I step aside to let him in. He walks in ahead of me, so I don't see his reaction to the few boxes in the living room or the open suitcase that is visible through my bedroom door. We go to the lumpy couch and sit, him at one end and me at the other. I fold my hands in my lap, trying to outwardly project a calm I'm most definitely not feeling.

For the first time, the silence between us is awkward. I'm waiting for him to start, seeing as I don't want to even think of why he might be here, for fear of letting that flare of hope turn into a flame that could burn me.

"Jesus. I had what I'd say all planned out. And now that I'm here, I can't stop staring at you."

My gaze bounces up from my lap to his face. Just as he said, his blue eyes are boring into me. It hurts to look at him and not be able to reach out and touch him as I have a thousand times over the last few weeks.

"Are you moving?" he asks the obvious question, finally breaking the silence again.

I nod. "Into Ali's place for now. Being alone is...hard."

His Adam's apple bobs up and down as he swallows. "Yeah. It is." Another second of silence, and then his head drops forward to hang down, his elbows resting on his knees. "I have to start with saying I'm so fucking sorry. That's not anywhere near enough, but it's the only place to begin." He lifts his head, and his eyes are so filled with pain it makes it hard for me to breathe.

"I pushed you away before you could leave me. That's the short version of how fucked-up I am. My entire life, I've kept everyone away, never letting anyone get close, simply so they couldn't hurt me later on by leaving. But I couldn't keep you away. I couldn't stop you from getting under my skin and into my broken black heart, no matter how hard I tried. And I guess at some point, I stopped trying. I let you in, and it felt good. Being with you, having you by my side, it felt good and right and easy."

He pauses, a sad smile lifting the corners of his lips. I want to trace the curve with my fingers, but again, I resist.

"And then it started to feel scary as hell. Because letting you in meant revealing my flaws. And I worried that when you saw them, you'd realize the truth that I was nowhere close to good enough for you. I'm a guy who had an abusive dad and a mom who died of cancer when I was a baby. I'm a guy who grew up bouncing around foster homes. I'm a guy who barely graduated from high school, has zero education, and only knows how to do one thing, play baseball. I gave my foster brother money, over and over, knowing it would probably be used to buy drugs, simply because I felt so guilty over leaving him in foster care when I aged out. I drove in an illegal street race and crashed a car because that same brother got caught up in a mess he couldn't get out of. I pick fights with assholes at bars. I don't have any friends except for the old guy who lives across the hall from me and a cat. I hate being around people, don't do small talk, and have never been in a relationship. There's nothing about me that makes me worthy of a woman like you, and I hurt you in an attempt to keep you from realizing that."

A lone tear spills from his eye, tracking slowly down his face, and I can't hold back any longer. My hand lifts to cup his cheek, my thumb wiping away the moisture. I shift closer to him as he turns his cheek into my hand, his eyes closing as he draws in a ragged breath.

"You're looking at everything all wrong," I murmur, my heart aching for this man who can't see how everything he thinks of as a flaw is actually a beautiful piece of what makes him so strong.

"You're a man who overcame a terrible childhood to become an incredible athlete who is admired by thousands. A man who is respected and valued by his teammates. You're a man who is so dedicated to his career, you'd do anything for it. And you're a man who defends those who can't defend themselves. Who gives everything he has to those he cares about, and has no clue just how big his heart really is. It's not broken and black. It's wounded and scared, but also capable of so much."

Tears are streaming down my face now. Maverick has lifted his head out of my hand to stare at me with an expression of innocent hope and wonder, like the little boy he once was can't believe the man he is today could be all I say.

"Eli came to see me a few days ago," he starts again, but his voice is stronger this time. "After you and he talked, he went and found a counselor who got him on the wait list for rehab. He said you were the one to make him finally realize he needed help."

My smile breaks free. I'm so happy to hear Eli took that step.

"But the wait could be months. So yesterday..." Maverick pauses, clearing his throat. "Yesterday I dropped him off at a private facility in the valley. He'll be there for two months. Colin and I are covering the cost." He slowly reaches over, glancing up at me first. Then, when he sees my smile, takes my hand and laces our fingers together. And that simple touch, the feel of his hand in mine, settles the ache in my chest. "He came to the apartment to thank you. You helped him in a way I never could. And I should have been falling at your feet in gratitude, not pushing you away in fear." His eyes close again, and he lifts our hands to his lips, kissing my knuckles lightly before opening his eyes and looking at me. "Can you find a way to forgive me?"

I lean in to rest my forehead against his, feeling his exhale against my skin. "Only if you can forgive yourself."

A choked sound close to a sob comes out of the big beautiful man sitting in front of me, and then he sags against me. His arms wrap around me like a vice, lifting me up to settle on his lap. We're pressed as close together as possible, and it's still not enough. I cup his scruff-covered jaw in my hands and press my lips to his, finally feeling his kiss fill my soul once again.

He pulls back, keeping it soft and short, and his eyes are still glistening with tears. "Sadie, I love you. I've been falling in love with you for weeks. Hell, probably for as long as I've known you. Everything about you is all I could possibly need. I never knew someone like you existed, much less could be with a guy like me. But I swear to you, I'll never let another day go by without telling you just how much I love you."

I'm speechless.

I'm staring at him through watery eyes, my mouth open in shock. Of all the things I imagined he would say if we saw each other again, those three words were never on the list. Even in my wildest dreams, where I imagined him coming back and apologizing, I didn't dare let myself picture him telling me he loved me.

I scramble to recover, knowing I need to say something before he starts to wonder if those feelings are reciprocated.

"I've wanted to tell you I was falling in love with you since the night of your first game. But it started long before that. You're not the only one who was scared. I was, too. So scared that I wouldn't be enough for you. We were both wrong, Maverick. We're more than enough for each other."

He leans in and kisses me again, his tongue darting out to trace the seam of my mouth. I open eagerly with a small moan.

This time when we break apart, the tears are gone and we're both breathing heavily. Maverick's head turns, and he zeros in on the boxes. "I'm glad you're getting out of this shithole, Specs." He looks back at me, tenderly tucking a piece of hair behind my ear. "But if you're gonna sleep somewhere other than here, it better be in my bed, where you belong."

"Mav," I murmur, running my fingers through the curls at the base of his neck. His eyes widen as he leans back slightly.

"What did you say?"

My brows draw together in confusion. "What do you mean?"

"Mav. You've never called me that, it's always Maverick."

It takes me a second to realize he's right. And another to realize why. "I think that was my weird way of not letting myself get too close. In my head, only people close to you called you Mav."

He's shaking his head, his smile so full of love. "Oh, Specs, you couldn't be more wrong. Everyone calls me Mav. Only the most important person in my world calls me Maverick." He kisses me again, deeper this time. And the world around us grinds to a halt. The only thing I'm aware of is the feel of his lips on mine and his arms holding me tightly, exactly where I want to be.

Suddenly, he stands up, making me squeak as he lifts me with him. "Maverick! What are you doing?"

He doesn't answer, just carries me into my bedroom. But my bed is covered in clothes and suitcases. Letting out a growl, he sets me down.

"We need to finish packing and get back to our apartment so I can show you how much I love you with my tongue and my cock."

"*Our* apartment?" I ask softly, and he looks down at me with such a tender smile.

"Yeah." His smile grows deliciously wicked. "If you think I'm gonna let you live anywhere other than with me, you're very wrong, Specs."

I wind my arms around his neck and go up on my toes to kiss his jaw, then his cheek, and then, finally, his lips. "I wouldn't want to be anywhere else."

CHAPTER THIRTY-EIGHT

Maverick

Unlocking the door to my apartment and holding it open for Sadie to walk through is right up there with hitting a home run in terms of how good it feels. She drops her bag on the table and immediately crouches down to pick up Cat, who nuzzles into her shoulder, his purr already audible.

"He's been grumpy ever since you left. Haven't heard him purr and he kept snubbing me." I reach out and scratch him behind the ears. "Guess I wasn't the only one miserable without you."

She turns slightly so I can kiss her upturned lips. Cat protests being squished between us and scratches to be let down, forcing us apart. That's fine because he'd just be in the way when I get to do what I want to her.

Taking her hands in mine, I start to walk backward in the direction of the bedroom. "We missed you. I'm pretty sure you should never leave again."

Her smile lights up everything around us. "Sounds good to me. But you have to be the one to tell Ali she needs a new roommate."

I don't bother responding to that, just pick her up and toss her on the bed. She props up on her elbows and watches me, unabashedly, as I pull my shirt off over my head and toss it to the floor. Shoes come off next, then my pants, until I'm down to nothing but my underwear, my dick already straining against the fabric. I step between her legs and she sits up, her hands immediately lifting to run up and down my stomach. I gather her hair in my hand and tug gently, forcing her head to tip back. My other hand circles her throat, and I hold her right there, feeling her fingers dig into me as I lean down and kiss her softly.

"I love you."

Her eyes are still closed as a dreamy smile covers her face. I can't help but kiss her again, deeper this time, sucking her lower lip in between my teeth. Not losing contact with her mouth, I drop down into a crouch, and slowly peel her shirt off, trailing my fingers down her bare skin and around to her back where I unhook her bra. It falls off and she instantly arches toward me. I can't resist the temptation, breaking away from our kiss to look down at her tits.

My hands cup them almost reverently, loving the way they overfill even my large hands. Her body is a fucking playground of soft curves, and it's all mine.

I pull one of her nipples into my mouth, letting my teeth graze it gently, teasing it into a stiff peak. Then I move to the other, giving it equal attention. She's squirming under me, her hands roaming my back, alternating between gripping tightly and stroking my skin. When I release her nipple with a pop, I bring one hand to the center of her chest and push gently.

"Lie back, Specs."

She does as I say, and I quickly tug her leggings and underwear down, finally revealing her glistening pussy. Trying to tighten her legs around me, her hips move on the bed. I trap her in place with my hands, waiting until her gaze meets mine.

"You're mine. All of you. I'm not gonna lie and say I won't ever fuck up again, but I do promise I'll never stop loving you. Never stop wanting you with every breath I take. My heart, whether it's broken or just wounded, black or scared, it's yours. Now and always."

She starts to lift up, but I press her back down, then lift her legs to drape them over my shoulders.

"And this is mine." With that, I open my mouth and lap up her seam, exerting enough pressure to have her arching off the bed, moaning my name.

Her thighs clamp around my head as I devour her, drinking down every drop of her arousal, finding every spot that makes her gasp, or sigh, or shriek. All too soon, she's arching off the bed, her body curling over my head as she chants my name, her pussy gushing her release as I lick and suck through her orgasm.

When she falls back on the bed, a delicious blush covering her skin, I kiss the inside of each knee before slowly lowering her legs and standing up. My cock is so hard it hurts. I'm desperate to be inside of her, to feel that sense of home I can only get with her.

But first, I walk around to the side of the bed and open the drawer, tossing a strip of condoms onto the mattress beside her. Her head rolls to the side, and she giggles when she sees how many I pulled out. "You're awfully ambitious."

I give her a wicked grin. "Nah. I plan on keeping you up all night, Specs. We've got a lot of catching up to do on orgasms."

I push down my boxers, my dick springing free. Sadie licks her lips, the unconscious movement so fucking cute I can't help but laugh. "Hungry, baby?" She looks up at me, the pink on her cheeks deepening. But then she nods and reaches a hand out to wrap around my length, making me groan. "Fuck. I'm not sure I can last very long if you do that."

"That's fine. Like you said, we have all night."

I lean over her and tip her chin up with one finger. "No. We have forever." She surges up somehow, reaching my lips and kissing me, one hand gripping my hair while the other continues to hold my cock.

"I love you," she breathes against my lips.

"And I love you."

Fuck, it feels so damn good to say that. I don't think I'll ever get tired of hearing it from her and I know I'll never want to stop saying it.

Her head dips down, those sweet lips wrapping around the tip of my dick. Her tongue traces a circle before she bobs down, taking half of me in. "Jesus, Specs. Look at you taking my dick."

She moans around my cock, the vibrations making me throw my head back, my hips starting to pump in short, shallow movements. It isn't long before I can feel my orgasm barreling toward me. I wasn't lying when I said I wouldn't last. Not when it's been so long since I had her.

I pull back, secretly loving her cry of protest when I pop free from her mouth. I bend down and kiss her puffy lips. "I need to be inside of you, Specs. Right fucking now."

She fumbles for the strip of condoms, tearing one off with an eager smile. "Yes, please," she says, her sweet tone at odds with the filthy picture she makes, spread out on my bed, her hair a mess, her lips looking well-kissed and her skin red from arousal and the scrape of my scruff.

I let her roll the condom down my cock, reciting my old Little League stats to stop from blowing just from the feel of her hand on me. When she's done, I grab her hands in one of mine, lifting them above her head and pinning them there. With my other, I grip her hip, lifting her thigh up to brace it on mine. And then, finally, I slowly push into her.

"Fuck."

"Maverick!"

Our groans are synchronized as our bodies come together at last. I pump my hips a few times, coating my dick in her arousal, making it glide more easily. When I'm finally in as deep as I can go, I still, releasing my hold on her hands and dropping my head to her shoulder. "Heaven. Fucking heaven. That's what you are."

She drags her fingers up and down my back, her pussy fluttering around my cock. "If I'm heaven, then you have to admit you're a good person," she teases, and I lift my head to see her impish grin. "Only good boys go to heaven."

"Hmm. Is that so?" I pull back and thrust back in, watching her tits jiggle. "But bad boys are so much more fun, aren't they?"

Her breathy sigh as I thrust again is answer enough. But her words lodge themselves in my heart. Somehow, she truly believes I'm a good person. And I'll be damned if I won't do everything in my power to live up to that.

I take her hand again, this time threading our fingers together before pinning it beside her head. My movements speed up as

I rock into her, watching her face as ecstasy takes over. She's so expressive in everything she does, and sex is no different. Every reaction is right there for me, and I can't look away.

"Mine." I growl out the one word before dipping my head down to kiss her again. She meets me, stroke for stroke, her hips rocking in time, her tongue chasing mine. This time, there's no holding back. No amount of baseball stats can hold off my release. But I'll get her there first.

I let go of her hand and lean back, changing the angle. Grabbing both legs, I lift them onto my shoulders and pull out slightly, only to slam back in. The new angle hits Sadie exactly where I meant it to, her hands clutching at the sheets as her head tilts back.

"Oh my God, Maverick. Yes! Oh God, right there. Yes!"

Her pussy starts to tighten, rhythmically squeezing my dick and making me grunt with every thrust.

"Give it to me, Specs. Now."

"Maverick!" she shrieks, her hands now gripping my forearms as I piston in and out of her. I feel her orgasm ripple through her, triggering my own as I groan, my movements now sloppy and uncoordinated as I come.

When I finally feel things slow down, I lower down on shaky arms to kiss her forehead gently. Then I climb off the bed and go to the bathroom to deal with the condom. When I crawl back in beside Sadie, I curl my body around her, pulling her back flush against my front. My hand finds a place between her breasts, her fingers tangled with mine. Her lips graze my knuckles, and I kiss her head.

"You belong here, Specs. In my arms, in my bed, and in my heart."

Chapter Thirty-Nine

Maverick

Catching a pop fly sent straight to my glove, ending the last game of the season feels pretty fucking good, not gonna lie. And I'm learning to actually enjoy the attention, the cheers, and the backslaps from my teammates instead of wanting to avoid it all.

But when Willow walks into the locker room and tells us all to hurry up and get presentable before some VIP season ticket holders come through for a meet and greet, I'm annoyed. That's beyond the limit of my peopling for today, and I just want to leave.

Standing in front of my locker, I stare at the snapshot of me and Sadie I taped up there last week. The guys gave me some grief, but it was good-natured. And honestly, I couldn't care less. Getting to stare at her face whenever I'm here is worth the ribbing.

Except, I tend to get caught up in looking at her beautiful smile and tune out everything else.

Which is why, when strange voices filter in, I glance up, not realizing the VIPs are already here. A bunch of white dudes are walking around with their chests all puffed out, thinking they're a big deal. *Yeah, okay.*

Lawyers. I remember Willow saying it was a law firm that paid for the locker room meet and greet. It goes to charity, so I'll suck it up, I guess.

Until I see him.

Dirtbag Dirk.

He notices me, and his face turns an interesting shade of purple-red.

It's fucking on.

I give him a wide grin, not hiding the malice behind it. Foregoing a shirt, I leave my muscles and tattoos on display as I swagger over to the group. Some other guy's mouth falls open when he sees me, and I turn my attention to him first.

"Maverick King. Nice to meet you. Did you enjoy the game?"

"Yeah, man, it was awesome. Great catch at the end."

"Thanks. Want a picture?"

The guy nods, and we take a quick selfie. Yeah, I'm shirtless and probably gonna end up on some idiot's social media, but whatever.

I make a point of ignoring the fucker who was dumb enough to walk away from my Specs as long as I can.

But then I notice Monty walking up to him, and I see my chance to truly mess with the asshole. Making my way over to them, I pitch my voice loud enough to be heard over the chatter. "Monty, you know who this is, right?" I ask, draping my arm over my teammate's shoulder. He looks at me but manages to conceal his confusion. I give him a wink before turning a sinister smirk toward Dirk. "It's Darren, right? Sadie's ex. Gotta say, man, I'm glad you fucked around on her, it gave me the chance to lock down the best fucking woman I've ever met."

Monty coughs out a laugh, catching on quick. "Darren, did you say? Wow, I don't know why anyone would screw things up with Sadie. She's top-notch."

"It's Dirk, actually." The asshole tries to appear confident, but his ears are still bright red, and he won't look at me. "And Sadie —"

"Nah, *Derek*, I'm gonna stop you there. You don't get to speak her name." I cut him off with a glare, moving away from Monty's shoulder to fold my arms across my chest, knowing it makes my muscles pop. By now, some of the other guys have drifted over, standing behind me. "You don't say her name and you don't go near her. In fact, it's probably a good idea if you never come to the stadium again. I mean, she's gonna be at all my games, and I wouldn't want security to have to toss your ass out for causing problems."

"Wait, this is the guy Sadie used to date?" Kai chimes in, snorting out a laugh. "Damn, Mav, she leveled up with you, bro." He holds out his hand for a high five and I slap it, never letting my stare drop from Dirk's weasel face.

"Thanks, Yami."

The bluster leaves Dickhead Dirk all at once, and he turns and slinks out of the locker room. And just like that, everyone goes back to whatever they were doing, not speaking of what just went down.

Of course, I know it was noticed. And not two minutes go by before Willow's standing next to me as I'm putting all my shit into my bag.

"You're really fucking lucky we didn't have cameras on."

I look over at the head of media relations with what I hope is an innocent expression. "I don't know what you're talking about."

She rolls her eyes with an amused huff. "Okay, Mav. Sure. Listen, the only reason I'm not giving you a lecture on how to properly handle VIPs is because that man is the worst scum of the earth and I absolutely loved watching you guys give him the shit he deserves. That, and judging by the lack of reaction from his colleagues, we're not alone in how we feel about him. But —" She lifts one hand and pokes me in my chest. "If you ever pull that with anyone else, you're gonna be in so much trouble you'll wish you were back on the IL."

"Message received. But just so you know, that was a one and done. Sadie doesn't have anymore trash exes I need to worry about, so we're cool."

I see Willow fighting a smile, but she eventually gives in with a shake of her head. "We're cool."

She walks away then, heading over to Sin and wrapping her arms around him. And I hurry to finish packing my shit so I can find my girl and get my own damn hug.

Soon enough, I strut out of the locker room, feeling really fucking good about things, despite it being the end of the season. Honestly, what just went down in the locker room with that twatwaffle was probably the highlight of the season.

Especially seeing as I get to go home with the woman he let get away.

Sadie's waiting for me in the hallway, and I walk straight up to her and lift her up into my arms before kissing her. I can feel her smile against my lips, and it's perfect.

"Hey, you. Good game."

I set her down after kissing her again. "Yeah, always good to end with a win." I sling my arm over her shoulder and we start to walk toward the car park.

"How did the VIP tour go?" she asks, and my grin widens as I start to chuckle. "What? What's so funny?"

"Guess what company did the meet and greet?"

We reach my car and pause.

"I have no idea."

"Stevenson and Schmidt," I say, naming the law firm Dick-face works for. Sadie's eyes widen and I see her biting back a smile.

"No way."

I nod. "Yeah. I know you want me to think before I act, but Specs, there was no fucking way I was gonna let the opportunity pass to tell him what I think, and just fuck with him. It was…" I kiss my fingers. "Perfection."

Sadie throws her head back, her laughter ringing free. "I wish I had been there to see that."

"You would've loved it. The guys all joined in. It was a thing of beauty, either way. Funniest shit I've seen in years. Although, I guess I should have thanked him. If he hadn't been such a fucker, I wouldn't have you."

She pulls me in for a hug, nestling against my chest. "I love you, Maverick. Thank you for loving me back."

"Always, Specs. Always."

CHAPTER FORTY

Sadie

> **MAVERICK: On my way back, Specs.
> I expect you naked for the next 24
> hours.**

A thrill runs through me at Maverick's text. The season is officially over, and after today, he won't have to go to the stadium for a while. He grumbled a bit this morning as he was leaving to go in for locker clean out and some meetings, but then I surprised him with the news that I was able to get the next two weeks off as vacation time.

We get two weeks with zero responsibilities, nowhere to be, and nothing to do, except whatever we want. The possibilities are endless, but Maverick made it clear what he wants to do.

When I suggested we go away somewhere, he simply laughed and said I was crazy if I thought he was going to let me get out of bed.

I'm certainly not going to complain about that idea...

So while he went to the stadium, I ran around doing some last-minute errands. Groceries, a leg wax, and a quick lunch with my mom, who badgered me about bringing Maverick over for dinner again.

I promised her we would, at some point. Just not anytime in the next few days.

Now I'm home, anxiously waiting for him to get here. And his text means I have less than half an hour before that happens. I double-check Cat's got food and water and move the wine I had chilling in the freezer into the fridge in case we lose track of time.

That makes me smile. *We're absolutely going to lose track of time...*

I hurry into the bathroom for a quick shower. When I walk into the bedroom, I close the door to keep Cat out and put on the dark teal lingerie set I bought because it reminded me of the Tridents' team colours. Then I grab one of his jerseys out of the closet and put that on top.

I know he said he expects me to be naked, but I have a sneaking suspicion he'll like this just as much.

With time to kill, I try to decide on a pose, flipping from my side onto my stomach, then over to my back. But nothing feels sexy or comfortable, and I can feel myself getting stressed out by trying to decide. And that's not sexy at all. I need to relax or I'll be a nervous wreck by the time he gets here.

Lying back on the bed, I open the bedside drawer and take out my favourite vibrator. Glancing at my phone, I figure I've got enough time to take the edge off before he gets here.

I tug my panties off, setting them to the side, and let my eyes close as I take in a slow breath.

"Okay. Just a quickie. Then I'll be fine."

The toy touches my skin and I sag into the mattress. Oh yeah, this is exactly what I need. I run it up and down my sex, keeping it on low, just teasing for a minute, the way Maverick does sometimes with his tongue. Of course, as soon as I think of that, of him, my arousal jumps.

"Mmm," I let out a soft moan as I circle my clit with the toy, alternating how much pressure I apply, drawing out the sensations. I play for a bit, not wanting to climb too high too fast. I have to bite my lip when I hold it in one spot for too long, feeling the familiar thrill of an oncoming orgasm start to flood my body. I lift the toy away with a gasp, blood rushing in my ears.

Smiling to myself, I lower it back down to edge myself some more. This feels deliciously naughty, playing while I wait for him to get home. It's something I never would have done before Maverick. But he's helped me discover this sexy side, and I absolutely love it.

My eyes have fluttered closed again, and I'm lost in sensation as I tease my clit, bringing my fingers into play, dipping in and out in shallow thrusts that feel good, but nowhere near as amazing as Maverick's thick, blunt digits.

I guess more time passes than I realize, because when the door to the bedroom opens, I shriek, my heart racing for more than one reason.

"What's going on, Specs?" Maverick growls and raises his hands to hold onto the door frame as he sears me with his gaze. "I thought I told you to be naked."

I let the vibrator fall from my hand, not missing the way his eyes track it, growing even darker with lust. I rise up on my knees and make my way to the end of the bed before giving him a smirk.

"You did. But I thought you might like this instead." I spin around, tossing my hair over one shoulder, revealing my back with his name on full display.

"Fucking hell," he croaks. Then hands land on my hips, gathering up the bottom hem of his jersey and lifting it. "And you're naked underneath?"

"Not quite," I whisper, turning my head to look at him. "But I took my panties off."

"Couldn't wait?"

I give my head a tiny shake, and he leans down to catch my earlobe between his teeth. "You're the sexiest thing in the entire fucking world, you know that?"

He backs away, and a whimper escapes me.

"Fuck. I love you, Sadie." His whisper is soft, full of wonder and so much adoration it's at odds with the dirty words he said a moment ago. Then his bare chest is pressed against my back, his tattooed arms that make me feel the safest I've ever been wrapped around me, and his lips have landed on my neck.

"I love you, too," I murmur back, reaching my hands behind me to tangle in his curls.

Together we fall onto the bed, and I let Maverick maneuver us until I'm on my back and he's on his side next to me. He hooks his finger in the front of his jersey, right above the top button. "Tell me. Did you choose this one so I'd have to open you like a present?"

I giggle because the thought did cross my mind when I looked at the jersey options. "Maybe."

He unhooks the first one, revealing a tiny patch of skin. "Good choice." Leaning in, he kisses the bared skin, then unhooks another button. A tiny bit of teal lace peeks out. "Hmm. What's this?"

I wriggle slightly. "Guess you'll have to keep going."

He lifts his head and gives me a smirk. "I don't plan on stopping, Specs. Not now, not ever."

The rest of the buttons are opened a lot faster, and he spreads the sides of his jersey wide, revealing my teal bra and...nothing else.

"Look at you. So fucking wet and ready for me. What am I gonna do with you?"

It's my turn to smirk and wiggle my eyebrows. "I can think of a few things..."

"Good thing we've got plenty of time to try them all out."

"Oh yeah? How much time?" I tease, but Maverick doesn't seem to find it funny. His smile is gone, and he seems oddly quiet.

"How about forever?"

I assume he's saying it offhandedly, the way he has a few times before. Talking about us being together forever. But then I notice the nervous expression that's come over him, and the way he's playing with my ring finger.

"Wait. Are you?" I start, then stop. "We're naked in bed and you're..."

"Asking you to marry me?" He lets out a nervous laugh. "Yeah. I had all these plans to do it up on the rooftop. I was gonna set up a romantic evening like we had before, but I can't wait any longer. I need you to know what you mean to me. I need you to know that I can't imagine life without you. And I'm dying to know if you'll do me the biggest honour of my entire fucking life and be my wife."

My eyes fill with tears, and he lifts a thumb to gently wipe them away.

"Are those happy tears?"

"Of course, they are," I cry, flinging my arms around him. "Yes, I'll marry you. Yes, yes, yes!"

Forever with Maverick King? Sounds better than any life I could have ever imagined for myself.

Our relationship might have started as a publicity stunt, but we're the only ones who know that. To the rest of the world, our love story started that night at the bar, when he saved me from my ex.

Come to think of it... Maybe that *was* the night it all began. The night my tattooed bad boy changed my life.

And made me fall in love.

Epilogue

Four Years Later

Maverick

Hoisting this trophy up in the air is the biggest *fuck you* I could possibly send to everyone in my life that ever held me back or made me think I wasn't worth it. The noise of the crowd is deafening. I'm jostled around by teammates and their family and friends. Theirs, not mine. There's only two people I give a flying shit about seeing right now.

As if the crowd can read my mind, it parts. And there she fucking is.

"Dude, are you smiling?" Monty slings his arm over my shoulders, and I don't even bother shrugging him off. Even now, after all these years playing together, he still gives me grief when I smile.

Like it's rare or something.

Maybe at one time it was, but not recently. These last several years, I've had nonstop reasons to smile.

"Fuck off, Monty," I say, but there's no bite to my words. His eyes light up when he sees Lark, and his arm falls away.

"You love me and you know it," he teases, but his attention isn't on me anymore. And I don't blame him. He's finally getting his forever with the girl he's wanted for so fucking long. And no one deserves it more than that dude.

Sadie reaches me, and I pass the trophy off to Monty without a second look so I can lift her up into my arms. She's a better prize than some fucking trophy, anyway.

"Hey, baby," I say, giving her the small smile that's just for her.

"I'm so proud of you." She's beaming. Happiness radiates out of her, bathing me in warmth and light, the way she always does. This is where I belong, with her in my arms, making me feel like anything is possible. Her love is the only reason I'm here, surrounded by people I respect and most of the time even like. She's the reason my teammates named me MVP and the reason I was fucking *happy* to sign a five-year contract with the Tridents last year.

"You know it's all because of you." I tilt my head to her ear, because even though it's loud with all the excitement and chaos around us, I don't need anyone hearing this. "It's because of this morning."

As expected, her cheeks turn bright red in an instant. "Maverick," she chides, but there's no heat behind her words. Well, not the angry sort of heat. A different kind, yeah. But that's my girl. I can read her moods like the pages of a fucking book written just for my enjoyment.

"I didn't notice you complaining this morning."

"It's not like you gave me a chance," she retorts, but her eyes are sparkling with mischief, and I know she's remembering the four orgasms I gave her before we got out of bed. Higher the orgasm count, higher the score for the game. That's what I figure. And seeing as we won the championship with a healthy three-point lead, I'd say those four orgasms were worth it.

Nothing beats seeing Sadie lost in herself and knowing it's because of me. Knowing that she only truly lets go with me.

"How soon can we get out of here?" she asks, but before I can answer, a voice cuts in.

"Not until he's done with the press conference."

Sadie slides down my body, her feet hitting the grass. But I keep her close to me as we turn to see Colin standing there with a wide grin.

"Well played, brother."

I slap his hand with mine and let him pull me in for a one-armed hug, keeping my other wrapped around Sadie. "Thanks, man." A moment passes between us. A moment not even Sadie is aware of. We've been through shit she can't even fathom, and I'm glad of that. Even though she knows everything about my past, it doesn't matter how deep our love runs. There will always be pieces of me no one understands like Colin does. And that means there's a small piece of today she can't appreciate the way he does.

Two kids from the wrong fucking side of the tracks. Two kids with fucked-up families and even more fucked-up childhoods. Two kids who rose the fuck above all of that.

His wife is standing back, and I bring her in for a quick hug as well. The only person missing today is Eli, but he couldn't get away from the treatment center he works at as an addictions counselor out in Manitoba. I'm proud of him for prioritizing his work and told him just that last night.

Besides, tonight I really only want to celebrate with one person. My wife. The woman who helped me realize the man I am today is the man I always wanted to be. Strong, steady, and open to what life brings.

"I love you, Sadie King."

Her beautiful smile is blinding, even under the bright lights of the stadium. "I love *you*, Maverick King."

We kiss and I don't give a fuck who sees or what camera catches us.

Let them.

Let the whole fucking world see me love the woman who saved me from myself.

To read a bonus scene with Maverick and Sadie, sign up for my newsletter:

https://bit.ly/JuliaJarrett_FTG_bonus

The next Vancouver Trident's book is Catch Her Heart:

https://bit.ly/JuliaJarrett_FTG

This book would not exist without a village of people. Chelle and Jess for their sports and injury related expertise, a different Jess, Kelly, Erica and Andrea for feedback, Becca for plotting, Chris for editing, Carolina for keeping me sane throughout it all, Alex and Theresa for dealing with my rambling voice memos about all the things, and Kari for creating the most perfect cover ever.

I never pictured myself as a sports romance writer, but here we are! Thank you readers, for loving my baseball boys as much as I do.

XOXO Julia

ABOUT THE AUTHOR

Julia Jarrett is a busy mother of two boys, a happy wife to her real-life book boyfriend and the owner of two rescue dogs, one from Guatemala and another one from Taiwan. She lives on the West Coast of Canada and when she isn't writing contemporary romance novels full of relatable heroines and swoon-worthy heroes, she's probably drinking tea (or wine) and reading.

For a complete listing of Julia Jarrett books please visit

www.authorjuliajarrett.com/books

Printed in Great Britain
by Amazon